© Marion Ettlinger

About the Author

R. S. JONES also wrote *Force of Gravity*
and was a recipient of a Whiting Writers'
Award. He was president of the New York
chapter of the ACT UP AIDS Awareness
Organization, and editor in chief and vice
president of HarperCollins Publishers.

Also by R. S. Jones

Force of Gravity

WALKING ON AIR

A NOVEL

WITH A NEW INTRODUCTION
BY RUSSELL BANKS

R. S. JONES

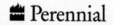

Perennial

An Imprint of HarperCollins*Publishers*

First Perennial edition published 2002.

Designed by Melodie Wertelet

The Library of Congress has catalogued the hardcover edition as follows:

Jones, R. S. (Robert S.)
  Walking on Air / R. S. Jones.
    p. cm.
  ISBN 0-395-74545-4
  I. Title.
PS3560.05249W35 1995
813'.54—dc20 95-17166 CIP

ISBN 0-06-051131-1 (pbk.)

02 03 04 05 06 RRD 10 9 8 7 6 5 4 3 2 1

Acknowledgments

I would like to express my thanks to the Mrs. Giles Whiting Foundation for its generous support in the writing of this book. And, of course, to Dawn Seferian and Alice Martell.

This book is dedicated to
LEWIS BRINDLE

and to the memory of my grandmother,
MARY SLATTERY CALLAGHAN MAHER

Horror is something perfectly natural; the mind's *horror vacui*. A thought is taking shape, then suddenly it notices that there is nothing more to think. Whereupon it crashes to the ground like a figure in a comic strip who suddenly realizes that he has been walking on air.

— PETER HANDKE, *A Sorrow Beyond Dreams*

The beautiful title of this beautiful novel is taken from a passage in *A Sorrow Beyond Dreams*, Peter Handke's memoir of his mother and her dreadful life and painful dying, and it's a fitting and illuminating allusion in several ways. Like Handke's small masterpiece of sorrow and memory, *Walking on Air* is a postmortem narrative, a recapitulation. It's the survivor's story of one who did not survive, reminding us at the same time that, even if we survive, none of us gets out of here alive. It is also the story of the awful burden placed by the dying upon those who love them.

And here it departs from Handke's memoir and becomes something more. For, even though the complex character of the man at the center of Robert Jones's novel, William Addams, is flawed to a terrifying degree, especially in the way he inflicts his long, drawn-out dying upon Henry and Susan, the two people who love him most, the novel is free of complaint and judgment. The novelist, his book, establishes and demonstrates the moral standard that his characters, Henry and Susan, and his readers, you and me, must struggle to meet. As if it were a test of his friends and lovers and our moral meaning, William's slow dying forces his final caregivers to endure humiliation, endless frustration, even cruel victimization by this brilliantly manipulative and calculating, albeit charismatic and lovable, man—to the point where they almost wish for his death to come. No, not *almost*. Henry wishes William would hurry up and die. Susan wishes it, too. And so do we. And we are horrified by our wishes and suddenly find ourselves walking on air. And then, as soon as we realize where we are, we fall like cartoon characters to the ground, where everything final is undeniably real.

It's a custodian's story, a family story, in a way, because we all are likely someday to find ourselves either in Henry's position or in William's and in many cases both, and though the context is AIDS, the cause of death, let us say, that's not the point; that's not what it's about, any more than Camus's *The Plague* is about the plague. I don't think AIDS is mentioned by name even once in the entire novel. This is a moral fable, a universal story, realistic and postmodern only in the sense that it is set in a time and place—the late eighties, New York City—where people insist on denying the illness and dying that everywhere surround them, and where, as a consequence of that denial, it grows ever more difficult for them to help one another. The novel is, in that sense, a deeply moving, metaphysical wake-up call. And though Robert Jones, the man, was deeply ironic at practically every opportunity, his novel is not. It is centered on his profound affection for his characters and his refusal to judge them. Or us.

The author's biographical note on the flap of the 1995 edition of the novel says only that "R. S. Jones is the author of *Force of Gravity*. The recipient of a Whiting Writer's Award, he lives in New York City." But, of course, he was much more than that, and not just to those of us who knew and loved him. As will be clear to anyone who reads *Walking on Air* or his first novel, the equally brilliant *Force of Gravity* (the titles are as intricately linked as the novels), Robert was well on his way to becoming what we like to call an "important" writer. At the same time, however, he had become by the mid-nineties an important editor, at least to me and to every other writer whose work he labored over at HarperCollins. We were, or felt we were, like family to him. For most of us, Denis Johnson, Oscar Hijuelos, Richard Bausch, Francine Prose, Mark Doty, and half a dozen others of that same high-quality (and perhaps high-maintenance) crew, he was our smarter, more disciplined, more spiritually evolved brother.

He seemed to have ceased writing around that time, and though he resisted talking about his own fiction, preferring always to talk about his beloved writers' current work instead, I recall a couple of times when, between long stints of editing the work of others, he spoke offhandedly of trying to get a little of his own writing done at his weekend house on Long Island. So I don't believe he gave up writing altogether, but he clearly knew that, as long as he was a more than full-time editor, he would not be able to write another novel. There was no lack of inspiration or desire, no lack of energy. For Robert, it was a deliberate, conscious sacrifice, made as if somewhere down the line he would have all the time in the world to write his novels.

PART ONE

I have never been anywhere but sick. In a sense, sickness is a place, more instructive than a long trip to Europe and it's always a place where there's no company, where nobody can follow.

— FLANNERY O'CONNOR

His body terrifies him.

There are two of him: a mind he has learned to control and then that body. His mind is who he talks to at night when he cannot sleep, the intelligence that translates what the eyes see of the world outside. While the body lies flat and useless upon the bed, his mind levitates above it, flying from one corner of the room to another, or farther out, to other rooms, other houses, other countries of memory, even other planets, other stars. Without it, the body is nothing: the mind's appendage, its artificial limb.

His mind has trained the body to follow its commands: to sit, to stand, to lie down like a pet. He can flex its muscles, swing its arms, make it jump, contort it in almost any direction. Sometimes he likes to test the body's limits, to cut it, scrape it, bend its fingers until each one crackles with pain. But even then he is only marooned on its surface. He can truly know nothing but its skin, its hair, its visible scars, the blue blush of its veins. Underneath, the body is a mystery of vessels, muscles, bones, a whole galaxy of parts as secret as the darkest star shrouded in clouds of deadly gas. He sees photographs of it in x-rays, but they are like shadows to the whole, only a hint of its dangers.

The body has its own life. The body to the mind is like a Siamese twin born inexorably hooked to one integral part, but desiring only to cut itself off and live free of the other. When he is ill, the body becomes possessed by an alien, just as he has seen in countless movies. *Then there are three of him: the mind, the body, and the disease growing larger and larger until it joins the body as one. Together they are bigger, more powerful than his mind can ever be. He is helpless to stop them. When his doctors give him drugs, they are the weakest battalion. They are shooting in the dark.*

His body is a bomb.

His body terrifies him.

His mind he knows.

The house where William was raised was built of rough white stone set on 1,400 acres of dried grass and cracked earth marked off from the surrounding wilderness by split-rail fences and rock walls that stretched beyond the visible horizon in any three directions. His family's nearest neighbors lived so far away that the only lights to break the darkness at night were the moon and stars or occasionally a truck driving past on the road 570 acres below. Even after their land withered from drought, forcing William's father to accept a job in the nearest town, the family never considered selling. They were raised to believe in the magic of owning so much land that they could claim a separate country for themselves, a state within a state, which they imagined safe from any invasion.

Every summer their well dried up, and they were forced to import water from town in plastic jugs. Each member of the family was permitted one bath a week in rainwater collected in buckets hung from the eaves of the roof. The water was always clouded with rust from the aged cans and left a film gritty as blood on their skin. Their only electricity came from an ancient generator that kept the lights inside the house no brighter than the glow from the hurricane lamps they carried to bed at night. William was born with a fear of fire and so he learned to creep his way upstairs with his candle unlit. He slept badly, even as a child, knowing that there was no light to comfort him if he awoke afraid in the middle of the dark.

His family shared a telephone line with five others spread

across the mountain. His father had to drive twenty-two miles to get their mail at the nearest post office, a distance measured only after he left the rutted, two-mile drive through three padlocked gates that kept their property closed against trespassers. In the rainy season, the dirt road to their house crumbled like cake, making its fragile ruts unpassable even in a Jeep. During those months William and his father had to carry their provisions through mud deep as their shins and more treacherous than ice. With nothing to grasp onto, they slipped and fell so frequently that they had to crawl uphill dragging their packages behind. From November until February, William's mother and younger sisters ventured only as far as the top of the drive, where the ground remained firm and safe, greeting William and his father with cups of steaming coffee spiked with chocolate and the aroma of breakfast frying on the stove.

At night the only sounds William heard were the grunts and snorts of animals or the singing wings of insects or the strains of music broken with static from his mother's transistor radio. Sometimes in the daylight, when he played along the rocky network of paths circling the foothills behind his home, he was stopped cold in his tracks by the rattle of snakes searching for shade in the summer heat.

Their warning was the most terrifying sound in the world, not a rattle at all but an electrified hiss that stunned the air so completely that even the plants and the breeze seemed to stiffen and the insects to freeze in midflight. No matter how close the sound, William could never see the pale brown markings and black diamonds cut like tattoos into its scales as the snake coiled against the dirt and leaves of the path. Its hiss seemed to come from every direction above and below and behind him. His father could always see the snake clear as a beacon against the ground. He would reach for a stick from among the debris of dead trees along the path and snap it once, beheading the snake with a flick of his wrist.

William's mother saved the rattles in jelly jars on a shelf by the kitchen window, where they paled and hardened in the afternoon sun. She glued them to silver ovals for earrings or next to turquoise stones on belt buckles that were sold as souvenirs at a local store. His father nailed the carcasses to the highest rafters of the barn until they desiccated and fell to the ground, like cardinals' hats hung in the spires of a cathedral.

To earn a living, they raised chickens for eggs and pigs for meat, generations of animals kept in interlocking corrals behind the barn. Every Sunday before dawn, William's father would drag him awake to help with the slaughter.

It was always cold when they rose at four A.M., even in summer, and the light was blue and purple as bruises. Before they disturbed the pigs, William and his father would build a fire under the bathtub filled with rainwater that they kept outside the shed by the pens. Twenty years later, William could remember as clearly as if it were the day before the stench of the pens mingling with the steam rising from the water in the tub. It was so quiet that the flames snapped like triggers as he stoked the fire, the sparks bursting with the brilliance of fireworks as they flew about his face. To keep him safe, William's father told him that each spark carried a soul to heaven, and if he touched it, he would block its passage to paradise.

When the bathtub bubbled with heat, his father would rise and whisper, "It's time," patting the pocket of his coat that held a knife as he stalked through the gate into the pen. The moment the pigs heard the hinge squeak, they knew to be afraid. They would shuffle their hooves in unison and cower against the opposite fence, heaving with grunts. Even in the dark they would avert their eyes, as if, by looking away, they could not be seen and would not be chosen. The pigs could not have known that the day before, William's father had selected the one he planned to kill. Already its snout had been painted with a green fluorescent triangle that was impervious to water and mud. Under cover of darkness, his father would switch the flashlight on and off, on and off, until its beam hit upon the animal with the triangle glowing brighter than any of the other pigs' eyes.

William was always struck by the knowledge that if the animals had bonded into a group they could easily have overpowered any man. Together they weighed thousands and thousands of pounds. But blinded by the flashlight and fear, they did not sense their power. They huddled together terrified, straining against the outside rails of the pen until the wood bowed and cracked with the pressure. When William and his father jumped the branded pig, the others screamed as they scrambled away, their faces slapping against the mud. Sometimes during the rainy season, the smallest pigs would drown in puddles that formed near their trough. With the flashlight on, their gray stomachs shone out of the sludge like moons.

After William and his father had trapped the pig they wanted, the others would hurry to the far side of the pen, all their eyes watching, but not one of them would make a move. The marked one would let itself go with a wail, like a musical note held impossibly long. With his hands around its neck, William could feel the vibrations grow so strong that his skin hummed.

As William looked away, his father would slit a vein in the pig's throat as easily as he might top a carrot. All its muscles would flail against William's grip. It was so dark he could see nothing as he struggled but flickers of the fluorescent mark catching crazily in the arc of the flashlight. Soon the animal's cries would slow to a cough, and a greasy film would slip over its eyes. As the pig grew limp in his arms, William could immediately sense the others relax. They would hunt around for food or nudge each other with their snouts, as if nothing had happened. Then his father would switch the light off, rendering the triangle invisible against the stiff hairs of the dead pig's snout.

After the animal was dead, they carried the carcass to the tub and let it soak a while. William's job was to cover his hands to his elbows with rubber gloves and pull off the skin that was steamed free by the smoking water. The trick was to wait just long enough for the skin to loosen, but not so long that the meat began to cook. William was always amazed at how easily the flesh and bristled hair fell into his hands with hardly a tug, impermanent as clothes. With his father's help, he hung the stripped pig on a hook fastened to the top of the corral gate. While William held the flashlight, his father would cut from its neck to the bottom of its belly. With a whoosh its organs plopped from the wound like rubbery, unconnected objects, leaving nothing but pink flesh scarred with patterns of dried blood, distinct as whip marks. Once they had finished, they carried the body to a walk-in freezer built in the barn and laid it atop a pile of frozen pigs stacked like logs against the wall. When William paused at the door before switching off the light, row after row of fluorescent triangles glowed back at him out of the clouds of icy air.

With a practiced hand, it took two hours from the moment they lit the fire until they locked the door to the cold storage. After their work was done, William and his father would sit on the ground outside the pen where the other pigs grunted peacefully again. As they waited for the day to rise, William listened time and again to stories about his father's childhood on the ranch. Rarely did he mention the people who had lived with him there: his parents, his brothers, his neighboring aunts. Rather, his histories were always enlivened by natural catastrophes: never heartbreak, but the ruination wrought by frost; never the lives of children, but the deaths of litters born premature, of horses with stillborn foals, of albino chickens with scarlet eyes, of scorpions nesting in shoes, of tarantulas jumping as high as his knees, and of rats that leaped even higher when cornered by a gun; of months without water, years without electricity; of crops that bloomed and others that failed; of drought, bountiful rains, perfect summers, of blizzards scattered so infrequently over the years that they became as memorable as births.

William believed that his father chose those moments to talk because in the particular cast of predawn light, caught between the fall of the moon and the rise of the sun, their land appeared at its most perfect and untouched. He knew his father wanted to teach him the things he was born knowing: to kill cleanly and with little fuss; to judge the weight of an animal at auction from fifty feet away; to sense a change in the weather hours before it occurred; to know the perfect dampness of soil for planting; the way to irrigate a field with a system of hoses as intricate as the corridors of an ant's cave; to know the exact time to the minute by imperceptible changes in the position of the sun or moon. Even inside with the shades drawn, his father always knew the hour, as if he could see shadows of light thrown on the ground outside through the hard stone walls of his house.

William knew that his father tried to teach him because he wanted the ranch to continue in the family through the next generation and beyond. But from earliest childhood William hated every moment of his life there: the drafty rooms of the house, which made him swelter in summer and freeze in winter, the poisoned leaves growing from every rock and crevice, which made his skin fester and swell with running sores, the incessant sting and bite of insects, the fatigue from constant exertion that made even the simplest chore seem an impossible task, the isolation from a world beyond his immediate family, which he learned to dread like a sickness.

There was no escape, so he dreamed of nothing else, the way he now dreamed of health as a country far beyond his reach. At eighteen he set out for the East to discover the cities he had read about in books, places of dreams he viewed with a longing as reckless as that of explorers who once dreamed of crossing uncharted territories to see firsthand the mountains of China, or of stowaways who dreamed of treasures buried on islands rising out of turquoise seas.

He disappeared.

He disappeared as far as a man can go without losing his mind or changing his identity.

The first thing he did when he arrived in the East was to add a second "d" to his last name. Forever after he spelled it "Addams." Even twenty years later, he grew impatient with salespeople and reservation clerks who automatically wrote his name with a single "d," as if they meant to tie him to a life he had never been part of. To new people he met, he lied about his past. He chose cities he had never been to as the place of his birth, sometimes other countries. He chose ordinary office jobs for his parents; sometimes he had no parents at all, but an aged aunt who had adopted him during her twilight years.

He counted his life's beginning from the moment his feet hit the city streets. He loved the buzz of traffic, day or night, and the darkness lit by neon with the glow of purple moons. He never missed the chilly nights with stars so bright that every curve of deserted hill and jagged edge of rock remained visible. He slept with the television on and a lamp burning at the end of the hall so that there was light and sound no matter the hour he awakened. He took two baths a day in blasts of hot water and had his groceries delivered to his door by the local market. Whenever possible, he stayed inside when it rained.

Two decades after moving to the city, William had no idea if his parents were still living and professed no desire to know. Despite the life he had made for himself in the intervening years, he still traced many of his best qualities to his childhood on the ranch: his self-reliance, his physical strength, his gift for gardening, his ease with animals, his ability to maneuver a car on the most treacherous roads. But what remained most vivid to him was the shock he had felt each time his father finished with a pig, a sorrow not so much for the animal itself, but for how effortlessly something as simple as a kitchen knife could cut the throat of a living thing and leave it dead. Whenever he felt his skin, he thought of nothing but how easily it could be floated off in water. Or, when he felt the flutter of his heart, how simply it could be pried loose and dumped into a can.

When William left the hospital for the first time after he learned he was dying, he stood with his suitcase on the avenue, only five blocks from home. The landmarks around him still seemed familiar, but he felt as if he had stumbled into a newly dangerous place: all the people going by were onto something, some kind of secret, and nobody was telling him anything. He waved his arms to hail a cab to get away from there, but taxi after taxi drove past, shunning him, as if a fluorescent triangle glowed from his forehead, visible to everyone but him.

3

It began with a fever that would not end and a vague but persistent queasiness that could have been attributed to exhaustion, or the beginning of a cold, or changes in the weather. But season after season passed, and the only constant in William's life was that he never felt well. Sometimes better, sometimes worse, but never as he remembered he had lived before. For a year there was nothing to catch hold of, no concrete ailment that would manifest itself as a nameable disease, simply fevers or the red shadow of a rash that crawled over his body like a phantom: from his arms to his legs to his buttocks, his neck, then around to his chest, never lingering long in one place, but never completely leaving. Often a soreness in his joints or aches that stabbed his lungs before vanishing, sudden spasms in his muscles, week after week of fleeting nausea like what he imagined morning sickness to be.

He kept his concerns to himself, but sometimes he would say to his friends by way of explaining his listlessness, "I think I'm catching flu," and be reassured when none of them expressed their own good health. Everyone he knew usually claimed to be on the threshold of a minor illness or crippling fatigue. Maybe the same rashes crawled under their clothes; maybe the same aches flashed and faded under their skin. Never did they say, "I feel great!" when he asked how they were. And even on days when he was too tired to rise from bed, he found reason not to panic: too much stress, fitful dreams, an inadequate diet. He convinced himself that he had simply forgotten what it meant to feel normal.

You're no longer young, he often told himself, now that he was almost forty. *This is all a sign of age.* Still, one worry haunted him that couldn't be dismissed as part of his former life. Every morning when he took his temperature, the thermometer registered no lower than 99.8 degrees, even on his best days. More often it rose to 101, 102, 103, sometimes even higher, as the mercury cooked to the edge. No matter how many cold baths or pills he took or juices he drank or extra hours of sleep he stole from his schedule, the fever clung to him like a shadow. Never again did his body rest at the mark from which other people define themselves as healthy.

During the times his fever rocked him with chills, his fear grew purer, but still he delayed a visit to the doctor. *It's a waste of money,* he told himself, although for years he had thought nothing of running to the doctor with the slightest ailment. Invariably, the moment his resolve weakened and he made plans to call for an appointment, his fever would break to a tolerable level, his rash would fade, his nausea would vanish, and his energy rebound enough so that he could again drag himself through the day.

In the news every week he heard stories of plagues of disease, of poisoned reservoirs and seas, of insecticides that tainted food, of radioactive earth and rain and clouds of exhaust that infected the city on the wind. *It's the price of living in the modern world,* he would think when he stepped outside and was halted by a hacking cough. *You cannot be protected.*

He examined other faces on the street to compare pallors, carriages, gaits, to his. He made bets, bargains, wagers, every time he moved. *If my taxi makes three green lights in a row, then I will be well. If it does not rain tomorrow, I will be well,* and on and on. He was amazed at how many bets he won, enough for a lifetime of luck. But still he felt ill.

Ever since he had learned to read, William had kept a book on the table by his bed that described the symptoms of every known disease. Whenever he felt a twinge in his body, he would work backward from the list of symptoms and diagnose himself. He had always imagined the worst. When he had a headache, he imagined a creeping brain tumor. When his eyes were tired, he imagined a permanent blindness darkening his vision. When he wobbled from the flu, he imagined a disease wrecking his neurological system.

Each illness had come like a curse, and each time he visited the doctor feeling certain he would be told terrible news. He begged in his heart for his life. And each time the doctor proved him wrong, he felt an indescribable exhilaration, like a prisoner who has been granted a reprieve. His serenity would last for months, but then his vigilance would catch something, some minor twitch, and worry would set in again.

There had been times when he had known a peacefulness in being ill, even delight in having his parents enter his room day and night to care for him. He loved the feel of their hands on his brow, sticking from the dampness of his sweat, the sight of their forms in the dim light of the hallway, bent with whispers. He loved the attention of tests, the thrill of the cure, the cool steel of the doctor's stethoscope sliding across his skin: a touch as fond to him then as a lover's would be later. And maybe never to be surpassed.

The revelation of his body's frailty struck him profoundly, the way some people see Christ and are forever changed. How could he believe himself to be a potent force in the world when he had known fevers that attacked out of the blue to cripple his body and lay siege to his mind? Or waves of nausea that left him lying helpless on the floor? Any human plan could be rendered meaningless by the attack of a single, fleeting illness. He learned early to treat disease with the respect and vigilance due his most dangerous foe. Although he worried, on days when his parts moved perfectly, when his breath was bountiful and deep, when he had enough energy for a roomful of people, he knew a jubilation in his body he believed unmatched by anyone on earth. He took nothing for granted, not one day.

Even when he found it difficult to stand, he never gave in. He believed it necessary to train for the final illness. When he felt sick, he forced himself to work, to do his chores, to visit with friends, so that he would know how to function when the time came. As he went about his business, he would say to himself, *This is how it will be; this is how it will be*, so that he might grow accustomed to it, so that maybe later there would be no surprises.

But it had surprised him. When the doctor on duty gave him the news, she spoke so quickly that the words slipped by him. *Me? Me? Who? Who?* William thought as he struggled to understand. He remembered looking at his slippers by the bed, the flowers in a vase, the view outside the window, trying to ground himself in something familiar. He stared back at her dumbly, fixated by the thick ridge of her upper lip visible under a smear of pink lipstick that made her mouth appear misshapen and grotesque. The doctor appeared grateful and relieved that he hadn't made a scene. She made her exit quickly, promising to return in the morning, straightening the brim of her crushed velvet hat as if she were rushing to a cocktail party. It was six in the evening on a quiet winter's day when she told him.

After the doctor had gone, William felt a panic such as he had never dreamed possible. He tried to shake it off like a hex. He telephoned his friends as if nothing had changed, hoping that stories from other lives might insulate him by their very ordinariness, as if somehow they might return him to the blessed circle of life from which he had been expelled. But the more he listened, the more he could only think, *This cannot be mine; this cannot be mine*, until he thought he might die, then, from hopelessness.

He settled down to sleep just as he had every night for forty years before. He curled around his pillow like a fetus. But when he closed his eyes, he felt as if he had been dropped from a plane. And when he hugged the pillow tighter against him, it was as if he were trying to wrap his body around all that plummeting air.

Nothing had stopped him, nothing had held him back.

When he was young and hypnotized by fevers, William used to think a lot about dying, but no matter how bad he felt, he could never imagine the exact shape of the end. Some of his illnesses had brought him close to death; a few times accidents had brought him even closer. Once, driving on a rain-slicked highway, he saw a car headed toward him in the wrong direction that did not veer. Once, diving alone in the ocean, he ran out of air one hundred feet below the surface. Each time reality had stopped like a breath, leaving nothing but a fear screaming through his body that obliterated everything he knew. He had time to think, *I can't believe this is happening*, and to repeat it again like a prayer. But nothing had made it any more real, and nothing had made it any less true.

For as long as he could, William pretended nothing had changed, because he knew there would be too much time later when it would be impossible to forget. He kept his visits to his doctor, his appointments for tests, secret with the vigilance of an extramarital affair. He had no idea what the disease would mean for his life, but already he knew that the times before had been nothing: the car had stopped; he had swum to the surface; his after-life had continued as before. But when he planned for the day he would tell his friends about his condition, he imagined saying, *Picture yourself trapped under the sea without air or hitting a skid pinned by those oncoming lights. Then take it even further: imagine that moment never ending; imagine living an eternity locked in that one grip of fear.*

When the moment came, he had no energy for explanations. He only needed help. He awoke one morning with a pressure on his lungs so heavy it felt as if elephants danced upon his chest.

"I am dying," he said to everyone he called, words that still remained mysterious to him, but by which he admitted he had reached the end of the world.

4

Henry raced for the lobby, juggling his brief-
case and a suitcase packed with William's mail, a clean change of
clothes, morning editions of the city's three newspapers, and a
Danish bought from his favorite bakery on the corner. He stepped
through the cool shadows of the hospital's towers into its maze of
tiled walls. Everywhere about him was the low hum of voices, the
quick squeak of rubber-soled shoes, and a repellent, pickled smell
that made him choke. He quickened his pace. He had only thirty
minutes until he had to leave for school.

Henry spent every morning before classes and every evening
long past visiting hours keeping watch in William's room. He had
kept his vigil for so long that he had come to tell the time of day
by the changes in the nurses' shifts. He imagined them charting
William's temperature, changing his IV, or counting the beats of
his pulse, even after he had returned to his apartment, miles from
the hospital, and was trying to forget what would become of him
now that William was dying.

When William was first admitted to the hospital, he was so ill
that Henry had thought nothing of his own life. Somehow he
found the energy and clarity to make a thousand impossible decisions about William's care. Now that the first crisis had passed, he
felt the strain of the last weeks creeping up on him. William was
due to be discharged the next day, but Henry didn't believe he
would last long on the outside. Although he wanted to believe that
his friend would recover, he worried that the longer William
lived, the more the hospital would become his home. Henry

needed to use this small remission as a chance to go away. He had arranged for their friend Susan to take William home. He had even cleaned William's apartment and stocked the refrigerator with food. But that morning when he called to break the news, William had slammed down the telephone.

William stood half a foot taller than Henry and weighed fifty pounds more, but the force of his character made him appear even larger than he was, somehow gigantic. His voice boomed, nearly a shout, whether he was angry or stating a kindness. The floor shook when he walked in and out of rooms. Even his furniture seemed to have been chosen for its massive scale: dark, wooden bookcases towering to the ceiling, overstuffed chairs, enormous rugs, a bed large enough for three men that required specially made sheets. And though Henry sometimes flinched before William spoke, as if warding off a blow, he also knew that no one in the world would ever be more loyal or would take on his battles with as much vigor as his own.

Henry tried to remind himself of that as he stepped out of the elevator doors and fixed a smile on his face. He hoped that if he entered cheerfully, he might subvert William's mood. But when he placed the suitcase on the floor and bent to kiss him hello, William glared up at him stonily. He sat in a chair by the window, waiting for the nurse to change his bedding, staring at the radiator as if it were his only company.

I'm still going away, Henry promised himself as he arranged the flowers in a vase by the window. He unwrapped the pastry and placed it within William's reach, resisting the urge to assist the nurse. As she expertly folded the sheet around each corner, it became translucent in spots. After she helped William to his feet and rolled him onto the mattress, he looked as if he were sprawled on a bed of ice.

When he was at the hospital, Henry wished the revolving

guard of attendants would continue forever: nurse after nurse greeting him as he held fast by William's bed. He dreaded being the only person in the room if William took a turn for the worse. Whenever the nurses left them alone and William grew too quiet, Henry would pinch his arm until his eyes popped open like a mechanical doll's, just to be certain he still breathed.

After so long together in the hospital room, sometimes hours passed when they had nothing to say. In the silence, Henry often had time to think about how the task of being William's keeper had befallen him. He knew that it had happened partly by default, partly by the compromises single friends make when they have no parents or spouses to usher them through trouble. But these reasons did not explain the extent to which his life had become saturated with William's. Of all the people he knew, Henry understood the least about his relationship with William. Everyone who did not know them well assumed they were lovers, but their friendship had always been something more, and less, than that.

They met by accident.

That night Henry had almost not gone out at all. He had left his apartment late, after midnight, feeling reckless when a man he was seeing failed to call. A mutual acquaintance introduced him to William only a few minutes after he walked through the door of his favorite bar. Henry had noticed him from time to time before, always standing alone with a forbidding expression and a loner's air, so he was surprised at William's spontaneous friendliness. They wandered outside to enjoy the first warm evening of that particular spring, drinking their beers as they perched on a parked car, listening to the catcalls from the barred windows of the women's prison on the opposite corner and the rude shouts of passersby on the highway across the meridian.

At the time, Henry believed he had never conversed so effortlessly with another man. It wasn't until later that he realized he had revealed everything there was to know about his own life, while William had offered almost nothing at all. William said he was a stockbroker and lived only a short distance from the bar; whatever else Henry learned about his past came later, mostly from gossip shared by Susan's and William's older friends. But that night Henry could not stop himself from talking, trying to forget, as the hour grew close to four A.M., his morning classes at the university more than one hundred blocks away. He didn't have money for cab fare. Late at night, it took a dangerous hour on the subway to get there, but still he talked until the metal grates screeched down over the door at last call.

William had cocked an eye as if to say "You coming?" and Henry had followed, detouring along the stretch of crumbling piers at the river's edge, then on past shuttered warehouses and meatpacking stores where prostitutes drifted in and out of the darkened corners. William seemed more comfortable on the street than anyone Henry had ever met, impervious to harm, not flinching even as they walked past packs of sinister boys huddled on the unlit streets. He trailed William eagerly, not knowing his intentions, but not wanting to leave. He was mesmerized by him. A decade older, William seemed to represent a confidence and easy familiarity that Henry coveted for his own.

At the door to William's building, Henry followed him in. He was stunned by the opulence of the apartment. Most of Henry's friends then were college students who used plastic milk cartons for bookcases and old boards balanced over filing cabinets for desks. They slept on sofa beds in studio apartments or on bunks in dormitory rooms. The walls of William's living room were hung with photographs of his friends. The red light on his answering machine blinked with messages. He seemed unusually beloved.

Henry had been so blinded by his studies that he had forgotten what a real life could be like. *I want to be part of this*, he remembered thinking, for it seemed as if William had a whole world and history that he might be willing to share.

That night was the only time they had sex, an event so silent and perfunctory that Henry always suspected that William assumed he was doing him a favor. He didn't bother explaining that his pleasure in meeting William had nothing to do with sex. At that time in his life, Henry went home with almost anyone who asked, as much from politeness as from desire. Sex was simply something he did, like eating or breathing or sleeping.

In the morning, William drove him to school. He called the next day to invite Henry to dinner. Succeeding days brought more invitations, including one for a weekend at his house at the beach. Gradually they moved closer and closer into each other's orbit until, without a decision being made, Henry felt almost as if he belonged to William.

He couldn't remember if he had ever wanted more from William, but years ago he had stopped questioning their bond. Over time, William became the only person he knew besides his family who seemed indispensable to his life. And yet, his secretiveness and hard reserve brought an edginess to their relations that often made Henry question where he stood.

William never mentioned his family. At Christmas and Thanksgiving he stayed home alone, refusing all invitations. He seemed truly to despise any reminder of what family life was like. "Friends are family," he said time and again, as if it were an explanation.

Like everyone else he knew, Henry told his friends secrets he would never dare to share with his parents. His family knew only the barest outline of his life. They had visited the school where he taught and had slept at his apartment, but they had little sense of his colleagues at work, his problems with students, the books he read, the men he loved. But neither did his friends have a true sense of his family. Henry never admitted to the mysterious ties that pulled him home every holiday, although he was almost thirty, or to his pleasure in his parents' weekly telephone calls. Although their conversations touched only the surface of his life, they deepened his confidence that his family would provide him with a haven no matter how low or degenerate he became. He had his own life and his family had theirs, yet the two circles somehow profoundly intersected, and Henry believed that whatever security he knew in the world stemmed from that unarticulated bond.

He could not believe that William never wondered what had become of his family, even in the idle curiosity of daydreams, when a person suddenly remembers a friend unseen for decades. But if he ever pried, William shrugged and let silence fall until the subject was changed. Henry worried that he, too, could be banished completely from William's mind if he ever displeased him. He suspected a secret hardness to William's character if he could so completely leave a whole life behind and never seem to care.

For a long time he didn't take William seriously when he said "Friends are family." But after William became ill, he began to address Henry more directly. He would say, "You are my family," and Henry grew to feel responsible for every detail of his life. When he was alone, he couldn't rid his thoughts of William, as if his every move were orchestrated from the hospital ward, in the way that some people believe they are guided by the hand of God. Henry began to fear he could never leave William. He began to feel stifled by the doctors who telephoned him at home with decisions about William's treatment and by the nurses who whispered information in the hallway about his condition. Now the rules had changed. At the top of William's medical chart it was written in ink that Henry was his next of kin.

William switched on the television news as the nurse left the room, keeping his eyes riveted to the screen. Henry sat in the opposite chair, staring out the window. He sneaked a peek at his watch while William's attention was diverted. There were only ten minutes until he had to leave for school. He listened to stories of storms threatening from the west, of a crack in a water main ruining the morning rush hour, of a student shot dead on a base-ball field, of a new scandal in the mayor's administration, hoping that some item would spark a conversation between them. But every time he started to speak, he stopped himself. William didn't care about weather, crime, or scandal when he felt himself to be more bereft than any stranger on the news.

Henry was sorry for William, but he also missed him. He was losing his best friend. One pleasure in their friendship had always been the freedom with which he discussed any subject that en-tered his mind. Before he was ill, William had given the best advice Henry had ever known: better than his teachers, his par-ents, his therapist, his other friends. He hoped, in time, that they could get those conversations back, but Henry had not yet learned the knack of speaking naturally while making it appear that noth-ing was more important than William's disease.

"Come on, William," he said at last. "Isn't there anything you want before I go?"

"A miracle cure," William growled. "A run in the park. A body not scarred by tumors."

Henry cringed. He considered shouting a list of all the things he had done for weeks on end without complaint: the hours he had spent organizing William's bills, keeping in touch with his office, arranging a schedule of visitors so that William was never alone. He knew that no one else among their friends would tolerate the demands he accepted as a matter of course. *Why don't I just walk out and let him stew?* he thought as he watched William turn serenely back to the television screen.

"I'm going," he said, trying to keep the tremor from his voice. He looked out the door into the hallway filled with scores of departing visitors. Nothing prevented him from picking up his briefcase and joining them. *I have a whole life to get back to,* he thought. *Classes to teach, articles to write, friends to see.*

He did not move.

Henry wanted to believe that without his help William would starve miserably in his apartment, that his doctors would abandon him, his telephone would be disconnected, his bank accounts would be overdrawn, his electricity would be shut off, but he knew it wasn't true. William would only find someone to replace him.

Henry wondered if there was a moment when he had actually chosen the position he now held with William, not consciously so much as naturally, the way two magnets connect. William had usurped his life, but how good had it been before? Had it been more than he remembered? Nights of pacing anxiously in his apartment, waiting for the telephone to ring; nights of staying at school fiddling with tasks that had no urgency; nights when he thought restlessness would make him jump out of his skin.

From across the bed William met his gaze in a way Henry remembered from a game he had played as a child where he raced into the path of an oncoming boy: the first to jump away had been the one to lose. Usually Henry flinched, but once he ran straight on, refusing to give in, and smashed his head so badly that he had to spend three days in the hospital. His young friends had celebrated his bravery, but Henry was never sure exactly what victory he had won.

William was convulsed by a racking cough. His hands flapped about his face, wildly; thick sprays of white spittle shot from his mouth and landed on the sheet like fog. Even as his body shuddered, he pinned Henry with an unrelenting glare. If William called his bluff, Henry imagined spending day after miserable day in the months ahead trying to go about his life, not worrying about William. Either the next day or two weeks or two months from then, he knew he would be the one to call. He blinked to signal his surrender, wiping an imaginary cinder from his eye. "Please, William," he said, pulling hard at the lash. "How about something I can do?"

William switched off the news and lay back on the bed. Henry tried not to read the expression on his face as a smirk. He stood ready to rush out onto the street to get William anything he wanted. He could take a cab to work and buy some extra time.

"Tell me something I don't know," William said, his voice muffled by the pillow propping the left side of his face.

Henry sat down. "Well, let's see," he said, happily. He racked his brain for some detail that would please William, something simple and to the point. "The speed of light is 189,282.5 miles per second," he said at last.

"That fast?" William laughed. "How'd they measure that last half mile?"

"That's nothing," Henry said. "Did you know our nearest galaxy is so far away that its light has taken two million years to reach us? Two point two million to be exact. Think about it. The light we see started coming at us long before the first man even walked the earth. I love this shit."

William laughed again. He picked up the Danish and took a

bite. He unfolded the newspaper and slid onto his side with his face to the wall. Through the slit in his gown, Henry saw a spray of strawberry-colored spots, round as nickels, dotting his back. They had not been there the day before.

He moved closer to the bed, resisting the urge to reach out and trace his finger around the spots. Instead he patted the smooth sides of his briefcase. "Anything you want to know about supernovas, white dwarfs, and the death of stars? I've got it all in here."

"Maybe not today," William said. "Sounds pretty violent."

"Tonight then."

"If you're free."

"Of course I'm free," Henry said. He leaned down to kiss him good-bye. Up close, William's skin was grooved and lined, like pale slate. Even the blond stubble of his beard had changed, grown yellow and stiffly curled, like dried moss. "Maybe I don't have to go away," he added. He could wait until William was settled at home. There were sure to be a few weeks before an emergency returned him to the hospital. He could steal some time then.

William looked up with crumbs of pastry plastered to his lips. His breath had a sour, cheesy smell. "Maybe we can go away together soon. Take a trip to the beach and visit the house. Forget about all this," he said, waving a hand at the table by the bed stacked with paper cups and a plastic pitcher of water. "Drink out of real glasses again."

"I don't know if I can," Henry said, his voice trailing off as he took in the empty bags of intravenous fluids on the floor, the sealed plastic box of William's contaminated waste, the heart monitor machine with electrodes hanging like tentacles against the wall. He couldn't conceive how they would ever be able to forget the hospital or anything that went with it.

"Fine," William said, slamming the newspaper against the

table so hard that cups flew into the air, landing on the linoleum with hollow pops. "Go alone. Go now."

"No, no," Henry said, hugging William's fist to his chest. "That wasn't what I meant. Of course I want to be with you. Especially there. It's your house."

"Not for long," William said, pulling his hand free and sliding it under the sheet. "Not if you're good."

5

It's getting harder for me to win, William thought nervously as he watched Henry scurry out the door. He knew he was close to exasperating him beyond repair, but he couldn't stop himself. At night he made lists of errands for Henry to do the following day, short-term things, to ensure that he had a reason to return. Sometimes he asked for music, sometimes for exotic cheeses to pad his weight, sometimes for magazines found only in the university bookstore at the far end of town. Sometimes he mused out loud about the plans he had made for after his discharge, hopeful things, to play on Henry's sympathy: plant tulips in his garden, take courses at night to perfect his French, travel around the world. But sometimes, when he was feeling most desperate that Henry might be slipping away, he couldn't resist mentioning the house.

William had bought the house near the ocean ten years before. When he had first come to the city, he had never wanted to leave, not even on weekends. He had learned the character of every street, reading every local history he could find, until each neighborhood became as distinct as a separate country. Over time his obsession cooled, like a new phase in a romance. He began venturing out beyond the city's borders, especially in summer when the streets grew hot and dangerous, driving the highways and back roads along the coast until he was stopped by the last spit of land: two huge, rocky cliffs marking a channel to the vast, open sea.

William began to dream of owning a home there, sixty miles from his apartment, but not so far that its remoteness echoed the desolation he had hated at his family's ranch. He saved for years until he had enough money to buy a large, decrepit house on the outskirts of a small village, the last stop on the train. From the back windows, he could see his neighbors' roofs and an alley lined with cars. But from the front door, the broad expanse of lawn and the thick, peaked trees gave the illusion of a place cut off from living things. From the upper floors, he could look past the branches to the ocean a quarter mile away, the roll of each wave white and distinct, but muffled by the distance, breaking softly through his windows while he slept.

The first winter he replastered rooms and stripped layers of paint from the moldings and stairs until the wood returned to a dark, polished gleam. In spring he planted the gardens and re-seeded the lawn. In summer he dug a swimming pool and tiled it with black ceramic squares. In autumn he reshingled the exterior walls and hung new shutters by the windows on all three floors. Within a year, he had made the perfect home. Its existence made every hope and dream he had ever possessed seem real. It was as much a part of him as any organ or limb.

In recent years, William believed that Henry had come to love the house as much as he did, spending hours worrying over the gardens, cleaning debris from the pool, feeding the squirrels and birds from long wooden troughs of seed outside the living room window. Whenever Henry visited, he packed photographs and books from his own apartment and set them on the shelves of the guest room, as if to make the space more completely his own.

Soon after he became ill, William offered to leave Henry the house in his will. Henry lived in a four-hundred-square-foot studio apartment in a marginal neighborhood near his school. He was dedicated to his students, but he barely made ends meet on his salary. He rarely had money for dinners out, and never for vaca-tions, unless William paid. He would never own anything unless he changed careers. By promising him the house, William wanted to reward his loyalty with something Henry could never buy, but he also hoped that telling him early might give Henry another reason to stay around.

For no matter how much of his care Henry assumed, William could never fully trust him. He was stunned at how quickly his life had dwindled to that hospital room with Henry as his most constant companion. Friends with other lives visited in the evenings, but they approached him as if they had been told to identify a body. As they neared his bed, they turned to Henry and relayed their messages through him, like people helpless in a foreign language.

William had begun to keep score in his head of the number of telephone calls he received every day. At first twenty, then ten, now sometimes only five. Three weeks before, his room had been so crowded during evening visiting hours that his friends had to pull in extra chairs from the lounge across the hall. Most nights lately, there was room to spare.

The sicker he became, the more William worried that there was a mystery to blood ties he had never understood that transcended the love any friend could offer. He knew many people who had abandoned their lovers, their apartments, everything they had become, at the last possible moment and gone home to their families to die, as if the life they'd led in the interim had only been a game. He had heard countless times that even the aged called out for their mothers in the throes of death, as if from first to last the mother was the one essential, irreplaceable thing. As a boy, William remembered pricking his finger with his best friend, Hugh. "Blood brothers," they would say as they watched the droplets merge, as if to render the bond of friendship something deeper than it could ever be on its own, as if a brother would be more vigilant, more loyal, than a friend could ever be.

William didn't know if he questioned Henry's faithfulness because he doubted his own, or if he had forfeited a security in leaving home, some natural acceptance of duty, which made family relationships more enduring than those a person could ever have with his friends. "You are my family," William said over and over to everyone he knew, repeating the phrase to himself when he dared not say it aloud, as if he could bewitch his friends into believing it was true.

He rose from bed and touched his slippered feet to the floor. As he stood, bright bubbles of light popped around his head. He inched his way to the window and leaned on the sill, looking at the street fourteen stories down. The windows of his room made a solid wall of glass, so he heard no sirens, no honks of traffic, no curses of pedestrians, nothing but the rattle of carts in the hallway beyond. It was as if he had been sealed within a glass box. He saw taxis pull up to the curb and drive away, small yellow squares of color. Scores of people filed through the hospital entrance, their heads small and round as pins. He was mesmerized by their quickness, the way they scurried in and out of the door like ants from a nest. From that height, it was impossible to believe that any of those figures had their own life or the troubles that went with it.

Although his view was partially obscured by the hospital tower, he believed he could see the flashing blue lights of the movie marquee on the corner by his apartment. At a run he could be home in five minutes flat, yet up there, his life seemed light years away.

In the morning Susan would come to take him back. His discharge left him sick with dread. He worried that his friends would find it easier to forget him once he was home. After a person left the hospital, everyone assumed his problems were over, but William didn't know how to convey that his were only beginning.

If he were able to choose, he would stay in the hospital forever, caught in that twilight between life and death where he needed no identity beyond his disease. He would miss the striped uniform of the hospital dressing gowns, the faceless nurses who attended him shift after shift, even the blandness of the institutional food arriving promptly at the appointed hour. One day became another, no matter how ill he felt: he arose at six A.M., when an aide drew his blood, and lay awake until eight P.M., when his last visitor was asked to leave. Back home, he would have to become something more than a patient, but he could never go back to being the person he had been before. His doctors had pronounced him out of danger, the most he could hope for, since there would never be a cure, but that only meant that the danger was sleeping inside him: haunting his body, like the ghost of a twin.

What will I do? he wondered in real confusion. His plans for the week ahead included lunch with Henry, two doctor's appointments, and a visit to his office. He couldn't imagine how he would work, see his friends, make plans for a future. Even slipping on his clothes would feel different, as if he were donning a disguise. For weeks he had tried to summon the courage he had found as a teenager to abandon everything familiar and remake his life without ever looking back. But sickness was different: being born into dying was like being the first person to walk the earth. There was no one to teach him. His life had less shape to him now than the feeblest of dreams.

The first summer after he bought his house in the country, William gave a party and invited ten of his friends. One night they got drunk after dinner and challenged each other to swim out into the sea at night.

William didn't join them. The water made him nervous even in daylight. He sat safely on the beach while his friends stripped and ran yodeling into the surf. Every few minutes he saw a foot kick into the air as one of them dove under a wave. There was no other sign that they had not been carried completely out to sea. The moment they lost themselves in the waves, the sound of the water smothered their voices. Even if they had called for help, William could not have heard them.

Despite his fear, he became obsessed with how it must feel to swim into the sea at night. Just before the end of the summer, he sat alone on a piece of driftwood for a long time to gather his nerve. Then he began to walk slowly out.

As he dove underneath a wave and immersed his body, he was surprised at how welcoming the water felt, so much warmer than the air. He swirled his arms and legs about tentatively, letting the current move him along like any piece of debris.

He began to relax. There in the moonlight, he watched the waves gather strength in the distance and roll inland, one after another, like hundreds of white fists saluting over the water. Each lifted his body up, only to set it down, again and again, until he thought he might sleep in the buoyancy.

Before he swam back to shore, he dove once more under the waves and touched the bottom. He opened his eyes. He felt the water break above him, maybe the way a blind person senses a change in motion, because when he looked around, he was held by the purest, swirling blackness. He kicked his legs and stretched out his arms, until his fingers dug into the sand. The water blew him about, weightlessly. Each shift in the tide, each gentle movement of the waves, held him suspended in the darkness a few feet below the surface. He concentrated on loosening every joint and muscle so that no part of his body fought the subtle ripples of current carrying him along so lightly that he felt himself become part of the water. He wanted to give himself over to it entirely, to relax his jaw and let the sea flow in and out of his mouth like air.

He pulled his legs to his chest and bunched into a ball. He opened his mouth and breathed deeply. The water shot into his throat like an arm jammed down his lung. In his panic, he became aware for the first time of how he was tossed about invisibly in all that dark water and how live things brushed against his flesh, and how he had no sense of where the surface was or where the shore might lie beyond it.

He flailed through the water as if he were scrambling up an embankment that couldn't support his weight. He was too desperate to breathe to choreograph his strokes, so he punched his arms into the darkness and crawled upward through the black spaces until he burst his head into the night air.

The surface of the water shone like phosphorescent foam, greenish white, seemingly radioactive, in the glow of the moon. It was impossible to distinguish the lights of the ships anchored at sea from those in the few lit houses nestled behind the dunes. He believed for a moment that he might never make it back, but he curled himself into the crest of the first large wave and rode it inland until his body scraped against the shore.

He lay panting, staring at the pockets of air bubbling up in the wake of each wave, as if the sand itself breathed. With his face pressed close against the ground, he could see no farther than a few feet away. When he pivoted his eyes and adjusted to the short range of vision, it was as if he were peering through a microscope, so separate and clear did everything seem. Each particle of sand was a different shade of brown or white or black, some the size of tiny pebbles, some thin as a layer of skin.

As it grew lighter, William watched insects skate in front of him, their transparent bodies sidestepping the troughs and indentations looming in the sand. They flattened themselves against the beach as each wave thundered upon them, then shook out their limbs and moved on, only to flatten themselves again as another wave rumbled near. As William lay there, scores of insects traveled past him in this manner, flying across the sand, then crouching in advance of the waves before skating off again, as if they had no memory of what had just happened. They went on like that, forgetfully, gracefully, until they skirted out of sight.

Often after he became ill, William thought about the night when he had opened his eyes under the water and felt the surf breaking overhead and the invisible pull of the current dragging him down, and how he had come to feel the same way now, even when it was light, even when he wasn't alone, even when his feet were planted firmly on the ground.

6

Susan flicked a cigarette onto the grass as she raced across the quadrangle. Her breath came in little gasps, but she patted the cigarette pack in her coat pocket, reassured. Although smoking was forbidden in William's room, she couldn't face visiting him without a full supply. When he behaved badly, she sneaked into the bathroom to steal a puff, choking back her impatience with thick clouds of smoke.

She rushed through the revolving door at the hospital's entrance, waving to the guard on duty as she made her way to the elevator bank. As she entered the car, her finger rose reflexively to the button for William's floor, but she pulled it back. She needed a few minutes to collect herself before she retrieved him. When she had called earlier that morning to arrange a time to take him home, he had let loose with venom and fear, claiming he was starving and abandoned, denouncing a custodian who had left his walls splattered with blood. He threatened to sue as he usually did, demanding that Susan advocate his cause with the hospital administrator.

Like everyone who knew him, Susan dreaded William's rages. Even when he was healthy, his anger had seemed personal and pointed. If he railed against the state of the government or a delay on the subway or a drop in his investments, his friends felt responsible for the failures of the presidency or the transit system or the disarray in the stock market. Sometimes his fury arose from a pure, moral conscience, but sometimes it was mixed with the fervor of a crank, leaving everyone uncertain how to respond.

Today Susan had no energy for battles. She pushed the button for the basement cafeteria instead. She bought coffee from a vending machine and joined a table of maintenance workers and a shame-faced nurse with fingers yellowed from nicotine. They shared a single turquoise ashtray piled high with butts.

From her corner, she watched groups of green-suited surgeons, secretaries, security guards, orderlies eating their meals. Small clusters of nervous couples sat silently clutching paper cups of coffee. Over the loudspeaker she heard the light, melodious tone of a woman paging doctors in a ceaseless stream of names: "Dr. Singer, Dr. Linden, Dr. Goldman, Dr. Pearl, Dr. Bellman," the voice chanted, as if calling attendance. Suddenly, in the same calm tone the woman called "Dr. Blue" twice, adding "Room 314" seemingly without urgency, but Susan knew from years of visiting hospitals that "Dr. Blue" was code for a patient in critical distress. Within seconds a woman set down her cup and ran, a stethoscope banging from her blazer pocket.

Susan drank in the sharp, medicinal smells mingling with the odor of simmering food. She closed her eyes, savoring it, mesmerized by the loudspeaker, the rattle of plastic trays, the whispered tones of her companions, the electric hum of fluorescent lights, the clank of coins in the vending machines, feeling so contented that she forgot William and his problems, fourteen floors away.

Susan owed her life to hospitals. As a child she had been diagnosed with a rare form of leukemia that killed more people than were ever cured. She learned afterward that twice her doctors had given her up for dead. But after months of chemotherapy and radiation she recovered, remembering little of her ordeal except a sweaty delirium and tissues seared by irradiated burns.

She had thrived in the hospital, taking strength from her doctors' and nurses' care, from her parents' untiring love. She had emerged from her illness much stronger than her peers, more fearless about her life. She never failed to bless her luck. Death had meant little to her beyond the stories of heaven her mother whispered as she kept a vigil by her bed. She wondered if she would feel the same calm now if the disease returned to haunt her life, as it did William's. As a child, she hadn't understood everything she was about to lose. When her own time came, she hoped her belief in God would temper her fear, but she kept that part of her life hidden, especially from William, who treated her weekly attendance at church as a defect of character, like a compulsion for shopping or a sexual quirk.

It was astonishing to her, but she had been friends with William for twenty years. He had been her neighbor in his first apartment in the city, a runaway, half starved and all alone. Susan had been young, too, just out of college, yet she immediately embraced him with a maternal flair. She ushered him through college, through the beginning of his career, through countless love affairs and schemes, keeping watch until he made his life his own.

At the time it seemed like nothing, the days they spent together that turned so easily into years. Only lately had Susan realized that she had known William longer, and at a closer distance, than any friend alive. There had been periods of estrangement since, often lasting for months at a time, and Susan had come to believe that their occasional fractiousness arose in part from such long familiarity. Having known William first and best, she was the only person from whom he could never hide.

Never before or since had Susan met anyone with a greater drive to succeed, a peculiar determination that made even his moments of leisure seem part of a larger plan. He had arrived in the city with a knapsack of clothes and his grandmother's wedding ring, stolen from a sock in his mother's dresser the night before he left. The money he received from the pawnbroker paid his rent until he got settled, although he found a job as a clerk in a grocery store by the end of his second day.

William won scholarships to every school to which he sought admission. He studied hard, making up for an ordinary intelligence with a tenacity that others saw as brilliance. He rarely slept more than four hours a night. Despite the impressive library he had collected over the years, Susan never saw him read anything other than magazines and newspapers, or paperback books about murder and other crimes, which he hid in a drawer at home.

At school he concentrated on subjects that would serve him well: economics, accounting, finance, tax law. For years he worked three jobs, living off a meager salary and hoarding his other income. After graduating from college, he went to work in a brokerage firm, where he remained for fifteen years. He mastered the stock market the way some people master a foreign language, and he applied to his own assets everything he learned from managing strangers' money. By the time he was thirty, he was living off his interest.

His secretiveness grew, the more confident and successful he became. At eighteen, William's imposing size, his resonant voice, his reticence, which hid a deeper immaturity, had made him appear to be an older man. But once he settled into his career, he never seemed to age. Until he became ill, he could have passed for a decade younger than his years. His skin remained glistening and smooth, strangely unlined, even as Susan saw pouches form under her own eyes. His hair was streaked with gold, even in winter, like someone who has spent too much time in the sun. She suspected it was dyed.

He made friends in abundance, but rarely let them leave their separate worlds. Once a year he invited former lovers, friends from school, colleagues from work, tricks from the bar, to a party celebrating the beginning of summer, first at his apartment in the city, later at his house at the beach. Although Susan liked many of the people she met at these gatherings, she never seemed to see them again until the following year.

Few of them were in evidence now. She had recognized some men in suits or leather jackets coming and going in William's room his first week in the hospital, but already it was clear that she and Henry would bear the burden of his care. She didn't know if William had discouraged the others from visiting, or if the distance he maintained, even from his closest friends, made it impossible for them to know how to behave now that he found himself in trouble.

Still, that very elusiveness had always been part of his appeal. His real warmth and affection seemed at odds with his underlying isolation, just as the independent spirit Susan admired was another side of his caginess and emotional reserve. Because of her own awkwardness in social situations, she was often quietly annoyed by William's ability to seduce everyone he met. His holding back seemed only to make people more eager to know him better. Even acquaintances eventually learned that he had left his parents when he was eighteen and had never spoken to them again. He had confessed the bare details of his flight the first week after Susan met him, but since then his teenaged guilelessness had been replaced by an air of more calculated mystery. He seemed to assume that his history would be shared by others in whispers, as though he had endured a tragedy too terrible to be spoken aloud. He allowed rumors to be spread unchecked by acquaintances who claimed confidences Susan knew William never would have shared.

After he announced one day that he had found a house he wanted to buy, something changed in him. By the end of every week, he seemed desperate to escape the city, when before he had never wanted to leave. He took more time off from his job. The life he had worked so hard to achieve began to seem a diversion from the place where he truly wanted to be.

The first year, Susan spent nearly every weekend at the house, helping with renovations. William settled happily into their new routine. He pressured her to leave earlier and earlier on Friday afternoons, and so delayed their departure on Sundays that she returned to the city exhausted, after midnight, unprepared to see clients in her real estate office the next day. She began to resent devoting her time to perfecting something that wasn't hers. William even designated a suite on the third floor as Susan's rooms and installed a separate phone number for her, but this gesture did not stop the house from coming between them like a lover. While she had cherished weekends in town with William, meeting him most Saturdays for lunch and Sundays for early dinner, she also loved the city for her own reasons. Her family had lived there for eighty years. If she had wanted to escape, she could have bought a house of her own.

She began to invent business trips, important meetings, bouts with flu, so that she didn't have to go with William. She found herself replaced by men more willing to do his bidding. Henry was only the last and most enduring, and her favorite among William's tribe. If she sometimes now grew nostalgic for the unbroken intimacy of their past, she wondered if what she really missed was only partly William and partly the promise their youth had held. For at forty, she felt her life had stalled.

Nothing was turning out as she had planned. In the last two years her parents had died: her father from a heart attack, her mother peacefully in her sleep, nine months later. She had no sisters or brothers. As she began to adjust to their deaths, she found herself drawing closer to William. He was so kind to her, so sympathetic about what it meant to have one's parents' die, that it seemed all the more strange that he had rejected his own. She had just become used to clinging to him again, to feeling his presence as the center of her day, when she learned that he was ill.

She stubbed out her cigarette and rose from the table. As she rode up in the elevator, her eyes swam with sadness and regret. She worried that she had loved William inadequately, that she had taken their relationship for granted. For whatever time they had left, she promised herself that she would make it up to him, that she would help him fight his illness just as surely as she had guided him through the city all those years ago, for though it was sometimes a source of shame to her, besides her father, William was the only man whom she had ever loved.

"You're late," William snapped as she walked in. He sat in a chair by the window, dressed in the clothes he had worn to the hospital four weeks before: jeans faded a powder blue, a black sweatshirt, a motorcycle jacket with a ruby-eyed salamander glued to its right shoulder. They fit him now like clothes borrowed from a larger man.

"You have an appointment I don't know about?" Susan asked, coolly. She pulled a cigarette from her pack and tapped it against her palm. She groped for her matches, then stopped, balancing the butt behind her ear.

"Home," he said, sounding fierce, but his voice caught on the word, drawing it out, nearly a stutter.

"Let's go, then," she said. She dug her heels into the floor to prevent herself from helping him out of the chair. He looked so fragile that she wanted to scoop him into her arms and carry him all the way home.

William pushed himself up with both hands defiantly. He rose halfway, bent at the waist, but spilled forward as he reached down to lift his suitcase, landing spread-eagled on the floor. "Fuck," he said, glowering at the tiles, trying to rein in his breath.

"William, it's me," Susan said gently, lifting him upright, holding him in place. She ran her hands along the length of his body as if smoothing wrinkles from fabric.

He cleared his throat roughly, half gurgle, half spit of disgust, but accepted her arm. She led him into the corridor and past the nursing station, then down in the elevator to the foyer, where she let him go, letting him push ahead through the revolving door, watching as he paused to blink in the light of the sun, willing him to stay erect with the full force of her mind, holding her breath as he moved recklessly into the traffic, his arms shooting into the air, wildly, as he tried to stop an onrushing sea of charging cabs.

7

Susan made no reference to William's white-knuckled grip on the door handle as the cab drew closer to his apartment. She watched his eyes open wider and wider as they drove past the movie theater on the corner, the market where he shopped, the dry cleaner's, the post office. "I like the city these days," she said, trying to distract him. "It was really horrible last summer, but now it's exciting again, like it's coming back to life."

"Maybe there's hope for both of us," William said as the cab stopped at the curb in front of his building. He waited on the sidewalk as Susan paid the driver and collected his suitcase. Through the glass entrance to the lobby he saw his favorite doorman reading a newspaper at the desk. A neighbor walking her dog waved from the sidewalk. The legless man who had lived for years in an alley off the street zoomed past in his wheelchair, drinking a beer.

William didn't know what he had expected, but when he had rehearsed his homecoming these past weeks, he imagined that something extraordinary would separate the passage of time from then to now. He hadn't decided what exactly. Maybe that the doorman would recoil from his thinness, or that new buildings would have sprung up on his street, or at least that there would be a different quality of light or air, some charge in the atmosphere, that he could point to when he stepped out of his cab. He didn't want to feel that the world was impervious to the changes within him.

Susan took his hand and led him to the elevator. He shielded his eyes from the sharp flames of light reflecting off the mirrored walls of the foyer. "Welcome home," the doorman said, as he had done every evening when William returned from work. Had the man even noticed he'd been gone?

Susan set his suitcase down on the slate tiles just inside the door to his apartment and swept her arm in welcome. Every wooden surface gleamed; every carpet seemed fluffed and beaten by hand; every glass surface and mirror were wiped free of prints and dust. "Henry and I cleaned things up a little," she said. "I hope you don't mind."

William nodded distractedly as his eyes took in his possessions, thing by thing. After the starkness of the hospital room, his apartment seemed fussy and overfull. Mirrors, candlesticks, wooden boxes, books, plants, bowls, trivets, lamps, crowded every surface. There were so many rugs that some hung from walls or were folded on tabletops. *All this junk*, he thought, remembering the years he had spent haunting antique shops and flea markets, searching the piles and dusty corners for treasures he had to own.

He heard the refrigerator door open and close; the kettle clanged against the stove. Susan hummed contentedly in the kitchen, as if she moved in her own apartment. From the clock above the bookcase, William saw that only ten minutes had passed since they'd arrived. Already it seemed like hours. He tinkled a scale on the piano keys with his left hand, straightened some books on a shelf, moved to a chair. Often in the past when he became agitated, he would spend the night cleaning his apartment, hypnotizing himself with the motion of cloth rubbing against wood or strokes of the mop soaping the floor. He rearranged furniture, sorted papers, moved lamps, mirrors, pictures, from room to room, anything to gain control over the space. Some nights he went even deeper, sweeping under beds, inside closets, even scrubbing under the refrigerator with a toothbrush until the linoleum shone. He craved a task to become lost in, but Susan and Henry had cleaned so thoroughly, there was nothing left for him to do.

He dragged his suitcase toward the bedroom, stepping carefully on the newly waxed floors. He caught a glimpse of himself as he passed the bathroom mirror — thin, pale — and turned quickly away, as if he'd encountered someone he wanted to avoid.

He clicked open the suitcase and sat on his bed. Fresh flowers bloomed in vases on his bureau and desk. The plants on his windowsill sprouted new shoots from every stem. He saw the book he had been reading set neatly on the nightstand. With the closet door ajar, he saw the sleeves of his coats and shirts, the piles of his sweaters stacked on the shelf above. He would have preferred to find the telephone still thrown on the floor as he had left it, the soiled sheets on the bed, the television screaming the news, the smudged drinking glasses on the bureau, clothes winding toward the bathroom like a rope: a room wrecked by his fevers in the days before he called his friends for help. Now it felt strange and unfamiliar, as if someone had erased evidence at the scene of a crime.

"William?" Susan called from the other room. "Want some tea?"

The dining room table was set with cups, saucers, even napkins tucked into silver rings. William took his place as Susan served him from his own dishes. She set a plate of cookies in front of him. As he stirred sugar into his tea, his spoon scraped against the porcelain rim.

"So," Susan said.

"So," he said, raising his cup. The tea steamed his cheeks. Susan's smile seemed smeared on her face. *She's awful*, he thought; then, just as quickly, *No, she's sweet*. At that moment he couldn't decide if he hated her or if he wanted her to move into his apartment and never leave, just as one moment he believed he would be cured and the next he believed he wouldn't live another day. The only impression that did not change was the anguish he felt at the waste of his life, but he kept that thought closed within his heart. Susan would only try to comfort him, and increasingly he felt numbed by his friends' consolations, for they offered less than flattery could to mend a broken heart.

Her sips were loud in the silence, almost slurps. William watched her eyes dart about the room, flitting from object to object, to the door, the window, the street outside. Something in him refused to help her.

Finally her gaze alighted on the opposite living room wall. "I've always liked that mirror," she said, pointing behind him, brimming with false cheer. "I don't remember where you bought it."

William turned to see a long rectangular mirror topped with an intricate wooden proscenium, like a miniature stage. He remembered the exact moment he had purchased it: October 1982 in Chatham, New York. He had been driving to Vermont for the weekend with his friend Edward, and they had stopped at an antiques barn to shop. William could still describe the clothes the dealer had worn and the smell of the basement where the oldest furniture was kept. Just before they left, he saw the mirror nailed crookedly to a wall, half hidden by a rack of dirty coats.

Edward held it high against his shirt as William examined it, wiping off thick coats of dust with his handkerchief and finding the name of the craftsman inscribed on the back: Howard Moore, 1848. As William wrote a check, the dealer told him that the mirror had hung for generations in the dining room of a summer house. He dipped a brush into a can of varnish as he spoke, expertly tinting a scratch along the base. It was raining that day, and William and Edward lingered longer than they should have. By the time they reached Vermont, they had lost their reservation and were forced to spend the night in the car. They had parked under the safety of a security light in a grocery store lot, using their parkas for blankets and their sweaters for pillows.

William considered telling Susan this story, but it hadn't been a remarkable day, particularly, nor one whose small pleasures could be conveyed to someone who wasn't present. An ordinary day not unlike thousands of others, yet one that the mirror kept distinct and intact in his mind, just as all the objects in his house each had a story to tell. Above the mirror hung an amber glass lantern that Susan had given him for his thirtieth birthday. They celebrated that night in a restaurant by the river, but Susan poured out her betrayal by a lover so obsessively that she grew bleary-eyed with drink and waved away the cake the waiter brought, as if it were an intrusion. William carried the lantern home unopened in its box.

As he looked around, each chair and book, each photograph and piece of furniture, flashed a fragment from his past. Even if they meant nothing to anyone else, he believed that the life of his things somehow held his own life together, as if every object in the room had its own memory.

He rose from his seat and unhooked the mirror from the wall. "Why don't you take it?" he said, holding it out to her. His arms trembled from the weight.

"Oh, no, that wasn't what I meant," Susan protested, blushing.

The paint on the wall behind where the mirror had hung was of a lighter, cleaner hue so an exact imprint of its shape remained visible. "I'd like to give you something for all you've done," he said, watching Susan search his face. He could tell she twitched to own it. He tried to smile warmly so she would accept the gift and leave.

"If you're sure?" she asked, rising from her chair to take it.

The moment he saw Susan touch the carved molding, William regretted what he had done. He hadn't meant to give the mirror to her, not yet, but now he couldn't take it back. *I have to learn to give things up*, he told himself. Aloud he said, "I'm sure."

An awkwardness came between them as if they had lingered too long after good-byes. "I'd better go, I guess," she said, reaching for her purse. "Will you be okay alone?"

"I have to be," he said, but he made certain she saw him stumble as he went to the closet for a sheet of padded paper. He wrapped the mirror carefully and handed it to her. "All yours."

"Thank you," she said, not meeting his eye. When she lifted the package, the frame hid her body from waist to head. She hesitated with her free hand on the opened door. "Do you want company to your doctor's appointment?"

William hitched her purse over her shoulder and patted her back. "Not yet. There'll be plenty of time for that later."

"Henry said to tell you he left some cash in your underwear drawer."

"Thanks."

"I'll call in the morning, but you call anytime if you feel the urge. About anything," she said. "Okay?" She puckered for a kiss. William brushed his lips against her cheek dryly, but he felt a racing of his heart as she began to slip away. He couldn't imagine shutting the door and being locked in his apartment alone.

Susan, too, seemed torn between staying and leaving. She kept propping the package in her arms, sometimes nearly setting it down, then lifting it up with a sigh. William was struck by an image of the mirror hung somewhere in her house, maybe against the pale yellow of her living room wall. If one day a stranger caught his reflection in the glass and asked where she got it, would she tell him William's story?

They stood for what seemed like minutes, half in and half out of the apartment. Susan swept the bangs out of her eyes repeatedly by throwing back her head. Her knuckles were mottled from the weight of her burden. William cleared his throat. "So that you know, I bought the mirror in 1982 on a trip with my friend Edward. He died two years ago this summer. I don't know why, but I've always associated it with him, even though he was only along for the ride."

From her expression, William could tell she had no idea how to respond. "Did I know him?" she asked.

"No," William said. "He didn't mix well. None of my friends knew him, really."

"Oh."

He felt ridiculous for having said anything, but for that moment he had wanted to believe in a connection among the people he had known, a link that could be passed unbroken from friend to friend, each object making something unseen remembered and thereby possible to hold. But Edward was only a name to Susan, just as William would be nothing but a name to the people she would meet in her life ahead whom he would never know.

His neighbor hailed them heartily as she exited the elevator, carrying a load of groceries. "You're home!"

"He's home," Susan said, beaming.

"Yes," William muttered, although he wasn't sure what it meant.

The neighbor reached inside her packages and removed a single yellow tulip from a small bouquet. She offered it to William, smiling. "I'm glad."

"I love you," Susan whispered as she started down the hallway, hefting the mirror over her shoulder like a board.

William heard the click of a bolt as his neighbor disappeared into her apartment. He watched the elevator doors slide shut after Susan. He stood in the corridor alone.

I am home, he said to himself as he closed his door, letting his hand rest on the frame for a moment, listening to the elevator open again and close, pressing the wood tight, listening, as if holding the door shut against intruders.

8

"William?" Henry called into the answering machine. He sounded nervous and edgy. "William? Are you there?"

William hesitated with his hand over the telephone, but didn't lift it. Henry had called twice since morning, and he had nothing left to say. It also occurred to him that if he didn't answer, a few hours of worry might make Henry more malleable the next day.

William paced about the living room. For a week he had done nothing except read and watch TV. He was sick of movies. He felt too well to stay in bed, but too dazed to start his life again. He didn't even feel ill at the moment: more thin and hollow, with the brittlest of bones. Mostly he felt too insubstantial to be real.

He moved to the window, lighting a cigarette, though his doctor had forbidden him to smoke. William had seen x-rays of his lungs, cloudy with scars from his disease, but he didn't care. He had given up too many things already.

When he looked out at the street below, he saw a stream of men, some in couples, some alone, walking in the direction of his favorite bar. In the soft light, their bodies shimmered with life. Even their shadows seemed to leap ahead of them carelessly. He had walked that same path a thousand times in the past ten years, memorizing every inch of concrete, every house and door frame, every struggling tree, spray of graffiti, broken telephone, and rat's nest, every abandoned car, the face of every drug dealer, from his apartment to the river. He never admitted it to anyone, but he had chosen his building for its proximity to the bar. He liked the fact that he had to pass through a seedy neighborhood completely unlike his own to get there, as if his journey mirrored the way he left his other life behind as he walked.

Every Friday and Saturday night for years, he set out for the bar after returning home from an evening with friends. He loved to dress deliberately, taking an hour to change his T-shirt and jeans, before leaving at the stroke of twelve, jumpy with the promise of love. He would meet his friend Alan by the side entrance to drink beer and gossip as they watched the men come and go through the door. Alan was tall and gray and into leather. He had lived in the city for so long that he claimed to know the sexual habits of every regular customer in the crowd.

William didn't know their names, but from Alan he knew their secrets. As they stood on the sidewalk and a particular man passed by, Alan would whisper, "He'll only have sex with a man wearing Keds" or "He's into knives" or "He's into bondage" or "He won the lottery" or "He has a portrait of his mother over his bed and a mirror set at an angle so that you see her face no matter where you lie."

William knew nothing of these men beyond what Alan told him, but over years of watching he had come to think of them fondly, as a part of his life. When he walked into the bar, he would take his place along the back wall where he was lit just right by a cloudy blue light. And as the night wore on, he would scan the room for the regulars. *Keds, knives, mom, lottery,* he would recite as he took an inventory of who was there.

Outside his window William heard hoots of laughter rising from the men on the street. The sound squeezed his heart with an unbearable longing. He wanted to return, just for an hour, to see if it was possible to reclaim the person he had been. He remembered how cold it had been the last time he visited the bar and how he had shivered violently under his coat, not knowing if it was the weather or a fever that unhinged him.

Once inside he had stood straight against the wall to keep his knees from buckling, refusing to give in until the lights flashed on at four A.M. and he was made to straggle out with the last drunken men. He remembered grabbing at parking meters for support as he struggled home, trying to forget how every person in the bar had kept a distance, clearing a circle around him as if they smelled his disease. After he was safely in bed, he sobbed with loneliness and fear, but even then he hadn't believed that his journey out would be the last for all the months to come.

He turned from the window and took a clean pair of jeans from his closet. He removed his shirt and stood in the fluorescent glare of the bathroom light. He wasn't accustomed to looking at his new body. He was stunned at the ways in which it had changed.

Even during the years when he exercised daily, William was disturbed at how his muscles would begin to shrink and lose their form if he rested for only a week. Now his chest sank inward as it never had, and his belly swelled softly out, forming a pouch at his waist. He traced a finger around a small, red tumor popping from his chest, rosy as a third nipple. He was afraid he'd lose his nerve if he turned around to see the cluster of tumors scattered across his back, so he pulled a T-shirt over his head. As he tucked it in, he noticed that the sleeves no longer stretched over his biceps as they once had, held perfectly in place by the expanse of his arm. He let the cloth flap loose, down to his elbows. He ran an ice cube over his face to pinken his cheeks and slapped himself twice.

He stepped into the darkened bedroom and examined himself in the full-length mirror. The diminished light disguised his shrunken look and softened the bony contours of his face. It would be no brighter in the bar: he could still pass for a person who wasn't ill.

A burst of energy as of old rushed through his body as he grabbed his leather jacket and ran outside, falling in step behind two men. Although he felt like an impostor, he followed them, taking comfort in all the familiar signs that marked his path to the river. The air outside was cool, unseasonably balmy: a night that in the past would have made him think the city was buffeted by the winds of paradise.

At the entrance to the bar, he paused for a moment as he always had, running a hand through his hair, adjusting his shirt in his jeans. Inside he was stunned by loud music with a frantic beat. Scores of men pushed against him, a sea of strangers. Alan had been dead since the previous autumn, and for a moment William wondered if everyone familiar to him had died, too. Finally he spotted the lottery winner and then, near the cigarette machine, the man who liked Keds talking to the bouncer. William sighed with relief, as if he had found something treasured.

He didn't know how to behave. Before he had stood for hours with the heel of his boot pressed against the wall, never moving except to refill his beer. Now he paced nervously, haunting the darkest corners. The other men looked right through him, erasing him with the same blank expression he had once perfected when someone unappealing tried to catch his eye. He searched for a man like himself somewhere in the room, someone with death in his eyes, but everyone appeared unburdened by cares. To his left, two men wearing only sneakers and jeans embraced, their bodies glistening with health. To his right, two men leaned over and kissed, then waltzed out the door.

A favorite song from years before pounded through the speakers. William felt his body sway reflexively to the rhythm. He watched the thickening throng along the bar, the arms raised in greeting, the glint of beer cans, the bartender tossing a towel into the air and catching it behind his back. The laughter rose higher than the music, a cacophony of joy. The dim, smoky light seemed to reflect each body to its best advantage, like photographs shot through gauze.

He moved even farther back into the shadows where no part of him was visible but the glow from his cigarette butt and the tips of his boots. His hair frizzed from sweat. Perspiration leaked into his shirt and pooled under his arms. He felt unwanted and hideous, suddenly deformed, as if he had been banished from a world in which he no longer had a place, and yet did not want to leave. He would have given anything to be part of it again.

He felt an ache, like a heartbreak, and found himself wanting acutely all the things he had given up willingly a thousand times before he was ill: love, permanence, a mate. Or maybe it wasn't love at all he missed but only the confidence he had felt in his old body and the thrill of a sexual score.

Of all the places he had loved to frequent in the city, William had been happiest in bars. He would lose the rest of his life in the weird light, the music, and the men all around him who had no identity beyond the clothes they wore and the shape of their bodies. He would stand for hours, mesmerized, usually going home alone, but sometimes leaving with a man whose chief appeal was that he never said his name. He kept parts of his life secret by design, not from shame or regret, but because he wanted to control what the world knew of him. He chose to tell his friends as little as possible about the things they would disapprove of, for he knew he would do them anyway, and he wanted to live free of their worry or scorn.

Desire changed him. Out in the world he discovered a race of men with secret lives who slipped in and out of different selves as easily as they shed their clothes. He grew to love best walking home alone at dawn after binges of sex and drugs, when the city was deserted and its endless streets seemed to form the perimeters of his own private world. And although he would admit to nights when his longing sometimes took the shape of a man, he knew that what he wanted was something a person was never meant to have: an eternal youth, a carelessness and invincibility, he had traded his life to buy.

He knew he had wasted a million chances because he had believed there would always be another and another after that. Because he had learned early the truth of the body's frailty, he should have wanted to protect it, but he played fire with it. He never gave it a chance. He wore it out to watch it recover, as if by springing back, it gave the lie to his mortality. It never occurred to him until too late that he might have made his body stronger to keep it safe through the decades ahead. He had squandered everything, like a fortune, but he knew that if a miracle gave him just a short reprieve, he would only rush back in and lose it all the same.

He zipped his jacket. He squeezed between the crush of bodies as he made his way to the door, feeling the brush of jeans against his hands, the warm touch of leather. His head ached from the noise. He walked home through the familiar streets, dazzled by the glow of the lights and the rustle of trees overhead; the comforting hum of traffic, cabs, couples arm in arm, every building sparkling the way he remembered it, the city nearly afire, giddy with life.

9

No one needed an appointment in William's doctor's office. There were so many emergencies among his patients that he had stopped keeping a regular schedule years before. Now that William was home from the hospital, he saw the doctor on alternate Thursdays. He tried to arrive in the morning to beat the afternoon crush, but often it was already so crowded that he had to be content spending hours, sometimes the whole day, waiting to be seen.

Every time William entered the office, the first thing he did was study the faces around him for signs of deterioration. There were five or six patients who had been coming on the same day for more than a year. Long before he was admitted to the hospital, they had become a fixture of his week. Although none were friends, they always greeted each other. As they said hello, their eyes would lock just long enough for a quick study of each slip and fall before they turned away. William wondered if they, too, saw in each uneasy smile a reflection of their own disintegration, as if each human face had become a small, round mirror.

Sometimes the receptionist offered an examination room early to the patient in the worst shape. No one ever protested, even if they had been sitting for hours. The patients treated each other with a deference and respect William had observed nowhere else. As they waited, they discussed the things that had come to define their lives as unhealthy men: drug reactions, diets, meditation techniques, funerals, visits from their mothers, the most comfortable fabrics to wear over their damaged skin, the best oils for their baths, rumors of new treatments from the underground. They never asked directly about another's health unless a person appeared unusually well.

Today almost everyone in the office looked pale with imminent death. The room was so crowded that William had to squeeze into an empty space beside the magazine rack. Coughs split the air around him; the walls swarmed with germs. William tried to keep his own breathing shallow so that he didn't suck the poisoned air too deeply into his lungs, but he felt every pore of his skin open, his body lousy with holes. He had read that bacteria attach to the flesh and thrive, invading the bloodstream when a finger simply touches the mouth or eye, so he stuck his hands deep into the pockets of his cardigan. He nodded to two men he knew with a tight-lipped smile. Sometimes when he was alone, he grew tearful with gratitude for the community he shared with the other patients, but often when he was there he felt entombed by their contagion, as if their every twitch and tremble made him vulnerable to another disease.

A man he didn't recognize came out of an examination room and stood at the receptionist's desk, writing a check. He was well dressed and deeply tanned, at odds with the blanched faces around him. As he signed his name, layers of multicolored bracelets slid down his arm, revealing a series of lesions of an almost perfect oval shape, clustered in groups of four or five, each the same dark strawberry color. There was something alive about the way they appeared to travel across his skin, as though his arm was overrun with leeches.

Then he's one, too, William thought as he counted the other patients. There were more than thirty people in the room, but he had never seen one of them in the neighborhood outside the office. Upon leaving, they seemed to vanish into thin air. Every once in a while, he would glimpse a phantom figure rushing through the crowd with the speed and invisible air of a celebrity. Then he would notice the peculiar downward cast of the head, the body swaddled in clothes too heavy for the weather, the eyes hidden by sunglasses even on cloudy days, and he would know it was only another outcast soul sprinting toward home.

William never felt more branded by his symptoms than when he walked alone at midday, his paranoia intensifying the farther he got from his apartment, believing he was the only person alive who was tainted, hating his shame and isolation, hating the strangers around him more with every step, yet worrying that they would devour him if they took his condition in, worrying that a sudden turn in their attention would unleash them into a mob. He knew he had to try to bear his illness proudly, but he saw revulsion and fear everywhere he looked: in strangers, in the eyes of his friends. When he visited his office, his coworkers made him feel as if even the unblemished skin of his face was pocked with open sores.

As often as possible, he did his errands late at night or asked Henry and Susan to do them. He had surrendered the street to the living, but for a moment he fantasized that if all the patients, with their ghastly pallors, wheelchairs, and canes, filed out of the office at the same time, they would outnumber the healthy people on the street two to one, causing pandemonium, as if the city were under attack by creatures raised from the dead.

"William? William?" he heard a voice call. The man in the next seat tapped him gently on the shoulder. The doctor stood in front of an empty examination room, his hands full of folders. William gathered up his knapsack and went in, taking his place in an upholstered chair. The doctor had decorated the rooms as much like a home as possible: rugs scattered on hardwood floors, sofas covered with lush satin fabrics, fresh flowers. William noticed a new photograph of the doctor dressed in a T-shirt and jeans hanging on the wall behind his head. He was shocked at how casual the doctor seemed in the pose, almost another person. In the office he always wore a suit.

"You okay?" the doctor asked.

"Oh yes, fine," William said. He tugged at his sleeve protectively. Underneath it was a new patch of blistered skin, bright red in the center, but outlined with a pussy white ring. He wouldn't mention it. The doctor had seen so many disasters among his patients that William felt spoiled and silly if he mentioned anything except the most extreme symptom. As his illness grew graver, he learned that if he brought up an isolated sore, a fleeting cough, or a fever below a dangerous level, the doctor would dismiss it without comment. William believed that he purposely withheld sympathy for smaller hurts to instill courage in his patients, because there was so much pain ahead that each would have to endure alone.

The doctor rubbed his eyes, the rims smudged with fatigue, nearly as dark as inked fingerprints. William knew he worked impossibly long hours without complaint. Every morning before office hours he visited patients in two hospitals at opposite ends of the city. He saw outpatients in his office until very late at night. In between, he worked tirelessly on the telephone, arranging for tests and deliveries, pleading for beds in the hospital and medicines in short supply. He even mailed birthday cards on time every year to each patient, with a handwritten message that sent his love. He had no other life. His kindness was muted by a slightly dazed look, even on his best days, like someone who has gone to war. From the dates of the diplomas on his wall, William had determined that the doctor was younger than he, but he seemed wiser and more mature. William always assumed that people with power over him were older, even policemen barely out of school.

As the doctor spread the pages of his chart across the desk, William saw a laboratory report of his most recent blood tests, neat lists of figures that tracked the progress of his disease. "A small decline, nothing significant," the doctor said. "How do you feel?"

"Tired," William said. "Nothing worse, but then none of this seems quite real."

The doctor passed the folder so that William could read the results for himself, but the numbers meant little to him. He had watched them fall steadily for months, from several hundred to double digits. It was only a matter of time before there was nothing left but a few solitary cells adrift in his bloodstream, like dim lights in fog. Once a week he lay on a couch in the back room for treatments with an experimental drug, but it had little effect except for a small burn as the liquid dripped into his vein. Since nothing else was available to him, he saw his appointments more as a way of touching base, just as in the days when he had continued to see his therapist although his life was on an even course, afraid to cut the ties entirely in case something went awry.

Before examining William's body, the doctor always asked questions about his life. If William had nothing to say, sometimes the doctor told him stories of other patients, of their miraculous remissions, but sometimes of their suicides, each moment orchestrated at home as carefully as a wedding: flowers, candles, music, a few chosen friends. Sometimes the doctor even shared his dreams. Often he said he dreamed of patients resurrected from the dead, of auras and blinding white lights, dreams of a religious intensity. Sometimes he dreamed of his body falling into crevasses, hanging helplessly at the end of a rope.

William squirmed whenever the doctor became too forthcoming about his private life. He didn't want to know his doubts and fears; he didn't want to know his dreams. The more human the doctor became, the less powerful he seemed, and William needed to believe he could summon the magic necessary to cure him. No matter how often the doctor urged him, William refused to call him by his first name.

"Let's take a look," the doctor said, indicating the examination table. William stripped and lay naked on his stomach. Out the window he saw an uneven row of apartment houses set against a corner of bright, blue sky. "Nice day," he said as the curtains billowed softly in the breeze.

The doctor grunted in response, concentrating on his work. William let his muscles go limp as the doctor's hands probed his glands, lingering here and there in the rocky places, then moving on before William could ask what he had found. His fingers ran over the lesions on his back, taking their shape. His nails scraped over the dried patches of skin. William felt strangely docile as the doctor worked. He turned over and opened his eyes, unblinking, as the flashlight moved close to his irises, then to his ears, his nose, drawing out the "aaaahh" in his throat, feeling his chest constrict as the doctor listened to the wheeze in his lungs.

"No cigarettes," the doctor said as he injected a needle to draw his blood. William looked away, growing dopey with pleasure, wishing the examination would continue for hours, hypnotized by the order and rhythm of the tests, believing his body safe from any invasion while he was in his doctor's hands.

He was completely without self-consciousness with the doctor. He dreaded his friends seeing him naked because they couldn't hide their shock, but the doctor had seen damage William could only imagine. He had worked in emergency rooms. He had watched hundreds of patients suffer and die. Never had he flinched when he examined William, being careful to call each disorder by its name — *tumor, rash, bacteria, virus* — so that they seemed distinct from his body, or only a temporary part. But after he was home, William blushed with shame at the way the doctor examined his skin, his touch no different from when he ran his hands over the shadow of an x-ray, as if it was simply a plain of deepening afflictions, not something that had ever been an object of desire.

The doctor turned his back as William slid down from the table. He scrubbed his hands in the sink. He never watched while William dressed, as if his body had become something private again. "See you in two weeks?" he asked over his shoulder.

"Yes," William said, slipping on his jeans. He lingered over his shoelaces, pulling each string tight. He had a question he wanted to ask, but he hesitated. In all his meetings with the doctor, William had forced himself to remain polite, never crying out even when he got his final diagnosis, never complaining during months of tests and uncertainty, never showing alarm, except, perhaps, in the tremor of his hands, the dryness in his throat as he spoke, the quick widening of his eyes. These were rules William had made privately. Often behind closed doors he heard other patients scream and sob, a hysterical pitch to their questions. He had seen the doctor step into the corridor, shaking with helplessness and rage. From the beginning William had decided to become his doctor's favorite patient, to seduce him completely with deference and charm. He hoped that if he made no trouble, the doctor would never stop working hard to save him.

There was one question about his illness that he had been afraid to raise in the hospital, or in all the weeks since, which had come to obsess him. He wanted to know how long he had to live. He had seen countless movies in which patients were given six months, sometimes a year, to survive. These limits were always stated with certainty, as if a sign from within the body revealed a definite date. William wanted to know if his own symptoms held clues his doctor hadn't disclosed. He had watched Alan die within weeks. From the first signs of his illness, his body had seemed to collapse completely around him, like an implosion. And yet William knew that some of the patients in the waiting room had survived in a tolerable state for years. It made a difference to him to know.

He tied his laces into neat double bows, keeping his head suspended halfway above his knees. "How long can a person expect to last?" he asked, feeling pushy in spite of his vagueness, as if he were pressing for privileged information.

He heard the doctor's chair roll on its wheels, its hinges squeaking as he rocked back and forth, stalling. William sat up straight as the doctor spoke, but still averted his eyes.

"I intend to keep working until we find a cure. I believe there will be treatments, but I can't predict when. Until then, we watch, we wait. I've got a lot of hope." His tone was warm and reassuring, but his hands gripped a pencil as if it were the butt of a knife.

"But I meant for me," William said, losing his shyness. On the examination table he saw the five vials of blood the doctor had drawn, each with a different-colored rubber stopper. The blood looked darker than he remembered, more black than red: thick, congealed, lying in the tube like sludge.

"I don't know what makes the difference," the doctor said. "Unfortunately, in many cases it's simply a mystery of genes."

"Then there's nothing to do," William said.

The doctor bristled, a sudden flush in his cheeks, a flash in his eyes. "I won't ever give up. I wouldn't call that nothing. I know a hundred men like you."

"I'm very grateful for your care," William said politely, as he would thank a person for dinner. When he stood to leave, the doctor squeezed his arm as he always did, then pulled him closer, stopping short of a full embrace. "Be good," he said.

"Be well," William said, his body tensing at the doctor's touch, smelling for the first time the stink of cheap cologne.

*

Out in the waiting room, the patients were fewer. Some sat reading newspapers, some stared into space. One fiddled with the silver knob of his cane, drumming his fingers, *tick, tick, tick*. His feet were encased in knitted booties with tufts of bloody gauze sticking from the edges. Under his jeans his legs looked shrunken and wooden, slightly askew, like the limbs of a marionette.

"Hi," William said to the puppet man, trying to put him at ease, but his voice barked in the silence. The man flinched, unsmiling. The others turned to look. No one spoke. William felt as if he were moving in slow motion, the room suspended in time, or as if he had stumbled into a chamber in a wax museum, so stiff and unreal did everyone seem. The only person who seemed alive was the receptionist, the telephone balanced against his ear as he scribbled in the appointment book.

"Two weeks?" William asked as the receptionist flipped through the calendar: March 22, March 23, March 24 . . . flashing past to April 6, each day already crowded with names.

"See you then," the receptionist said, adding William's name to a list that ran halfway down the page. The telephone rang, then rang again. A man entered from the street and headed for the desk, pushing William aside. The doctor opened the door to his office and beckoned a bald woman in. He looked at William as if to say "You still here?"

As William turned to the door, the doctor's words slammed back at him: *I know a hundred men like you.* He wanted to believe that what was happening to him was the most cataclysmic event — an atomic blast, a slaughter of children, the collapse of a galaxy when two planets collide — but there in the waiting room, he felt for the first time as if it were nothing. If anything, that made it harder to bear. He was no one special, a name inked on a page, a patient in waiting, just another man who was dying.

10

The first thing Henry did after he learned William was dying was to have his upper right arm tattooed with a pale blue dragon. He sat for hours in the artist's studio studying portfolios with every conceivable shape and design. Henry tried to hide his shock at the photographs of tattooed body parts: not just arms and backs, but whole torsos, with serpents bursting from breasts, penises coiled with black barbed wire, buttocks with fanged wolves, scalps with arrowheads and mystical charms, shins, thighs, ankles, calves, wrists, fingers, the palms of hands, no inch of skin that hadn't been inked and drilled. He finally chose a dragon copied from one worn by Celtic warriors. The figure was drawn with soft, feathery outlines, more like clouds than scales, and a knobby head with a forked tongue of the deepest red that licked across the bony top of his shoulder. In time he thought he might have his entire body tattooed: with serpents, lions' heads, different dragons, a whole slew of nature's fiercest creatures to adorn him like evil eyes.

His body was changing.

All his life Henry's natural thinness had never fluctuated, no matter what he ate. He never considered his body's shape as anything but a given. He rarely exercised, preferring to spend his free time preparing for classes, reading, or visiting with friends. But since William had become ill, his own weakness had obsessed him. He had seen patients in the hospital worn down to nothing but diapered bones with skulls. He had watched the nurses flip their bodies when they changed the sheets as easily as children toss a doll. Their shrunken bodies made Henry newly aware of how little there was of him to withstand a disease. William had always been large and meaty, but already he was growing thinner, layer by layer. Although Henry held no illusions about becoming invincible, he hoped, at least, to grow stronger so that he would have the resources to fight whatever his future might hold. Before William's discharge, he paid his first visit to the gym.

He felt ashamed to enter, daunted by the men and women who moved confidently through the racks of weights and intricate machines. At first, he hid under baggy sweatpants and a billowing shirt that covered his arms to his wrists, but after only two months he was astonished by his progress. Nothing he had ever done in his life had produced such tangible results. His muscles swelled, his arms grew thicker, a body he had never imagined could exist began to emerge from his soft mounds of flesh, like a form sculpted from clay.

As he worked the weights, he emptied his mind of everything but the cool feel of steel in his hand, each breath timed perfectly to the rhythm of each exertion. Away from the gym, he dreamed of returning in the way he had once dreamed of telephone calls from useless men. He sneaked in visits between classes and trips to William's apartment, telling no one of his secret. He walked differently now, with a kind of swagger that had less to do with vanity than with a heady sense of control, as if he were creating himself from nothing. Out in the world he could rarely sustain this sensation of power, but when he grew uncertain, he would run a hand under his shirt to stroke the newly taut skin, and feel his own presence, barrel-chested and coiled with muscle, where before his body had seemed hardly to ruffle the air as he moved.

Henry sat up from the bench, dizzy with fatigue. He returned the barbells neatly to their rack and wiped his brow with a towel. It was time to meet William for dinner. He skipped the shower and pulled his jeans over his shorts. As he walked to the subway, he slung his gym bag over his shoulder, carefully carrying a present for William in a shopping bag at his side.

Lately Henry had become obsessed with the idea of buying William a pet. William rarely consented to go out, even to restaurants. He went to his office two mornings a week, but seemed to have lost all interest in his job. He claimed to have problems with vertigo and a clouding in the sight of his left eye that gave him headaches when he read. He complained of unending fatigue. Henry didn't know if William exaggerated some of his afflictions for sympathy, but he had noticed that he walked more cautiously, sometimes stumbling with the boozy gait of a drunken man. Henry worried that all the hours William spent alone only aggravated his problems. He talked of nothing else, the way a person with an eating disorder speaks only of food.

Growing up, Henry had lived in a house with more animals than children. Every night he slept with his arm around his favorite dog, sharing the pillow, feeling its heart beat against his own. The tenderness he felt was different from his love for any member of his family. He wanted nothing more than to protect it. William hated surprises of any kind, but Henry hoped that if he arrived unannounced with a dog and William deigned to let it stay, it might distract him from his symptoms. It would give him something to care for besides himself, even a reason to go outside.

That morning Henry had stopped at the local pet store. He stood before the pens of puppies for a long time, deciding. The dogs yipped and barked and bit the bars of their cages. They ran in manic circles around the floor. As he watched, his enthusiasm waned. There, away from daydreaming at his kitchen table, the puppies seemed too helpless to be used as an experiment to modify William's behavior. He would never have the energy to care for so robust an animal. And if William died, the dog would be or-phaned. Already Henry knew he didn't want to adopt it. He was sick of responsibilities. After William, he didn't want anything else to hold him down. He had fantasies of moving, of leaving the city for another job. He had no idea what his new life would be, but he knew it would never happen if he kept too many burdens from his past.

He returned the dogs to their pens regretfully, loath to aban-don entirely the idea of a pet. At the back of the store he saw a wall of aquariums filled with fish of every conceivable kind. He was tempted by the miniature sharks and skittish piranhas that swam menacingly toward his fingers, but he decided to begin more modestly. He chose four silver tetras that shimmered with a rain-bow of colors, and he bought a small rectangular tank lit by a pale purple light. It would hardly occupy a square foot of space. With fish, at least, William would have other creatures inside his apart-ment to remind him that he was still alive.

As Henry set his packages on the floor of the subway car, he peered down at the fish trapped inside their clear plastic bag. Each time the train rocked on its tracks, the water splashed to one side, as if swept by a rough tide. *This is the stupidest thing I've ever done*, he thought as he watched the fish dart back and forth in their few inches of portable sea. Now that he had bought them, he couldn't imagine how he would explain his gift. He would offer them without comment, like a bouquet of flowers. If William hated them, Henry would take them home. Fish were as fragile as in-sects. They wouldn't live long.

At each stop, so many people crowded into the car that Henry had to straddle the bag so that no one would crush it. He wasn't used to traveling at rush hour. His classes began at seven-thirty and ended at three, too early to share the car with anyone but nannies and schoolchildren. He observed the expensively suited men and women enviously as he thought of them returning home from their jobs. He fiddled with the hem of his sweatshirt. He bent down to straighten the cuffs of his jeans. He felt ridiculous and underdressed, like a teenager, among all these professional people his age.

More and more he worried that his life had taken the wrong course. He had gone directly from his graduate studies to teaching at a private academy for boys. He had never considered any career other than teaching. He liked the security of classrooms and the long vacations. He especially liked how teaching gave him an excuse to explore any idea that interested him and share it with his students.

Since childhood Henry had run to libraries to understand everything he could, especially about subjects that frightened him. After all his years of study, it seemed a miracle to be paid for something he did as second nature. But as he grew older, he watched his contemporaries advance in careers in business, medicine, law, lives he could only imagine. They bought houses, traveled, married, had children, divorced, while he stayed in school. Even worse, he was old enough now to have seen his first students return to campus heady with careers that made him envious. He had been privileged and intelligent enough to do anything he wanted, yet he had chosen the easiest thing that it was possible for him to be.

He was always the poorest among his friends. Living in the city on his salary, he could only eke out an existence from paycheck to paycheck. If not for the free meals William offered, by the end of every month he would have no money left for subway fare.

At the beginning of their friendship, Henry would reach slowly into his pocket for an imaginary roll of bills whenever they dined out, praying that William would pay. He always did. Over time, they had stopped pretending. He sat motionless as William passed his credit card and signed the check. William never made him feel that he was taking advantage of his generosity. Henry did what he could. He often paid the tip. He bought extravagant presents he could ill afford for William's birthday and Christmas. He was always willing to do errands that William found unpleasant: shopping for groceries, servicing his car, firing the boys who tended the garden, the women who cleaned his apartment in the city. He did these favors without thinking twice, in the same way, he assumed, that William paid for their meals and weekends away.

After William became ill and began to dangle the promise of the house, Henry questioned his own motives for the first time in their friendship. When he got angry with William, he couldn't decide if he tempered his response out of a natural reticence or from fear that William would change his will. Although Henry had said time and again that he didn't want the house, he also hoped William would ignore him. Short of a miracle, it would be his only ticket out. Sometimes when he stared, daydreaming, at the framed photograph of the house enshrined on his bookshelf at home, he had to stop from marveling, *One day it will all be mine.*

His greediness confused him. He wanted the house, just as he wanted to win the lottery or make a fortune gambling at cards, but no more than he wanted to retain his sense of selflessness and self-respect. If he was to receive any reward, he wanted it to come unheralded, at the end. Now he couldn't help but wonder if William was merely upping an ante that had always been part of their bond, if over the years they had both allowed their good will to be bought and sold. He didn't know if it mattered, if a person could find an imbalance in every relationship that could be reduced to different forms of barter, but it had not occurred to him until recently that there might have been a reason he was drawn to William other than simply companionship and love.

Sometimes when he looked back upon the course of his life,

Henry was stunned at how its most significant events seemed to have evolved from chance encounters. Often he wondered what would have happened if he had stayed home the night they met. William might have forever remained one of the nameless strangers preening at the back of the bar. Often, too, he wondered at the life he might have missed by surrendering too early. After William, he never found time to meet other people. His friends were William's friends. His best possessions were gifts from William. Even the decor of his small apartment was a flea-market version of William's taste in antiques.

His lack of ambition had never worried him before William was ill. Now, when he thumbed through the biographies and memoirs on his shelves at home, he was reproached by the fullness of those other lives: love affairs, financial ruin, physical collapse, multiple marriages, vengeful children, tragic deaths, decades of sacrifice, triumphs in work, religious conversions, madness, alcoholism, drug addiction. Henry had never risked anything. He had lived for years in the same claustrophobic apartment. He had worked for years at the same unremarkable job. He rarely traveled. Although he pretended otherwise, he had never sustained a romance beyond a couple of weeks. He would never admit it, but William's illness was the most exciting thing that had happened in his life. His usefulness thrilled him. The crises gripped him like a drug. Often his joy in helping William so obscured the truth of his disease that he had to remind himself that it was probable his friend would die.

Ever since he learned William was ill, Henry had read every book he could find on death: philosophical treatises, guides for the sick, manuals for self-healing, histories of religions and funerary rites. He studied autobiographies of people facing death so that he might understand the stages a person endures when he or she approaches the end. He read the diary of a man who tracked his own disintegration as his body was consumed by a disease. No matter how much he read, these stories seemed as distant to him as newspaper headlines about people killed in fires or murdered in their homes. It wasn't that he didn't believe something terrible could happen, for he saw evidence of that every day, but more that he couldn't imagine his own life ending, despite the grief that experience might hold.

Henry closed his eyes and rocked with the speed of the train, holding tightly to the center pole. He heard the screech of the wheels against the metal rails, the murmur of the passengers, even the crinkle of the bags at his feet, moving with the vibrations. He could imagine the train crashing, even see in his mind the splintering of metal, the implosion of glass, the bodies tossed screaming — an accident in slow motion, bloody and violent — but in the silence after, he still saw himself observing the wreckage as the last person alive. He could imagine himself in pain, broken, crying for help, but he couldn't make his way to the final moment when he did not move, did not breathe, did not think. He couldn't make what *dead* meant real for himself, when all around him everything breathed, everything jumped with life.

During graduate school he had worked as a secretary in the security department of the university hospital. His office was deep inside the basement, so he was far removed from the daily dramas played out in the corridors above. Upstairs, he knew, people died every hour, but he never saw bodies on stretchers or even patients in their rooms. He could have been working in an office anywhere. But in the middle of one night he bribed a security guard to take him into the morgue. The room was small, no larger than a walk-in freezer. Six corpses lay on metal shelves built like bunks along the wall. Each was covered in a beige plastic bag that became translucent where the body strained against it: the knob of an ankle, the crook of a knee, the mound of a breast, a fisted hand.

The bags were pulled so tightly around the heads that the faces were stretched and distorted, like thieves wearing sheer stockings for masks, each mouth agape in a perfect O, but stiff, frozen, as if they had been murdered while singing.

Those six figures in their darkened vault returned to him now in dreams, sometimes wrapped exactly as they had been, but sometimes sitting, sometimes moving about the room in their vinyl shrouds. They were the only images of death Henry had seen for himself, but they were still so unreal, even in nightmares, that they didn't seem to have ever been alive. They were more like mannequins packaged for garbage.

Even with everything he had learned in the past months, some part of him still rebelled at the idea that a life could come down to that, especially now when he felt his new body so powerfully about him, his blood pumping through his veins, his brain alert, his breath steady and deep. He had read that a human heart beats three billion times in a lifetime, so many times that it seemed close enough to infinity to still imagine that he was immune.

The throng of commuters propelled Henry up the subway stairs. He clutched the bag to his chest to keep the fish warm in the cool spring air. As he hit the sidewalk, the lights in the buildings around him began to blink on against the darkening sky, first one at a time, then three, four, five at once, small explosions of color that seemed to mark his passage to William's door. The stores were packed with shoppers. The restaurants were full. A line stretched around the block in front of the movie theater on the corner. He watched people climb out of taxis and wave to their friends, then embrace, chattering with the news of the day.

He quickened his pace. As he turned onto the circular drive to William's building, he lifted the shopping bag with his left arm so that he felt his biceps strain against his sleeve. In the lobby a man caught and held his eye, pausing as he waited for Henry to snatch the bait. For a moment he considered following, maybe calling William from the pay phone on the corner to say he'd been delayed. But as he smiled back, he was stopped by an image of his friend bundled in blankets on his couch upstairs, the windows of his apartment shut to the noise of the world below. Despite his regrets at the mistakes and miscalculations he had made, Henry knew he would have time later to cut his losses and begin again. Although he struggled to understand the full meaning of William's illness and fear of approaching death, something became clearer as he looked through the huge, vaulted windows of the lobby to the bustle of the street outside: for imagine losing everything, imagine the sadness at leaving a whole life behind.

"Is there something wrong with your feet?" Susan's voice was faint and indistinct, as though she were calling from a foreign country.

"Hello?" William pressed the receiver closer to his ear. The sound of waves crashed from every corner of his living room. The glare from the setting sun shone directly through the window onto his aquarium, throwing huge fish-shaped shadows against the wall.

"What's that noise?" Susan asked.

"Nothing," William said, pulling the cord across the room to turn down the stereo's volume. He was embarrassed to tell her that he had spent the last hour listening to a recording of surf breaking on an ocean shore. His doctor had lent him a whole library of nature sounds to help relieve stress. He had serenades of crickets and cicadas, of squealing porpoises at play, of birds flapping in flight, of wind and snow and rippling water, of rushing streams, waterfalls, and pounding rain, so that sometimes his apartment seemed to be rocked by a howling storm.

The doctor believed that drugs alone were not enough to cure him. He had advised William to meditate on the tapes four times a day to release his body's healing powers. William was unsure exactly what quality in nature was meant to help him, but he was willing to try anything. He had played the tapes religiously for the past two weeks, filling his waking hours with the sound, even as he rode the subway or walked down the street. When he listened at home, he imagined his couch as a boat floating in a sea warmed by a Caribbean sun. Each time he exhaled, he imagined sending his body's poisons out into the atmosphere, where they were lost among the black clouds of exhaust from city buses and factories. He imagined the clumps of deadly cells within him as handfuls of sand being obliterated by a torrent of waves. He worked hard to lose himself in the hypnotic rhythms and lush crescendos of sound pouring into his ears, but he didn't feel any better. As each day passed, he felt increasingly that some inner part of him had failed.

"I'm calling you in the city, aren't I?" Susan asked, confused. "It sounds like you're at the beach."

"I'm not," William said. "I'm here."

"Good. So how was your day?" She sounded giddy and somewhat overwrought. William wondered if she was drunk.

"Fine," he said. "And yours?"

"I thought you'd never ask," she said, giggling. "Don't laugh, but I went to this psychic a friend at work told me about, and it was incredible. He called out your name the moment I entered the room. Henry's too. He knew about my illness as a child. He knew my parents were dead. That I live alone. About my job. But what really freaked me out was the way he seemed to know things I've never told anyone. Not even you."

"What *things?*" William asked, spitting the word like an obscenity. Though he guarded his own privacy zealously, he was offended that Susan might keep secrets from him. *What has she done that I don't know about?* he wondered, resentful that his friends were getting on with their lives too easily without him.

"Well, like . . . ," Susan said. Even through the telephone, William could feel her enthusiasm wane. She paused, then began again, her voice hardened with a defensive edge. "If I didn't think you'd sneer, I'd call them parts of my soul, but it doesn't matter.

The point is, he was right on target. He even knew the color of my living room walls."

With my mirror smack in the middle, I bet, William thought, but aloud he only said, "I wouldn't sneer."

"Well, let's not take our chances. The important thing wasn't what he said, anyway, but what he could do. His gift, or whatever you want to call it. He knew everything, like he was reading my mind. I can't tell you how exciting it was. People aren't supposed to have that kind of power. It was creepy, too, in a way, but now that I'm back home, I don't have a clue what any of it means."

William lay back on the couch. On the console against the wall, he could see the red and green lights of the amplifier pulsing soundlessly to the beat of the tape. As Susan spoke, he imagined hearing the rainstorm that came near the end of the recording, a whistling wind, a flapping of lush, wet leaves. He had tried so hard to rouse whatever magical quality of mind lay dormant within him that he wanted to believe what Susan was saying about the psychic. He knew it was possible. He himself had proof of a patient or two who had achieved miraculous remissions with treatments no different from his own. Their successes were the only news that gave his doctor hope, but he also knew the world abounded with charlatans and frauds.

"Do you think it was some kind of trick?" he asked as he watched the tape click off and the flashing lights abruptly stop. Although the volume was already down, an energy in the room seemed simultaneously to freeze.

"It couldn't have been. He was too specific. And he doesn't know anyone I know. He's just this guy."

"I've thought of going, but I don't know how to tell the quacks from the real ones. If there are real ones . . . ," William said. When he browsed in the city, sometimes there seemed to be tarot readers and fortunetellers on every block. Often he was tempted to buy a prediction for the ten dollars advertised on the sidewalk sign, but he was afraid someone he knew might see him as they passed on the street outside.

"I've never been to one, obviously, but I swear he was legit," Susan said. "My only other experience was the Christmas I threw the tarot cards I got in my stocking before I left on vacation. I drew the card for death. My father forbade me to leave, but I went anyway. My car crashed into a snowdrift only an hour down the road, but I always figured it was just nerves that did me in."

An image of a car sliding on a storm-slicked road flashed through William's mind. He saw it crash against piles of snow, then flip, spinning, into the air. He sank lower into the cushions, propping his feet over the arm. "Did he tell you anything bad?" he asked.

"A few things." She hesitated. "He said he saw death all around me. Rooms lit with candles, coffins, that kind of stuff, but nothing specific. Not surprising these days, I guess."

It's me, William thought in a panic. *He meant me.* He tried to find a message in Susan's tone, some hint that the psychic had seen him marked for death, maybe only weeks from then, but she sounded matter-of-fact, almost studied in her restraint. If she sensed his alarm, she would only lie to pacify him. "But I could have told you that," he said, trying to match her casualness. "And you don't have to pay me."

"But it was the way he did it," Susan said, her words spilling forth again, nearly a babble. "I had barely shaken his hand hello before he asked, 'Who's William?' He shut his eyes and gave these capsule descriptions of everyone, like he was in a trance. He said Henry was sweet, a good soul, a bit too eager. Nothing we don't know, but my point is, he couldn't have known what Henry was like unless he'd met him or —"

"And how did he define me?" William asked, cutting her off.

"Difficult but worth the trouble," Susan said without missing a beat.

"True enough, I hope," William said, reaching for his package of cigarettes. He still believed he couldn't think clearly without them, but he had limited himself to one an hour, setting a portable timer so that he didn't smoke again until freed by the ping of the bell.

He flicked his lighter and inhaled deeply. He suspected that Susan was withholding information. Surely the psychic must have told her something more than just William's name and a summary of his personality. As he summoned the courage to ask, his whole body tensed, just as it did in the seconds before his doctor flipped open a report containing the results of his most recent tests.

He was exhausted by his daily battle between wanting to know the worst and wanting to know nothing at all. So far he had managed to walk that tightrope without falling into complete despair, but the threat was never far. *I will hang up the telephone if she says too much,* he told himself. He shut his eyes, flinching, but managed to ask, "So did he know I was sick?"

"He was very specific. He claimed there was a problem with your feet and that you believe it's your circulation, but it isn't. It's neurological and you should have it checked. I couldn't decide if I should mention it, but if I didn't and something bad happened, I'd never be able to forgive myself. Do you mind my asking? Is there something wrong?"

William disguised his gasp with a cough. He curled his legs under his buttocks and covered his lap with a cushion. For days his toes had felt oddly numb, even when he wore thick, woolly socks, like bare feet dipped too long in snow. He hadn't yet told his doctor, but it was the first new symptom in weeks that had caused him concern. So far he had managed to live with it, pretending his feet were only temporarily asleep. He soaked them in pails of hot water. He walked in circles around his living room so that his legs didn't wither from disuse.

When he listened to his tapes, he imagined the blood in his body cascading from his shoulders like a waterfall, collecting in rich, red pools at his toes. He still hadn't given up hope that the numbness would vanish. He was afraid that if he admitted the truth to Susan now, he would surrender whatever strength of will was preventing the paralysis from flourishing unchecked. He hoped denial, even half believed, could slow its onslaught.

He stubbed out the cigarette and reset the timer. "Not that I know of," he lied. Snuggled within the cushions, his feet sparked with sharp tingles of pain, like phantom limbs.

"Well, that's good, then," Susan said, relieved. "He wasn't right about absolutely everything, you know. By the way, he said there was something wrong with Henry's bladder. I'm about to call him."

"Lucky you. A whole evening ahead of spreading good news."

Susan laughed. "So you want to get some dinner?"

"Not tonight, but maybe later in the week."

"You've got plans?" she asked, hopefully.

"Just tired," William said with a yawn. He stretched his arms over his head with exaggerated movements to prove it, as if Susan could see him. "Besides, I've got to feed my fish."

"Yes, I heard."

"I think they're supposed to baby-sit."

"Consider yourself lucky. You almost got a dog."

"Really?" William said, wistfully. "I love dogs. I had a great one when I was a child. Big, black, and dumb. She was my favorite member of the family."

"Not much competition there," Susan said.

"True, but I've never come close to loving a human being as much as I loved that dog. For years after she died, I was sick with grief." As he spoke, quick, fragmented images of his dog came back to him as vividly as if he gazed upon a series of photographs: her cocked ears, her lolling tongue, the curve at the tip of her tail, the solitary oval of white fur, like a dab of paint, at the base of her chin.

He heard Susan's feet tap on the kitchen floor, heard water run in the sink, the clink of a glass, as she wandered with her portable phone. Although he knew it wasn't fair, he was annoyed that her call had shaken his reserve and made him sentimental. He wished she would hang up, but they had been friends for so long, she wasn't unnerved by silences between them. In years before, they often did the crossword puzzle over the telephone on Sunday afternoons, not speaking for long stretches of time, or watched movies in bed late at night, hooked ear to ear.

Tonight her familiarity oppressed him. Soon Henry would make his nightly call. And later, maybe other friends. He needed time to get his balance back before regret took root and haunted his sleep. "I need to go," he said.

He heard her set a glass down on the counter. She slammed the refrigerator door. "You could get another dog," she said, ignoring him.

"No."

"I'd help walk it. I wouldn't mind." She gulped into the receiver, her voice thick with stifled tears.

William turned to see the fish swimming in their tank, right, left, up, down, right, left, up, down. They were so robotic in their movements that they seemed unreal to him. He couldn't imagine how a person could ever grow fond of fish. There was nothing to do but feed them. They couldn't be touched.

"That's not the reason," he said, sharply. He didn't want to explain that there was a mournfulness he remembered in his dog's eyes whenever he left the house that used to break his heart. A long time ago he had decided that the only way to endure his illness was to sever his affections one by one. A dog would only destroy the indifference he had worked so hard to achieve. He wanted nothing in his life that would make it harder to say good-bye.

"Maybe I'll get one and you can borrow it," Susan said. "You could be its uncle or something."

"You hate dogs," William said. "Remember?"

"I never said that, exactly. I said I hated them messing up my apartment, but I don't know why I cared. Nobody sees it except the cleaning lady. I haven't had a date since last Halloween."

"Really?"

"Sad but true."

"I'd marry you if things were different," William said.

"You've been promising that for years," she said, laughing. "Maybe it's time to call your bluff, before I'm ruined by middle age."

William bristled in spite of himself. He wouldn't allow her even this offhand nostalgia. "I was middle-aged when I was nineteen, it turned out."

"William," she said, the word like a sigh.

"It's true."

"Maybe, but you can't know for sure."

"Yes, I can," he said. He didn't mean to drive his point home unkindly, but he refused to let anyone forget that the newspapers couldn't write of his disease without using adjectives meant to amplify its danger: *incurable, fatal, lethal, deadly, terminal* were trumpeted in every report, day after day. But even as he played the words repeatedly in his head, he often felt that they described someone else. Or that he had become not one, but two: the living, breathing person he had known for years, and then another, half-conscious, half-formed, but maturing wildly, like a demon child with a whole future to behold.

"I've had enough for one evening," Susan said. "It's been a long day." Even through the static, she sounded both angry and bored.

"I'll be nicer tomorrow," William said.

"Don't make promises you won't keep," she said, but her tone had lost its sharpness.

William untangled his legs and set his feet on the floor. He massaged his heels, trying to coax the blood to bring some feeling to the skin. He marveled again that Susan's psychic had guessed what no one else could possibly have known. "You never told me his name," he said.

"Who? My date?"

"No. The guy you saw. The psychic."

"Oh. You were so depressing I almost forgot that I had a great day. He's called Jim Benton. Just a normal name, but I've got to tell you, there's something about him that's amazing."

William set down the telephone and stretched his legs across the coffee table. He wiggled his toes. The weird sparks shooting from his nerve endings terrified him. He dreaded becoming paralyzed. He dreaded that the faltering sight in his left eye meant that soon he would be blind. Sometimes he felt a dangerous rumble in the beating of his heart, sometimes a burning in his lungs, sometimes a pain in his ear as sharp as if an ice pick were being driven through the drum.

There was so much still to come, afflictions more horrible than anything he had yet suffered. Some people died so quickly, snatched by a sudden ailment in the middle of the night, but others lingered intolerably, their bodies refusing to surrender until they were almost decomposed. He didn't know which he hoped for or what his death would be.

He had assumed there was nothing to do except wait while his body turned against him, part by part. But while he could still keep his own secrets, while he could still keep most signs of his condition hidden under his clothes, he wondered what, if anything, the psychic could divine about his life. Since his doctor could tell him nothing, William wanted to know if a gifted stranger might warn him of the danger in store, maybe map out the territory ahead so that he would be less surprised, as if he were planning the itinerary for a trip. Or maybe some part of him still hoped to be told that it was all a mistake, that he was dreaming, dreaming still.

He picked up the telephone book. He felt their meeting was fated when he found that out of the millions of names in the city, there was only one James Benton. He dialed the number, excited for the first time in weeks.

There were so many things he wanted to know.

"Come in," Jim Benton said as he led William through the entrance to his studio. A black map of the universe with white, glitter stars took up the entire wall behind a long desk made from a wooden door balanced on two black filing cabinets. On a small shelf next to the desk, William saw a pile of multicolored rocks, each twinkling with white crusts, like fossilized jewels. Placed in a circle around them were four crystals, blue, white, pink, and green, cut in the shape of pyramids. Sticks of incense smoked from their midst and from every windowsill and tabletop, so that William choked on the perfumed air.

"I see you've got all your bases covered," he said, indicating a large, three-dimensional portrait of Jesus with rays of light shooting from his arms. On a table in front of it a polished jade Buddha sat in the center of a wreath of eucalyptus leaves.

The psychic laughed as he offered a low black chair. He was younger than William had expected, with a pale, freckled face. A rope of clear crystal beads sparkled against his pale sweatshirt, nearly the same hue as his skin. He had hairless arms and the pure, poreless skin of a boy. He looked remarkably untouched for a person William guessed to be past thirty.

"Interesting chart," the psychic said as he pulled some papers from a folder.

The week before, William had left the date, place, and time of his birth on the psychic's answering machine. March 3, 1956, at 7:03 A.M. in Greenfield, California. He couldn't believe that any qualities unique to that particular time and place had forever determined the course of his life, but his doubts didn't keep him from adding that he had been born a month premature. Perhaps he had been drawn out of the womb early, by the movement of the stars and the inexorable pull of a Pisces moon, like a current or a tide.

His mother had spoken of a glass-walled nursery filled with bassinets of squalling babies. Out of so many, there must have been another born the same instant as he. If they were to meet, what would their differences be? During high school he had known a girl named Carol Sweich, who shared his birth date. They had been nothing alike. But often now William wondered what had become of her and if their common stars made her suffer as he suffered now.

The psychic kept the papers facing him, but with his one good eye William could see two pages printed from a computer. At this distance, they didn't appear much different from his laboratory reports. The first sheet had two large, perfectly drawn circles with each center filled with words. The other contained a list of astrological signs followed by columns and figures. William could read "positive" and "negative" written next to each entry. Even upside down, he could see that his negatives outnumbered his positives, two to one.

Jim closed his eyes and slowly waved his arms above the paper. Then he smiled, blinking. "You are Pisces with a moon in Aquarius. That means you are a very nice person."

"I'm not, actually," William said. He didn't want compliments. He wanted to see a whole life ahead of him printed on those charts.

"You better lay off the cigarettes," Jim said with a stern look. "Your lungs are terrible."

William stiffened. He had showered carefully before he left home to erase the odor of smoke and had worn newly laundered clothes. "I quit," he lied.

A look of disbelief flickered on the psychic's face, as if he could see beneath the layers of William's clothes and skin to his lungs gooey with tar. "Well, you need to take care."

"Yes," William said politely. The tumors burned on his back like hot coins.

"Whew!" Jim said as he studied the chart. "Your life is really changing." He traced a finger along the edge of the larger circle. "Pluto is in the house of death. It's very strong here," he said, lingering over one particular spot. "I see you backing off from many of your relationships. You've been staying close to home lately to protect yourself. I'd say it's been a very transformative year." His voice was breathy and light, but he stared at William with concern. "Am I right? Has there been a tremendous change?"

"I have been overwhelmed by things lately," William admitted, leaning closer to the table.

Jim pointed to a box in the corner of the chart. He mentioned the name of a moon, which one William couldn't remember later, but it was in the position of that particular star that Jim saw the most cataclysmic change. Then, with a flutter of his hands, he pointed to moon after moon rising on the chart, so many that William couldn't keep track of them: some receding, some coming present, so that if he hadn't been preoccupied with his illness, he might have taken comfort from the predictable rise and fall of those signs ordering his life. Now that he lived with little hope, he felt the moons' rise and fall like nothing but a curse.

"What's there? What's there?" he wanted to ask, peering anxiously at the signs snared within the circles, but he was afraid to know.

"I see you moving," Jim announced. "Do you have plans? A new apartment maybe?"

"No," William said, nervously. "What exactly do you see?" He knew he would never move again, except maybe back to the hospital.

"Lots of bright white space," Jim said. "Much sparser. You're cutting down. I bet you own a lot of things."

"Yes," William whispered. He scraped his chair away from the table and looked around. He noticed, scornfully, for the first time that the clay flowerpots arranged in groups about the room were painted gold, as a child might do in school.

"I see a new circle of people around you," the psychic said. "In the past you've spent your time taking care of your friends, but now you're letting people take care of you. Does that make sense?"

"In a way," William said, thinking of all the doctors and nurses who had been unknown to him only months before. He pictured himself abandoned to the hospital by his friends, left entirely in the care of strangers. He was horrified that the psychic seemed to see the truth of his present life. He tried to imagine if the same words would apply to anyone who might come there, like Henry or Susan. Henry had met the same patients and doctors as William. Henry was much more likely to move. His life might have changed these past months in any number of ways without William knowing.

Jim smiled. "I see love, a new love."

"No," William said, relaxing. "In that you're wrong."

"But you've already met him. Mickey . . . Mick . . . something like that. The name is very clear."

"Believe me. You're wrong."

The psychic shrugged and pointed to a break in the chart. "Here I see month after month of frantic activity that peaked in January. Since then your life's been more stabilized. Am I right?"

William fidgeted in his seat. January was the month he had entered the hospital. He picked up the pink quartz crystal and tossed it idly back and forth. "I can't think of anything in particular. What exactly do you see?"

Jim took the rock from William and set it on the table, out of reach. "Nothing concrete," he said, "but I can't help thinking it's been an amazing year. The next months will continue to be bumpy." He poked a finger at the bottom curve of the second circle. "And right here, about a year from now, I see an enormous change. I can't tell what exactly, but the energy's intense. I don't mean to freak you out, but you need to be careful. If you don't, there's a danger you'll explode." He glanced away as he spoke, as if to soften the blow.

A breeze from the opened window sent a cloud of incense fluttering into William's face. He waved the smoke away, madly. "Could you put that out?" he snapped, indicating a pyramid-shaped brass holder that held three smoldering sticks.

Jim wet two fingers with his tongue and pinched the red-hot tips of the punks serenely. "Sure."

"Sorry, but I hate that stuff," William said. Beads of sweat collected on his brow. His lips felt stretched over his teeth, chapped and thin. Did the psychic mean he had only one year to live?

If I believe him, I am doomed, he told himself. Maybe the psychic had tricked information out of Susan. Maybe he was feeding it back to William now, pretending those details were secrets he had divined.

Everyone William knew was in danger, one way or another. Just living in the city meant taking one's life in one's hands, day after day. It occurred to him that any prediction could be proved true simply by the power of suggestion. Jim could tell someone he saw a different occupation or a new love; it could put ideas in their head or make them more receptive to something they had wanted to do for years. And if the advice he offered encouraged them to make a change, they would believe he had predicted it all along.

"You okay?" Jim asked, reaching for William's hand.

"Yes, fine," William said, trying not to surrender to a dizziness that made the psychic's features blur and the room spin as if tilted on its axis.

"Okay, then, I want you to write down the names of the most important people in your life," Jim said, passing him a legal pad.

William tore a page into separate bits. Quickly he wrote *Henry*, then *Susan*. He scrawled the names of his doorman and his former boss to stack the deck. He hesitated before adding *Edmund* and *Rachel*, the names of his parents. He tensed as he wrote, like someone who has accepted a dare.

Jim waved his hands over the paper, then raised them higher, as if singed by its heat. "Sorry, nothing," he said as he hovered over William's boss. He moved past the doorman, shaking his head. "A coworker, maybe?" he asked, frowning, barely pausing as his hand shot to William's parents. He lifted the names between two fingers and shut his eyes. "I feel a separation stretching for years. Or something worse than that. Some sort of betrayal, maybe?"

William leaned back, aghast. "If he can see that far back, then how clear the present must be," he thought, dreading the horror of what was to come. He pictured the white stone house on the ranch more clearly than he had in years, then an image of his parents grown white-haired and wrinkled with age. They would be over seventy now. He never dreamed of reunion, even in his most desperate moments, but he couldn't help but ask, "Are they dead?"

"No," Jim said. "They're very much alive." He shuddered briefly, letting the torn corners of paper float to the floor. "I'm sorry about what happened. It needn't have turned out that way."

William shrugged. "Too late now," he said, but the psychic seemed to look right through him, lost in another place and time.

"I see Brendan," he said, finally. "Who's he?"

William racked his brain, thrilled that he had never known anyone named Brendan. He couldn't even think of a classmate from his distant past with that name. He beamed, believing that if the psychic could err so completely in one regard, then later he could discount any bad news. "I don't know a Brendan," he said. "Never have."

"Blond? About your age?" Jim asked in a tone of voice that reminded William of his therapist's when she believed he was resisting.

"No. You're wrong."

"Odd that I would feel the name so strongly when it's such an uncommon one," Jim said. "Well, maybe you'll remember later." He chose another slip of paper and read, "Henry," aloud. "He's intense, but very much your friend. Be nicer to him. He really cares."

Before William could speak, Jim retrieved Susan's name. He closed the paper in his palm, speaking in clipped staccato tones. "She's like a sister. You were once closer but have grown apart. She wants to talk to you, but she's afraid. You need to give her an opening."

William was surprised that his lip trembled. For a moment he was afraid he might weep and confess his reasons for coming. He composed himself before he said, "You met her two weeks ago."

"Yes?"

"I wondered if you remembered."

"Yes."

"Well, she told me some things you said that made me worry, and well . . . that's partly why I'm here."

"She shouldn't have," Jim said. "It's impossible to reconstruct a session for someone who wasn't there. It gets a different spin." He cracked the joints in his fingers, loud as snapped twigs.

William indicated the chart separating them and moved forward to touch the pages, as if they were written in Braille. "But are you always honest about what you see?"

"You mean, do I ever give bad news? Sure. I give warnings if I see a dangerous period ahead, like I did with you. But remember this: if you believe in another, deeper plane, as I do, then what's to say that every spirit is good? They're like people everywhere. Some could be evil, liars, anything at all. That's why I don't like my clients to believe that what I see is irrevocable. It takes away any possibility of chance. Or maybe even a miracle."

"I don't believe in miracles," William said. "I'm not even sure I believe in chance."

"Miracles are a part of life," Jim said. His sincerity withered the half-formed smirk on William's face. At that moment, he wished that he, too, were able to believe.

"Either way," Jim continued, "everything I do is just an interpretation of something intangible. Call it an educated instinct, maybe a gift. It's not like reading a script."

"But let's say that something terrible was about to happen to you, maybe even that you were about to die, could you read it in your own chart?"

The psychic hesitated, but he engaged William fully with his friendliness. "I'm not sure, because I don't do my own chart. It's like cutting your own hair. I might see a pattern for the coming months, maybe the next year. Nothing concrete. But look, you could leave here and be shot on the street. You could go home and jump out a window. What do I know? Anything I see is intelligible only to a point. And even if you were killed the moment you left, your chart needn't have an end. I might see an energy racing through the dark that could be simply the movement of your soul. There's nothing here that simply tracks the course of your body. To me it's just a thing, like meat."

William saw an image of his soul shooting like a meteor into the galaxy while his body lay lifeless on a bed. He couldn't decide how far to press this man. He certainly was kind; he could ask Jim anything and no one else would ever know. But if he were to admit his true reason for coming, Jim might return to the charts and tell him that he saw his life stopping cold at one specific moment only months from then. William wasn't ready to know more; maybe he never would be.

Get out now, a voice told him as he dug into his pocket and peeled a roll of bills, slipping five twenties under the corner of his chart. "Thank you for your help," he said, standing.

Jim winked and squeezed William's arm. "Anytime. I'm always here."

William let his fingers brush against the psychic's hand. "When do you think it's reasonable to return?" he asked, shyly. Despite his doubts, he felt so warm in Jim's presence that suddenly he wanted to come back the next day, and the day after, to maintain a kind of vigilance over his life. In the old days, he would have tried to seduce him.

"It's up to you, but usually not for nine months at least, usually a year. I don't like people to think they can't function without a chart to guide them."

"A year?" William laughed to himself. He could well be dead by then. But maybe the psychic would not have suggested such a distant date if he'd envisioned William's death. "I'm not interested in crystal balls," he lied.

"Good. They don't exist."

"I'd be afraid if I thought I could see every moment of the rest of my life," William continued. "But part of me also wants it. I want to know."

"You already know," Jim said. "Trust me. You've got it all inside."

As William walked through the foyer, he tripped on a small rug at the threshold. He caught his balance by slamming his hand against the wall, disturbing a square, framed mirror. He straightened it carefully, shocked at how pale he was, even under the flush of his embarrassment. He looked old.

Jim followed him to the top of the stairs. William regarded the landing at the bottom of the three steep flights dizzily, praying that his feet would carry him there. After an hour sitting immobile in the chair, they felt useless and near dead. No longer concerned with keeping secrets, but more from a sense of wounded pride, he didn't want the psychic to watch him struggle down. "Good-bye again," he said, delaying. "Maybe see you next year."

"I hope so," Jim said. "Take care."

William managed the first step as the psychic turned back to his apartment, then another, leaning hard against the banister. He paused when he felt a pair of eyes peering over the railing at the top of his descending head. He looked up, catching Jim's stare.

"You really should tell your doctor about your feet," the psychic said, gently, before he moved into the shadows and disappeared.

Dusk was falling when William walked outside. He turned left onto a southbound street, limping among a crowd that knocked against him, hissing at his slowness. He veered off the sidewalk, creeping along beside the cars parked at the curb. He kept his eyes on the pavement so that he did not trip on the bumps and rutted tar that threatened to send him sprawling to the ground. *I hate this place*, he cried to himself, but he could have been anywhere and known the same despair.

The psychic had undone him, not by anything he said, but in subtler ways, for William was even less sure now what he wanted. It made no difference to know how much longer he had to live; his illness had already broken the spell. He remembered what Henry had told him one day in the hospital when he read from the notes for his afternoon class: that when Prometheus stole fire from Olympus, the gods sought their revenge by stealing from all mortals a gift they believed to be precious: the knowledge of the date of their death. A theft for a theft. By taking this certainty away, they meant to mock all humans by deluding them with the false hope of immortality, the misbelief that they could be like gods and live forever. But what kind of punishment was that?

Every time he fell in love, William needed to believe that the emotion would last forever, even if it never had before. The possibility of endlessness filled him with a kind of hope. And even when the love lasted no longer than a week or two, the same hopefulness returned each time desire claimed him. This illusion was necessary, just as acting as if his life would never end had empowered him with purpose, even if it had never been fulfilled. If he had known from birth the exact moment of his death, he would only have become paralyzed by the passage of time and marked each day with an x on the calendar, just as he was doing now. Before he became ill, time always seemed to be moving. Afterward, it stopped. What he regretted most about his disease was the way it had stolen from him the ignorance upon which promises were built, and which he had left too far behind to ever feel again.

A truck honked meanly, startling him so that he stumbled against a car. He jumped back as a bus blew by, ruffling his hair. He raised an arm to hail a cab, desperate to get out of there. Within seconds one screeched to a stop and he tumbled in. He gave his address to the driver, then slumped down, mute and trembling. He tried to distract himself by counting familiar sights as they whisked through the traffic — past the opera house, the museum, his therapist's office, a favorite store, then into the park and through the narrow tunnel that brought them out to the other side of town.

In another time, he would have walked the whole way home to clear his head, but his feet, his back, his eyes, burned with pain and fatigue. He tried to shake off his panic, but with the radio blaring music with a salsa beat and the swerve and rush of oncoming cars, he felt trapped against the lumpy seat. Three fat-faced children leered at him from a gallery of photographs taped to the dashboard. A bulky, silver-plated crucifix swung on a chain from the rear-view mirror. He swelled with rage at the foreignness of the driver, mimicking his name to himself with a racist sneer, stopping just short of railing insanely about how his kind polluted the city and made life there impossible to bear.

I want out, he was going to shout, but through the window he saw the avenue stretching for miles in front of him, flat and in a perfect line. He felt his body flinch with a kind of hopelessness he had never experienced before. He might as well have looked out upon the earth from the edge of the visible universe, marooned, adrift, for the distance that separated him from where he sat to the door of his home was no less far than that.

PART TWO

The only thing grief has taught me is how shallow it is. That, like all the rest, plays about the surface, and never introduces me into the reality, for contact with which we would even pay the costly price of sons and lovers. . . . An innavigatable sea washes with silent waves between us and the things we aim at and converse with. Grief, too, will make us idealists. In the death of my son, now more than two years ago, I seem to have lost a beautiful estate — no more. I cannot get it nearer to me. If to-morrow I should be informed of the bankruptcy of my principal debtors, the loss of my property would be a great inconvenience to me, perhaps, for many years; but it would leave me as it found me, — neither better nor worse. So it is with this calamity; it does not touch me; something which I fancied was a part of me, which could not be torn away without tearing me nor enlarged without enriching me, falls off from me and leaves no scar. It was caducous. I grieve that grief can teach me nothing, nor carry me one step into real nature.

— RALPH WALDO EMERSON, *Experience*

13

He feels awful all the time.

When he is not in crisis, his friends assume he feels the way they do, as if his disease were a sporadic interruption, a cold or flu, instead of an unstoppable assault, a wearing down. At night, when his brain refuses to let the body sleep, he thinks of ways to describe to his friends what it feels like to be dying, the day-to-day process of the body wasting from the inside out. Hour after hour he spins sentences in his head, but he despairs of ever finding the right words. He feels as separate from his friends as if illness had taught him a new, untranslatable language they will never speak. Still, he cannot stop. The need for sympathy, the need for them to understand, rattles his sleep.

The closest he can get is: imagine the aftermath of the worst flu you've ever had, the first day beyond two weeks of vomiting and fever, before you believe you will ever really be well. The body is spent, shaken — a cottony mouth, palsied limbs, bruised bones, the head a dull ache, the stomach thin as paper, hollowed-out — so that every organ, every vein, every muscle and tendon reels from an unending seasickness, a poisonousness that sticks to him like webs.

That is the best he ever feels.

Then imagine your skin in revolt, the skin like a map of the ravages of the interior. Its rashes and blisters bloom in long, tentacle-like clusters. Tumors inch down now to your arms, your wrists, your hands, permanent as scars. Patches of eczema cover your shoulders, your back, with white crusted craters that remind you of other things: a field of day-old snow, a spoiled custard, a long-distance photograph of the surface of the moon. Except the thing you see is not something other. It is your body.

That is the best he ever feels.

He is so tired. Every step is an effort, even if he pretends otherwise. The farther he ventures out from home, the worse he feels, for movement only excites the disease. When he walks too long a distance, he becomes desperate, as if he were lost alone among the dunes of the Sahara, a mountain range in winter, the middle of the deepest sea. When he eats dinner with friends, he chews, he smiles, he chats, but he isn't listening. He wants only to lay down his head and go to sleep. He longs for bed. He longs to give up.

That is the best he ever feels.

The closer he gets to death, the less he understands, for it is harder to comprehend than the terrain of an undiscovered universe. He cannot picture it, cannot even guess, for all his energy is taken up by dying. He had not anticipated that the fear would escalate, day after day, growing in tandem with the disease. He wants to say to his friends: imagine awakening from a deep sleep to hear a window being jimmied in your house, a shatter of glass, footsteps on the stairs, the click of a trigger. You rise, trembling, look around. The steps inch nearer. You want to act to save yourself, only there is no escape: no telephone call to summon the police, no cry for help to the street outside, no weapon to fashion from the objects in your room, for the sounds you hear are your own heart beating. The intruder is already part of you. It has stolen inside.

That is the best he ever feels.

*

Each morning when he awakes, he opens an eye. During sleep he forgets, and there is a brief, nearly conscious moment when he hopes a miracle has occurred. He yawns, tentatively; raises his head. He doesn't feel so bad. But when he starts to stand, the poisons move, churning through his system like factory smoke, thick clouds of it, that knock him flat before he gets two inches from the bed. Then it all comes back, the infinity of his sickness, every morning a reminder that he lives something that will never end.

Even if he never tells you, that is the best he ever feels.

14

There was something about Henry's blood that could help William, or so his doctor believed. He had read about a revolutionary machine invented by a colleague in a neighboring state that withdrew plasma from a healthy donor and pumped it directly into the patient's vein. The theory was that infusions of perfect blood could rebuild an immune system and thwart the progress of the disease. Only one machine existed in the country. The treatment was too experimental to have been proven right or wrong, but already swarms of patients had flocked to the doctor's office. William broke through the waiting list with a few well-placed telephone calls and an offer to pay cash. All he needed was a healthy donor willing to travel once a month for the transfusion.

When William called to ask if he would participate in the experiment, Henry jumped at the chance. At last he was offered a way to help his friend directly, not just by companionship or love, but by something tangible, a part of his own body that could be fed straight into William, as if Henry himself had become a miracle drug.

The morning they met at the train station to travel to the doctor's office, William was strangely silent, almost shy, but Henry embraced him joyfully, as if after a long separation. In his back pocket he carried a letter from his doctor proclaiming his blood free of any impurities or communicable disease. In his knapsack: a bag of pastries and two cups of coffee, the morning newspaper, a book with a handmade, brown paper cover, and a stack of magazines, as if the journey ahead would take all day instead of an easy hour along the river.

William immediately settled into the first double seat and closed his eyes. Henry arranged the magazines and newspaper on his lap. A bell sounded. The conductor shouted a command. Henry flicked on the overhead light as the train slipped into the dark maze of underground tunnels beneath the city streets. He broke a corner off the plastic cup and sipped his coffee. "Hungry?" he asked, crinkling the bag of pastries temptingly, but William didn't stir. His eyeballs flitted under his lids as he pretended to sleep.

The train made one stop in the heart of the ghetto, then traveled north along the river, stopping every few minutes at towns so small that their stations were nothing but shacks, with vending machines and pay telephones set outside by the rails. Henry was stunned to see trees in every direction ablaze with flame-colored leaves. He couldn't believe summer had come and gone without his noticing the change of seasons.

He counted back from the date on the newspaper: nine months had passed since William had entered the hospital. It seemed to be as recent as yesterday and as far as forever since that day, so completely had their lives been changed. Soon it would be a year. Henry had never told William, but in the hospital the doctor had whispered that he could expect to survive for eighteen months with the drugs available then. He had kept that information secret from everyone except Susan, not wanting to jinx William with its finality.

Already they were halfway there.

Despite the miracle the new treatment promised, Henry hoped it hadn't come too late. Over his and Susan's protests, William had resigned from his job and taken disability. He spent almost every moment in his apartment alone. Even acquaintances had noticed a change in him. He had become less volatile, often even sweet, with a slightly befuddled quality. Sometimes now in conversation his words broke forth, sudden and disconnected, like a person shouting in his sleep. One lung had collapsed without warning and had been intricately repaired. After months of failing vision, William had gone blind in his left eye. He wore glasses for the first time in his life, with tortoise-shell frames that gave him a studious, distracted air, and lenses tinted gray to obscure his eyes. But Henry could still detect a slower flutter of the left lid, a single blink to two of the unafflicted one.

Sometimes when he was alone, Henry held one eye closed in an attempt to understand William's diminishing sight. He practiced turning his head around to compensate for the loss of a sideward glance, even stumbled to within inches of street signs and posters to focus on the words. Still, he knew his experiment was nothing compared to the truth of William's life, for he lacked the fear that his other eye would follow after, leaving him helpless and struck blind.

From the window of the train, he had a clear view across the river to the villages nestled along its banks: white clapboard houses, neat lawns, church steeples rising from sloping slate roofs into a blue, cloudless sky. He breathed deeply and closed his eyes. Even sealed within the car, he felt as if he could inhale the crystalline air.

Until William's illness intervened, Henry hadn't realized how much he had come to depend on visits to the house for whatever sense of peacefulness he could claim for his life. Now car alarms and police sirens kept him awake until dawn on weekend nights, no matter where he slept. The longer he went without escape, the more the city felt like an alien place, so thick with black molecules of dust and exhaust that he could see its air. He was tired of crime and constant vigilance, of days of ceaseless inconvenience and preposterous expense, tired of the crunch of cockroaches under his boot and of rats racing across the sidewalk at every turn, sometimes brushing against his feet.

He missed the time alone in the country with William, but he also missed the ritual of leaving promptly at four every Friday afternoon, the vast expanse of farmland, sea, and sky, the familiarity with shopkeepers that he never found in the city, even the sound of the house in the middle of the night: the echoes of its rooms, the creak of the wind against the walls that sometimes made him feel as if he were caught inside a living thing. Over the past eight years, the hours he spent at school or home had begun to seem like an intrusion on the two days of bliss he spent each week at William's house. The joy he had known in being there was exactly how he wanted the rest of his life to be.

He wasn't sure why, but William hadn't asked to visit the house since his last day in the hospital. When they remained in the city during the first weeks after his discharge, Henry assumed he was simply waiting for his energy to return before making the trip. But in recent months, William had begun to talk of taking vacations, even flights to Europe, and still he never suggested going to the beach. Although Henry missed the house, part of him was relieved. The moment William told him about his will, the serenity it offered was ruined forever. He couldn't imagine what it would be like to return now, setting his books and photographs on the shelf in his room, walking through the downstairs after William had gone to bed, sitting awake until dawn in the chair by the living room window, knowing that it was to be his. With William watching, it would be impossible to stay a moment without being crippled by self-consciousness.

The last time they had gone there was New Year's Eve, only two weeks before William entered the hospital. Henry had just returned from Christmas vacation with his parents, giddy after so many claustrophobic nights sleeping on the sofa while his married brothers were given the spare rooms. He had taken a bus to William's house directly from the airport, not bothering to stop at his apartment, counting the exits impatiently as he rode closer and closer.

As time went on, that weekend grew more perfect in Henry's mind: five inches of new snow preceding a crisp winter night lit by the moon and the twinkling colored lights of holiday decorations reflecting off the neighbors' whitened lawns. William had claimed to be catching flu, so Henry held his arm when they took a walk after dinner. With the feathery drifts beneath their feet and the vapor of their breath mixing with William's cigarette smoke, he had felt as if they were floating among clouds.

Back inside, they built a fire and lay on cushions on the floor, their faces, the rugs, the dark, burnished wood of the walls, all seeming to glow orange-red in the flames. They had kept the TV on to watch the ball drop in Times Square at midnight, raising their glasses to toast the New Year, even tipping a glass to Susan, who had fled the cold for a week in the sun.

After William drifted off to sleep, Henry tiptoed about the room, looking again at his opened presents under the Christmas tree, stoking the fire until it roared, then peering out the frosted windows to watch a snow-thickened wind whip across the yard. He remembered thinking how contented he was to have returned. He loved his parents, but he had been bored by their endless meals and celebrations for the first time he could recall, crowded by relatives who never stopped talking, yet asked no questions about his life. Feeling flushed with love, and freed from his usual inhibition by the bottle of champagne he had finished alone, Henry leaned down to shake William awake. He told him that he would never again go home for the holidays, even began to make a list of guests to invite for a party the following year, until William raised a hand and said, "Slow down. I hate Christmas, remember? Let's just keep it you and me."

Henry had felt both pleased and chastened, but later he was ashamed at how stupid he had been. William must already have known that the disease had taken hold of him, for within two weeks he was in the hospital and their familiar world was over.

The house grew larger in Henry's mind, whiter, more idyllic against the freshly fallen snow. Sometimes he wondered if he would ever see it again, or if it had been ruined for William, too, in different ways, and so had become part of a past to which they could never return. Often now he dreamed of sneaking off to some underpopulated place on his own, especially when he felt crushed by William's demands. But he was afraid that guilt would haunt his life forever if he were to be so mean as to leave his friend to die alone.

As if he read his mind, William shifted in his seat, bunching his knapsack like a pillow against the window. "Thank you for doing this," he said simply, for once not growling to undermine the gratitude he wanted to express.

"You're welcome," Henry said, but he felt a sinking in his heart, because he knew that as long as William lived, his disease would dictate the boundaries of both their homes.

When the train arrived at the station, William seemed overwhelmed by the few disembarking passengers. Henry helped him down the two metal steps onto the platform and out into the street. They stopped at a line of waiting cabs, not yellow with the familiar stenciled markings of those in the city, but black and sleek, like limousines. They climbed into the first idling car as Henry gave the driver the doctor's address. The man snapped his head around, then turned back to the road, gripping the steering wheel with both hands, not moving. All Henry could see were his mean, green eyes glowering in the rear-view mirror.

In the old days, William would have challenged his look of hatred and disgust with an unflinching stare, maybe even raised his voice in protest, but now he bent his head down quickly. "There goes your tip, asshole," Henry muttered as he leaned forward to catch the driver's glare. He kept his gaze steady and unafraid, though he trembled inside, until the man blinked and they drove away.

Henry wanted to kill the driver, but he couldn't entirely blame him. He had become so accustomed to the sight of sick people roaming the city streets that he had forgotten they were not in evidence everywhere, not even in newspapers or on TV. He had to admit that in the bright, suburban light, William's skin appeared more ghostly than ever, faintly tinged with green.

They rode in silence, broken only by William's ragged cough. He clapped his hands to his mouth to stifle the noise, as a person would do in a theater, until his fingers glistened with spit. The driver lit one cigarette, then another, obscuring his head in thick veils of smoke. After several miles, the car slowed and turned into a parking lot. Henry tensed, thinking the driver planned to leave them stranded in an industrial park. Then he noticed the correct address printed on a small wooden sign tucked within a manicured circle of sodded lawn.

"We're there," he said, bewildered by the low rectangular building with black, mirrored windows rising before them, nothing like the quaint brownstone on a tree-lined street where William's doctor had his office in the city.

Henry paid the fare with exact change, down to the nickel. He led William through an electrified door, past a security guard, and down a long, gray-carpeted corridor to the doctor's suite. The door swung open on a well-oiled hinge. They tiptoed in.

Only two couples occupied the four rows of upholstered chairs. Henry gave his name to the receptionist before joining William in a double seat. He chose a magazine from his knapsack and pretended to read as he studied the four other men. He had no trouble distinguishing the donors from the patients: the two sick men slumped like sacks of bones within their chairs. William seemed almost sprightly by comparison. One man wore a wrinkled pajama top over a pair of filthy jeans. His jaw hung slackly open, revealing a fat, cream-colored tongue. He seemed incapable of speech. But suddenly he smiled at Henry and croaked, with a fungus-thickened slur, "Your first time?"

Henry nodded, fanning the magazine across his chest in a kind of hug.

"My third," the man said, flashing two fingers in a victory sign, but he wheezed harshly, as if no air reached his lungs.

"We'd almost given up hope until news of Dr. Beck's treatment came," his companion said breathlessly, like a pilgrim come to drink at the waters of Lourdes.

The other patient nodded in agreement, but his movements were slow and stiff. "Me, too," he whispered, his eyes bulging.

This isn't possible, Henry thought as he fidgeted against the chair. Maybe his expectations had been too high, but when he imagined coming to the doctor's office, he pictured a room filled with recovering patients, rosy-cheeked and brimming with promise, not these freaks nearly demented in their optimism. It was impossible to know how bad they had looked before their treatments began. Maybe they had been rolled in comatose, on stretchers, but today they seemed to be hopeless cases, cadaverous and half alive. *If this doesn't work, what will we do?* he thought. He turned to William for reassurance, but his face was buried in a fashion magazine, with an expression as concentrated as if he were studying for an exam.

Over the loudspeaker a man called Henry's name. He squeezed William's hand as he rose to follow a secretary into a large paneled office lined floor to ceiling with shelves of medical books. Each volume was bound in soft, red leather with gold letters stamped into its uncracked spine. Henry barely had time to scan the first row of titles before a man barreled in from a side door.

"I'm Alan Beck," he said, extending an arm as if throwing a punch. Henry took two steps back as he shook the doctor's hand. His nails were white and perfectly trimmed, as shiny as his expensive suit. He smelled clean and freshly showered, perfumed with lavender talc. He reminded Henry more of a preacher than a physician, one who had made millions on TV.

"Make yourself comfortable," the doctor said. "I asked to see you first to explain the procedure, so you'll know what's in store."

"It seems pretty straightforward," Henry said, sitting in a chair that matched exactly the red of the leather books. "My only concern is that it work." He smiled the way he did with the parents of students he hated at school.

The doctor took a pencil from a brass cup and braced it between his thumbs, as if to snap it in half, then stopped teasingly, pointing the tip at Henry's face. "I don't have enough data yet to disprove the skeptics, but I'm convinced I'm onto something. You would be, too, if you'd seen the results I've achieved in only six months. By next year I expect to publish a paper that will change the face of therapy."

His enthusiasm seemed at odds with the two ruined patients Henry had met in the waiting room. "But those other men . . . ," he began haltingly, pointing toward the outer door. He wondered if they could possibly have been as bad as he remembered.

The doctor shrugged, unfazed. "Some begin too late, but I've got over one hundred patients in treatment, and more than half are in complete remission. Nobody else alive can beat those odds. My only problem is finding dependable donors. And necessary funds."

Henry felt pinned by the doctor's eyes. In the light from the window, his pupils glittered with specks of gold. Henry stopped himself from volunteering to travel there on alternate weeks to donate his blood to strangers. He knew he would only become dangerously entwined in their lives. "How soon will I see a change in William?" he asked instead, looking down at his lap to break the lock of the doctor's stare.

Beck flipped the pencil into the air. It landed perfectly in the center of the cup, with a pop, spinning two revolutions around the rim. He leaned back, smiling, as if pleased by something more than just his aim. "By tomorrow, I hope, or the next day for sure. My machine mixes the plasma with antihistamines to prevent allergic reactions, so tonight he'll sleep it off. By Wednesday or Thursday, you'll notice an increase in his energy. After two weeks there'll be a gradual return to his previous state.

"But . . . ," he paused for emphasis, leaning halfway across the desk. "With successive treatments, the good days will grow longer every month. A year from now, there's no telling what will happen. I hope it's the beginning of a whole new world. For all of us."

"Me, too," Henry said, feeling a new wave of hopefulness rise on the crest of the doctor's conviction. He reached into his pocket for the letter confirming the health of his blood, eager to get started. "I'm supposed to give you this," he added, passing the envelope across the desk.

The doctor scanned the letter, eyes gleaming, then slipped it into William's folder. "If you ever find yourself with a few extra hours, we could use a man like you. I've got so many patients desperate for donors, they could form a line around the block."

Henry imagined himself trapped within a crowd of hundreds: men, women, and children pecking at his clothes, tapping at his body with canes. He couldn't dispel the feeling that a decent person would somehow find the time to help. "Don't ask me that," he said. "Not now, anyway. I barely have time for my friend."

"Then let's go meet him," the doctor said curtly, rising and stretching to his full height so that Henry felt dwarfed and childish in his chair.

William dozed alone in the waiting room, the magazine dropped at his feet. The doctor leaned down to shake his arm, gently, with a kindness Henry hadn't believed he possessed. He ushered them into a cavernous chamber with cinder-block walls and a polished linoleum floor. Two rocking chairs were placed to the right and left of a gleaming beige machine. Except for long plastic tubes emerging from each side, it looked more like a clothes dryer than a miraculous device, but Henry tried to keep his spirits high.

"Meet the monster," the doctor said, affecting a B-movie accent. He smiled broadly, pointing to his left just as a middle-aged woman entered the room. Confused by the doctor's intention, Henry looked from her lean, blond features to the small glass window in the center of the machine framed with polished strips of metal. Then he heard, "And meet Elsa. She'll fix you up."

As the doctor left, the nurse snapped on a pair of latex gloves and swabbed Henry's arm with an alcohol pad. He made a fist that popped a network of veins over his muscles, fat, supple, and blue. "Nice," Elsa cooed as she slipped the IV in. He watched her lift William's arm with a tight-lipped smile. His veins were squashed and mottled with scars from months of different treatments, overused as a junkie's. In the places between, dark red tumors clogged the skin. The nurse pinched expertly along the flesh until she squeezed a thin, squiggled inch and secured the needle with a strip of tape. She dusted her hands, pleased, then flicked a switch on the opposite wall.

"Back in thirty," she said, tapping her watch as she marched out the door. Henry felt a slight tug in his vein as the machine whirred, like a fan accelerating. He gripped the arms of his chair, trying to keep its rockers firmly on the ground. "Do you think Elsa moonlights at the prison?" he asked nervously, but William stared ahead, white-faced and stony, like a man strapped to his seat as a plane ascends, scared to death of flying.

A music video flickered on a television screen hooked to the ceiling above their heads, but the volume was too low to be heard over the sound of the machine. The singers seemed to sway to the *clatclatclat* of the motor. Henry tried to concentrate on their dancing feet, but out of the corner of his eye he saw the plastic tube darken with a spurt of blood, and he turned his attention there, praying for its healing powers.

The engine revved into higher gear. After several minutes, a clear, syrupy substance leaked out the other end, inching toward the needle in William's vein. "Ready?" Henry asked. His voice echoed off the chilly cement walls. *Ready?*

William crossed two fingers as he raised his free arm. He rocked back, once, twice, as if bracing himself, then dropped his hand and fished a tape player from his bag. "Sayonara," he said, placing the earphones on his head.

Henry's legs shook on the raised balls of his feet, while William sat completely still, betraying nothing, as if napping on a porch in the open air. *What is he thinking?* Henry wondered, amazed by the calm demeanor of his friend. Excitement, fear, hope, charged so palpably through his own body that he would have leaped from the chair had he not been bound by the needle in his arm.

He closed his eyes and imagined lying with William in a deep, feathery bed, their bodies curled into its center, the tubes encircling them like arms. He pictured his blood, stripped free of color, like a pure and liquid sun. He let the hum of the machine run through him until he felt its sound pump directly from his heart. *Please work,* he pleaded silently as he stroked his swollen vein, as if it alone were capable of bestowing all the grace he sought for both of them to have.

"Beach, sea, sand," William muttered twice, flat and off-key, as if he were singing a refrain along with the tape, forgetting Henry was near.

What song is that? Henry remembered thinking as he drifted off to dreams, dreaming more in thirty minutes than he had in the last nine months of fitful sleep.

He awoke with a start when Elsa touched his arm. She moved between them silently, detaching both IVs and pressing thin strips of gauze and tape over their bubbling wounds. She poured orange juice into two specimen cups, pausing to steady William's trembling hand.

"Wait a few minutes before you stand," she said, wiping the counter with a towel. She gathered some papers for the trash and wound a yard of rubber tubing around her arm. "I wish you good luck," she added, passing each of them a miniature candy bar, like those given a child on Halloween.

"William?" Henry asked. The room seemed oddly quiet in the nurse's absence, as if they were locked inside the building in the middle of the night, totally alone.

"I'm here," William said. He rubbed his fingers over the bandage on his arm.

"How do you feel?"

"I don't know. Dopey, but otherwise the same."

"The doctor said it would take a few days," Henry said, munching his chocolate. Now that its motor was silenced, the machine looked amateurish and preposterous, the invention of a crank. "He claimed he had a hundred men in treatment," he added, forgetting what the doctor's point had been.

"They all say that," William said. "I think it's code they learn in medical school."

"Let's go home," Henry said, rising to his feet. He stumbled as William leaned heavily against him, 150 pounds of dead weight. He propped him in a chair in the waiting room before scheduling their next appointment, exactly one month from that day. He wished it were sooner. He didn't want to wait to find out whether the treatment would or wouldn't work.

On the way back to the city, William slept for real, snoring loudly as commuters poured into the aisles. A dribble of drool, the color of plasma, collected on his chin.

Once he was certain William wouldn't awake, Henry removed the book he had secreted in his bag. He had stripped off its dust jacket at home and fashioned a cover from a paper sack, as if he were hiding pornography instead of a history of death in other cultures.

He lost himself in funerary ceremonies and strange rites of burial, whole catalogs of precautions from ages past that protected the living from the dead. He read that sometimes the deceased's house was set on fire to obliterate the spirit, or strung with nets to trap the escaping soul. He read of animal and human sacrifice, of corpses draped with coins to buy safe passage across the river of death, of crematoriums and ovens, of mummies embalmed with aromatic herbs. He read of pyres piled high with burning sticks, of burial grounds ringed with flaming ditches to keep loose souls contained, even of bodies buried aboveground, hung swinging from the limbs of the trees.

As they traveled, the murmurs of the other passengers receded, until Henry became lost in the worlds contained in his book, lulled by the steady rhythm of William's snores and the gentle vibrations of the train. He was amazed at how in other times the dead were treated as living things, not just as memories, but as fearsome, sometimes vengeful souls. The more he read, the more he realized that what he dreaded most about William's death was the opposite of his spirit's return: he feared that it would mean the complete extinguishing of everything familiar, that there would be nothing to prove William had existed except a jumble of discarded things.

The dead were gone too quickly. In the hospital Henry had heard stories of warm corpses sneaked out of rooms in secret compartments at the bottom of supply carts, so that no visitors might see them. If William was going to die, Henry longed for a ceremony equal to those he read about in his book — a procession of mourners, a blazing fire, even a slaughter of gladiators to mark the event — but he knew nothing about how even simple arrangements were made: undertakers, plots, reservations for a church, eulogies, a slab of marble for a tomb. To ask William's advice would mean that he had given up too early, but there was so much more to death than one man's dying, Henry felt incapable of managing alone.

He heard a whistle as the train sped into a tunnel and out the other side. Light to dark then back to light so quickly that his vision faltered, as if he had stared too long at the sun. He blinked twice to banish the grayness that swept through the car, waiting as William's form was restored slowly to his sight, like a body emerging from clouds. In sleep, the creases of worry that lined his mouth and brow relaxed, so that he seemed younger, but also less alive. His head slumped to one side, making the glands in his neck swell oddly out, like second cheeks, but with his eyes closed, his face seemed blank and hollow as a rubber mask. Although Henry could see William's chest slowly expand and contract with every breath, he thought, for an instant, that he'd seen an image of what his friend would look like dead.

He wondered if the time would ever come when William admitted he had abandoned hope, so they might plan together for his death, or if they would continue the charade of his living long past reason, even after William lay wasted on a bed. He didn't know why such gloom had swallowed him, when the treatment should have buoyed his spirits with their last, best hope. Maybe it was the memory of those two men in the waiting room who had made such faith seem a lie. Or maybe it was the books he had been reading that made death seem more certain than anything else he could dare to dream for his life.

"Tell me something I don't know," William said suddenly, opening his eyes. He grabbed Henry's knapsack, rummaging for leftovers from that morning's food.

Henry dropped his book with a start, as if he were the one who had been awakened. Just before becoming lost in daydreams, he had read that crematorium ovens were heated to 1,800 degrees. He racked his brain for any detail from the magazines and newspapers he carried in his bag, but his mind was blank of everything except images of burning bodies. "My mother told me on the phone the other night that there are only thirty-seven classical music stations left in the whole country," he finally said.

William yawned. "You're slipping," he said cheerfully, biting the corner from a stale crust of bread.

"Yes," Henry admitted, and let it pass, for he couldn't think of anything else to say. He turned to look toward the shore of the river, banked with huge, green expanses of field and lawn, dotted with clusters of oak and birch and pine. On another day, the sight might have made him eager for a simpler life, but suddenly it seemed like nothing more than acres of virgin burial sites, play-grounds for the dead: the circling birds watchful as vultures, the shadows of approaching dusk thick as mummies' shrouds. And that fire of red, orange, and yellow leaves was merely waiting to be stripped bare by winter and hung with corpses, like Christmas ornaments, swinging from the limbs of the trees.

15

In the shadow of a hill on the back quarter of the ranch, William's family had maintained a cemetery for generations, laid with the graves of their ancestors. Publius Virgilius Adams, Eber Hendrix, Mary Brewster, Elijah Hubbard — a multitude of names and interconnections that had been tied to the same plot of land for more than a century. Each family in turn had kept meticulous records of every detail known about their relatives in wooden boxes stacked by decade in a cedar closet in the attic. Albums of photographs, diaries, letters, birth certificates, marriage licenses, passports, account ledgers, badly typed autobiographies, were passed from patriarch to patriarch. Framed and protected by a double layer of glass was the original deed to the property, hung over the mantel in the living room, like a coat of arms.

At the western edge of the cemetery, just inside the property line, a large, untouched field of grass had been saved for William's immediate family and their descendants. His father used to worry about having enough space for future generations, as if he envisioned graves scattered over every inch of the visible mountainside for centuries to come.

As a child, William liked to play within the rusted, wrought iron fence that surrounded the older section of graves, pretending that the weathered stones were remnants of a ruined city. The older markers appeared to have been frozen in a moment of violence: some tipped to one side, some shoved to within inches of the ground, like bodies pushed over. The rest lay flat, overgrown with weeds and crumbled into pieces. Only one tombstone remained perfectly upright. It sat off to the side, rigid and untouched, as if it had somehow been spared the event that leveled the others. The lettering was worn off its face, leaving it bleached and smooth as a bone.

The landscape had always appeared oddly posed to William, like a photograph that captured some calamity out of time, just for an instant, but that threatened to spring back to life at any moment. He spent hours peering at every stone, wiping the surface with the back of his hand and scraping dirt off the faded indentations for traces of a date. Even then, he was obsessed with determining who among his relatives had died young. When he crawled on all fours to read the inscriptions, he felt as if the whole place might suddenly be set free from the weird gravity that held it in suspension and come crashing down around him.

Just inside the gate was a separate plot with four gravestones stretched across a dried patch of grass, two large slabs in the middle with a smaller one on either side: the father, Avery; the mother, Charlotte; the daughters, Elizabeth and Sarah. They had died within a month of each other in 1872. From the dates on the tombs, William determined that the mother had died first, followed by the father a week later, then the eldest daughter, leaving the last alive for five, long days before she joined them. Family legend held that they had been killed by a smallpox epidemic that had wiped out most of the surrounding county within a year.

Because that family left no direct heirs, the ranch had passed to cousins who began the line of descendants on William's father's side. His great-grandfather had been an itinerant farmer, barely scraping by. He had left Ohio with his wife and daughter, later followed by his brother, and built the house in which William would later be born. A plague even then had changed the course of their history.

The night before he left the ranch for the last time, William stopped to visit the four graves, sitting for an hour in the moon-light. It was so bright that he could read the inscriptions without moving close, the marble seeming almost electrified in the dark-ness. He remembered a large root which grew out of the center of the father's stone and rested along the top of the mother's, like a petrified arm. A colony of ants swarmed near the youngest daugh-ter, devouring a crust of bread in a quivering mass, then breaking off one by one to rush back into their nest, perhaps dug as deep as a grave. He scattered the ants with his boot before filling a small jar with dirt, which he packed in his knapsack, along with his clothes and his grandmother's wedding ring. He had kept the jar safe through all the years he lived in the city, from apartment to apartment, until he bought his house at the beach.

On his last weekend there, he sneaked outside after Henry had gone to sleep. He stood swaying in the storm in the back yard, his mind so exhausted by fear of what was happening to him that he felt strangely becalmed, nearly hypnotized by the twinkling lights on the houses all around him: blue, yellow, red, and green against the white night sky. Before he went back inside, he bent down and sprinkled the dirt in the vial around the base of a willow tree, unable to clearly see what he was doing, yet feeling the particles disperse against his skin before they vanished in the swirling gusts of snow and wind, as if they were ashes of a loved one thrown from a cliff into the sea.

William's grandfather had spent his life researching the family's history back to ancient Anglo-Saxon kings. He believed that this heritage confirmed a kind of nobility upon them, as if only acci-dents of birth or nationality had kept them from ruling. In all his conversations, he referred to the queen of England as "cousin."

He spent his free time poring over huge sheets of yellowed paper that traced the family's descendants in America back to the

Mayflower. Before he died, he hoped to visit the grave of every ancestor not buried at the ranch. He traveled from state to state for decades, recording the address of every cemetery he could find, even sketching maps of the exact position of every grave. He kept these drawings in a leather folder so that no one after him would ever get lost if they tried to make their way there.

Before he was weakened by several heart attacks and strokes, he found the grave of every relative for the past three centuries except one: a second cousin twice removed on his great-great-grandmother's side named Ruth Babcock. The only fact he knew about her was that she had died in 1787. Until William's disappearance, she was the only missing link in the perfect chain he had drawn from Charlemagne to William and his sisters. He scoured death records throughout the country, stopping at town halls in every state where the family had settled. He returned to all the places he had visited on earlier trips, never trusting maps, driving on back roads until he discovered even the smallest and most obscure burial sites. He could never learn if Ruth had married or even the year she was born. She seemed to have dropped off the face of the earth.

When he was bedridden and could no longer travel, he offered a reward to the person who could find Ruth Babcock. Her absence seemed to throw the whole effort of his search into question, as if without her, the family's history had no meaning. He wrote letters to even his most distant relations, repeating his theories about what could have happened to her. "Please find her," he always added in a postscript written in a spidery hand under his signature, as if he could no longer sign his name without thinking of her.

When William's grandfather was dying, he called out to her in his delirium, shouting, *Ruth, Ruth, Ruth,* in wonderment, as if at the last possible moment she had appeared to him after all his years of searching.

16

Susan sat smoking at her kitchen table, sorting through a large packet of letters that had arrived in the morning's mail. She slit one envelope open with a butter knife and began to read: "My name is Peter and I've been divorced for seven years. My former wife . . ."

She put that one aside and chose another, frowning as she scanned its perfectly formed, round letters written in turquoise ink. *Too compulsive, and a little fey,* she thought as she set it down unopened. The telephone rang, but she didn't answer it. She would allow no distractions from her morning's work.

The month before, Susan had taken out a personal ad in the city's glossiest magazine. It wasn't her nature to keep secrets, but she had told no one, not even William. He would have wanted to read every letter and make a joke of them. She already regretted her boldness, less from fear of the danger of meeting strangers in the city than from the humiliation of advertising for love. She had always assumed that the columns in the back of magazines were a bastion of the last resort, a place for fat girls and cripples.

Maybe that's what I am, she thought the day she mailed her ad, but she didn't care. A woman her age was meant to wait patiently until she stumbled upon an available man, but she didn't know another way to find one. The professionals who gathered every night in the local bars were at least a decade younger. Whenever she ventured in, she felt washed-up and ugly, older than her years. She didn't know many men outside her office, and the men there were either married or gay. Younger men no longer flirted with her; if she asked a question in a department store or movie theater, they always called her "ma'am."

She studied the listings in several magazines until she knew the different styles of the ads by heart, from the flippest to the most sincere. She spent a long time deciding the most flattering way to describe herself. The statistics were easy — single white female, 5'7", 135 pounds, straight dark hair, green eyes, forty years old — but she didn't know how to make her personality emerge in three short lines of type.

Nearly every person in every ad wanted companionship, a friend for dinner or walks on the beach. Many described themselves as sexy. It had been so long since her last date, she had no idea if an average man would find her attractive. So much depended on chemistry that she didn't see the point in describing herself that way. Often friends were driven wild by men who left her cold. She also suspected that "sexy" was a code people used to advertise for sex, and she didn't want to fuck anonymously with strangers, as William and Henry did. Still, she longed for other things that went beyond the lure of a human touch: a home, children, love, friends who weren't dying. Because she didn't know how to express the emptiness she felt without sounding desperate or misused, she had only added after her description, "I want to change my life."

Before sealing the envelope, she decided to shave five years off her age. Depending on the day, she could still look younger than most of her contemporaries, especially those who were raising families. To stack the odds further in her favor, she subtracted ten pounds from her weight. She hoped it would give her an incentive to diet in the weeks before she met her date. But she didn't lie about everything. She made sure to say she smoked.

Counting the envelopes, she was astonished to find that she had received forty responses to the first appearance of her ad. A few letters were photocopied, as if they had been sent to every person advertising in the magazine, woman or man. After skimming each one, she arranged them on the table in two piles: those she would never answer and those she might. She saved a space for any letter that might set her mind to dreaming.

She was surprised that almost every man had sent a Polaroid proudly, even though she hadn't asked. She would never have done it herself. She didn't want strangers passing her image around for inspection. Many were pleasant looking, not the freaks and losers she had expected. Only a few were overweight. All but two were divorced. Many had children in college. One was a recent grandparent.

How are they old enough? she wondered, forgetting her own age. Their lives seemed full, or almost completed, while she couldn't claim an enduring relationship since her first year out of college. Unless, of course, she counted William.

William's disease had brought both boredom and a kind of panic to her life. During the first months of his illness, Susan had postponed making long-term plans. She worried that her ability to move freely would seem insulting to him, and as time went on, it became easier to make no plans at all. She rarely went to movies or restaurants. She never exercised. She attended church on alternate Sundays, if she had the energy to rise from bed. She lost touch with most of her other friends. Her outside world consisted of her office, the grocery store, the dry cleaner's, and William's living room. She might as well have lived in the suburbs, so seldom did she explore the city's unfamiliar neighborhoods. Whenever she had occasion to venture off her usual path, the newness of the streets and shops was as startling as if she were traveling in a foreign country.

Susan knew that all the fault for slowing down couldn't be blamed on William, but one way or another, she had lost her forward motion at the same time he lost his health. Even at her office or safely back at home, she felt oddly suspended, as if nothing more would happen until after William died. She was so eager for a change that sometimes when the telephone rang, she prayed it was the doctor telling her that he was dead.

She had never planned to spend her life alone. She was no lover of solitude. She had always assumed she would marry, in the same way she had assumed she would have a successful career. She had expected nothing more than a conventional life. Love had never seemed to be something a person looked for, like an apartment or a job, but more like a bolt that struck from nowhere, an accident or revelation. And while she waited, she created her own world. She made money and friends. She was never unhappy.

Looking back, she couldn't point to the moment when she lost control of her life, but its easy rhythms, its comfort and familiarity, had lulled her into a dangerous routine. She poured her spare energy into her family and friends, coddling them like children or lovers. She turned twenty-five, then thirty, then was on the cusp of middle age. She worked still harder at her job, selling more apartments than any other agent in her office, crowding her schedule until there was no room for romance. She told herself she didn't care.

As her life grew fuller, she lost her ease with strangers. She began to boast that her friendships had an intensity that rivaled any lover's; she came to draw from them a physical, almost sexual thrill. She and her friends shared meals and secrets. They celebrated holidays and anniversaries. They took vacations and planned for their futures. Sometimes they bickered and grew bored, but never to a degree that threatened the steady course of their day. Over time, whenever she left her circle to go on a date, she grew anxious and disoriented, like a child who has wandered off, too far from home.

One attraction of her friendship with William had always been that he was rarely distracted by a lover's demands, so they gave to each other their own best selves. Even during the years when they had grown more distant, she never seemed to fall in love, but only sought to replace him with another, constant friend. Sister to brother had been the ideal she valued in all relationships, but now she worried that her great devotion had simply disguised a deeper fear of connection, something hard and superficial at her core, that left her bereft of any real capacity to love.

She cherished her independence, just as she cherished her friends, but she had come to think that she had paid a price for her separate life. Some unspoken barrier to love and need was never crossed when she returned home at night alone. Once she closed the door to her apartment, some truer part of her mind was opened, a self that thrived in privacy and isolation, unwilling to compromise or bend. Home became a space of secret thinking. She grew selfish by default. She didn't know if these patterns of heart had become so ingrained that it was too late to learn to love another way, but lately she dreamed of an intimacy she hoped existed, the kind that comes with years spent sleeping next to someone, naked in a bed.

From the stack of letters on her table, she chose one from a man whose reply was reticent and shy, but shot through with a sly humor. His name was Stephen. He hadn't enclosed a photograph, so immediately she began to imagine his appearance from his brief description: 5′10″, gray-black hair, 155 pounds, 42 years old. He worked in a law office, but didn't claim to be an attorney. He didn't say if he'd ever been married. Later she might choose a different man, but for now she stashed the other letters behind a stack of dinner plates in the upper cupboard. Even the cleaning lady would never find them there.

Stephen had typed his telephone number at the bottom of the page. She lit another cigarette before she dialed. As she waited for the connection, she prayed he wouldn't answer. She wasn't sure why, but it made a difference that he call her back, unexpectedly. She made a bet with herself: if she was able to leave a message without speaking to him first, they would meet and fall in love. She waited one, two, three rings. The machine clicked on.

He wasn't home.

She listened to his taped recording, preparing what to say. She was pleased to hear that he had a tenor voice, with no lisp or odd impediment. She kept her message brief, but in the few seconds it took her to speak, her mind teemed with preposterous dreams: a handsome man with gray at the temples, a wedding party, three dark-haired children, a shingled house, a sleek blue car. She hoped Stephen would return home before too long, but for the moment she savored the sick, giddy feeling in the pit of her stomach. It had been so long since she had waited for a man to call, she had forgotten how unnerving it was. Everyone had lost something because of William's illness, but she realized that what she regretted most was the way her sense of anticipation had become confused with the expectation of a new disaster. She had forgotten what it was like to look forward to something with pleasure.

Hit the showers, you pig, she thought, glancing down at her baggy sweatpants with a cigarette burn in the thigh, her dirty sneakers. Her bangs stuck to her forehead, dull with grease. As she rose from the table, the telephone rang again. Her heart quickened. She let it ring three times, gurgling roughly in her throat so that her voice had a raw, sultry quality when she answered. "Hello?"

It was only William.

"Susan? What's the matter? Are you sick?" He coughed into her ear.

"No," she said, swallowing hard. She tried to keep her disappointment from poisoning her tone, but just hearing his voice oppressed her. For a moment, guiltily, she considered confessing what she had done, but she stopped herself. She didn't want to risk having him ruin her pleasure. "I just got up," was all she said.

"Gray day."

This was her cue to be amusing. Outside the window, the sky was scattered with clouds, blue-white, broken by hints of sun. The air was crisp and clear. "I haven't been out yet," she said, looking around for something to do. Sometimes when William called, she tried to read the newspaper as he rambled, but often he reprimanded her in midsentence if he heard the turning of a page. Today she risked annoying him. She wrenched the faucet on and began washing the breakfast dishes.

"Me either." His voice cracked, barely audible over the water.

She swiped the sponge over a plate, dreamily. *Maybe he only stepped out to buy the paper*, she thought, imagining the man returning home to hear her message. If he called that afternoon, should she play hard to get or admit the truth and say she wasn't busy?

"You there?" William asked.

"Yes. Sure." She let the rushing water fill the silence.

"What did you do last night?"

"Nothing much. Stayed in."

"Me, too," he said, companionably. "Two peas in a pod."

"Yes," she said, bristling. She had been worn out from running his errands all week and had collapsed early into bed. She scrubbed hard at a piece of gluey yolk congealed on the blade of a knife.

"You going out later?" he asked. "I was wondering if you could get a few things."

"Sure," she sighed. She dried her hands and picked up a pencil. It wasn't necessary for anyone to do William's shopping. He could afford the delivery charge from the market on his corner. His lists were just another way to hook her in. As she wrote

"William" at the top of the page, the pencil point snapped against the pad. "Shit."

"What's wrong?"

"Nothing. Just tell me what you need."

"Milk, bread, vitamin C. A new video, if you don't mind an extra stop. Maybe you want to stay and watch."

"I've got to go out later," she said, too sharply. "But I'll be over soon."

She kicked hard against the cabinet door as she set down the telephone. She knew that once she stopped at his apartment, he would convince her to stay. Before she knew it, the day would vanish. Later, back at home, Henry would call to talk about William. Then it would be time for bed. The two of them had closed her in. The one evening recently when she refused to return their calls, her telephone had rung ceaselessly until well past midnight, Henry after William after Henry after William pleading into her answering machine, *"Susan, are you there? Are you all right? Susan, are you there?"*

I'm so sick of him, she thought as she walked into the living room. She felt a pang of remorse as she caught her reflection in the mirror William had given her, bought the day he shopped with his now dead friend. What was his name? David? Stephen? No, that was the man in the ad. Edward, maybe. She ran her finger tenderly over the ornate frame, trying to conjure her love for William.

It isn't his fault he's so depressing, she told herself, but in her heart she believed she would behave differently if she were ever ill again. At the very least, she would pay strangers to do the chores that she and Henry did. She would never make another's life stop just so she had morbid company. Even the mirror seemed less a gift to her now than a bribe. It wasn't hers, not in the way the desk from her mother, the bureau from her aunt, the dining room table that had stood for years in her grandmother's house were hers, because William never gave anything for free.

In the bathroom, she ran water for her tub. *I will shop. I will visit, but only for an hour*, she promised as she stripped off her clothes. When she slipped under the suds, she felt her anger fade, but not her lingering depression. She was frightened by the ease with which she forgot the complex ways she loved William. The whole history of their affection was in danger of being wiped out by the tedium of his disease. She knew that on another day, in a better mood, her old attachment would return, but even then she couldn't deny that the friend she loved was going, if not gone. Still breathing, still conscious, still needful of her time and care, he had outlived himself, while she had the chance of another forty years. She was desperate not to waste any more of them.

When they first met, she and William had often played a game called Truth. Late at night, after hours of alcohol and drugs, they would take turns imagining dangerous circumstances. Which friend did they secretly desire? Which parent would they rather have die? Sometimes they upped the ante and imagined themselves in real peril. If both were trapped in a fire with the chance for only one to escape, who would it be? William always admitted he would save himself, while Susan wavered, for she didn't believe she could bear the guilt of choosing her own life at another's expense.

As she kicked out her legs and looked down at the wrinkling flesh magnified below the surface, she was shocked by how much she had changed. Or maybe she hadn't changed at all, but had simply never been tested. It had been easy to believe in her own selflessness before she had a self to lose. She sank lower in the water, submerging her ears, then lower still until her hair floated above her face like weeds.

She imagined drifting in a sinking boat with William, only one life preserver to share between them. As they jumped off the side to swim the miles to shore, she imagined buckling the jacket safely to her body, letting him hold onto the straps until he began to drag her down. Once she would have liked to believe that she would fight to keep them both afloat, or they would die together, but now she saw herself paddle off to watch from a safe distance, horrified yet still unmoving, while he thrashed about the surface, gasping for air, and then was gone, leaving her alive and free to mourn.

17

There was a homeless man outside William's apartment who cried all day in loud despair, *"Please somebody help me! Please somebody help me!"* He had huddled in the doorway of an abandoned store for more than a year, day and night, through all four seasons. His sobs pierced every window in the neighborhood, interrupting every conversation, every solitary walk, every nap, every meal, every moment of repose. He whined. He brayed. He moaned. He sobbed. He had no dignity whatsoever.

The way he sat shirtless in the rain or left his coat unbuttoned in the snow so that he would look more pathetic, made William hate him. He had observed a similar hostility in passersby on the street. No one ever gave the man money. Sometimes when he walked by, William bunched a fat wad of bills in his fist so that it was level with the man's nose, close enough to sniff. Though William was sure the man lacked shelter, food, and any form of human companionship, he felt an uncontrollable urge to punish him. The man invaded his solitude every time he left his home, demanding spare change for food or cigarettes, even when it was clear that William was struggling breathlessly with his own packages. But the man's endless cries were much more than a daily annoyance, for they made any plea for help seem repellent, a nightmare of calculation and need.

All his life William had avoided people who poured out their troubles without invitation the moment life struck them a blow. His own diffidence was only partly a desire to keep his life secret; it was also a hedge against boring his friends. He believed that people wanted most to be courted and amused. They would tolerate trouble only sparingly. Henry was the one person he had ever met with whom he felt free to rant and rave, but even with him, William's rages barely touched the surface of his life's regrets.

William had been raised to believe that suffering was a private matter, more secret than sex. When he was a child, his mother had walked for three days on a broken leg before seeing a doctor. And his grandfather had lived for decades stooped by arthritis, his knees as wrecked as broken hinges, never once complaining. His father worked with heavy tools for years despite an arm shortened by a fused and shattered bone, wincing without comment whenever he struck a hammer to a board. None of them believed in medication. When his mother was blinded by migraines, she pressed ice cubes wrapped in washcloths over her eyes and dozed in a shuttered room. Whenever William's skin erupted with poison ivy, his father scrubbed the rash with steel wool before immersing the sores in a bucket of bleach.

Although William grew to hate his life there, when he left he went according to his family's silent code: quickly and without complaint. Because of the intricate rules that governed their conduct, he thought it possible that in the twenty years since his flight, his parents had mentioned him only casually, if at all, as though he were a distant cousin once met at a reunion and never seen again.

He wanted to be different, but he carried their reticence within him like an inherited gene. Like them, he possessed a chilling ability to shut himself off completely from trouble. When he was unable to pay a bill, he stuffed the envelope unopened in a drawer. When he ended a relationship, he simply stopped answering the telephone. He always preferred to be thought heartless and cruel rather than endure an anguished confrontation.

From time to time in the past, several of his friends had surrendered to exhaustion and despair in ways they never had before, either sobbing hysterically about a broken heart or, once or twice, threatening to take their lives. The next morning William would brush their embarrassment away, but though he wouldn't admit it, there was something shocking about these scenes that made it difficult to return to the way life had been. Some secret part of the person's soul had been revealed that undermined the self they presented on ordinary days. Everyone had doubts, especially about the meaning of their lives, but these wild cries that went beyond polite despair threatened the balance of civility that made William comfortable in human relationships. And because he knew himself so well, it was impossible not to notice a similar wariness imprinted on the faces of his friends from the moment they learned that he was ill.

He didn't blame them. In the past, when he tended to friends laid flat by flu, his benevolence would wane after a few attentive days. He would begin to make excuses — feigning illness, problems at work, unbreakable engagements — so that he wouldn't have to visit. By the end of a week, his expressions of care would give way to perfunctory telephone calls or flowers sent by messenger. Even when he castigated himself for his selfishness, he never believed that his responses were any worse than those of an average man. So after months of his own crises and remissions, he wasn't surprised to find his own visitors fall away like leaves.

Still, he had lost so many relationships so quickly, he couldn't decide if his own retreat was responsible or if he had, in fact, been abandoned by most of the people he had known. In recent years, many of his closest friends had preceded him in death: Edward, Robert, Alan. A kind of unreality had overtaken him as they, and others, began to die. He hadn't been able to adjust to what this destruction would mean for his own life by the time he was taken by the same disease. Afterward, he didn't care.

Because his energy was limited, he made his own decision to

let go entirely of people he had kept in touch with primarily by mail: former colleagues and friends from college who had moved away. He saw no one from the bar. In the bright light of his apartment, dressed in daytime clothes and stripped of any sexual charge, they seemed like strangers. For a while he continued to see people from work, many of whom he had known for fifteen years. They fought to take him out to lunch whenever he went to the office. They had even celebrated his discharge from the hospital with a surprise party, complete with cake and funny cards. After he retired, their meetings quickly dwindled. He hadn't heard from one of them in months, although if he lived that long, he was sure he'd receive a stack of Christmas cards.

It became easier to stay at home alone. No matter how sick he was of thinking about symptoms and disease, if someone tried to distract him or failed to inquire about his health, he grew quickly aggrieved, as if already they didn't care. If he heard of someone's plans, he felt a sadness that nearly crippled him with regret. And when he watched his friends thrive and grow without him, he felt a desperation and envy unlike any he had known before. He came to hate their awkwardness, the cheap bouquets of flowers they brought, or the boxes of candy he would never eat. Sometimes his mind howled with fury at their abandonment, daring them to endure half as well as he had the long assault of a terminal disease. Sometimes he was kept awake by waves of hatred and resentment, wishing each of them would die.

He knew that any number of his friends, even those to whom he had not spoken in months, would rally when a real crisis came — a trip to the hospital, a dash for medicine in the middle of the night, intervention with his doctor, even money, should he need it — but it was in the abyss of ordinary days that he felt most alone. Often he longed for a crisis to break the monotony of his listlessness and lingering fatigue.

What he missed most was talking on the telephone late into the night, gossiping, planning, recapping the news of the day. But soon he hesitated to call if he only wanted to hear the purr of a familiar voice. He grew accustomed to the catch in even Henry's and Susan's voices, a hollow pause as they waited for him to state what he needed, as if he had no other purpose than to ruin their days with emergencies. No matter how willing they were to bring groceries to his door, take him out for a meal, spend an evening watching videos or playing cards, he knew they would only retreat further if he belabored his illness. He had decided he could safely express his horror at his failing body, his great fear of death, only once to each of them. There was so much time left to be afraid, months, maybe years, that he felt the need to parcel out his fear slowly so that they would remain comfortable in his presence. He had to pretend as much as possible that he didn't care, as if losing his life was nothing to him. But the rage that lay between his private terror and the silence he imposed upon his heart, made his personality wither and grow small.

His doctor had urged him to join a support group for the dying so that he might find a sympathetic circle of new friends. He had attended one meeting, held in the apartment of a stranger, where six pale men sat drinking chamomile tea. Some told their stories with false bravado. Some convulsed with sobs. Some spoke of desertion by their families and the fear of dying alone. Others gave testimony to the charity of their friends, as if that quality defined a beauty in themselves. One spoke of plans for his funeral and his wish to have his ashes sprinkled from a helicopter over the Arctic Circle, dusting the snow like a gray-black rain. All evening William kept mum. He knew the other men assumed his silence came from shyness, but it was more from boredom and a vague contempt. It might have been a meeting about any affliction: alcoholism, overeating, or a problem with drugs. By speaking their fears aloud, they reduced dying to the pettiness of a small complaint. William didn't want to find death in their aches and moans and problems with bills. He needed to believe it to be a great adventure beyond human comprehension for its suffering to be endured.

At home, alone, he kept his demons to himself as much as possible, but they ate at his reason. He tried to convince himself that he had been given more in forty years than most people found in lifetimes of disappointment and regret. It had become his habit to study the obituary pages the moment the newspaper arrived, studying the biographies of those who had died in order to place himself in relation to them on a scale of sorrow.

For years he had been haunted by the story of a man tormented by his captors in a death camp. As his punishment for a minor infraction of the rules, he was made to stand in a field ringed by armed guards. Although weakened by months of beatings and starvation, he was ordered to hold two buckets brimming with sand straight out from his body and not let them drop. If he moved, even to wobble an inch, he would be shot. And so the man stood, not wavering, for a day and a night, first in the sun, later in the cold.

William could never remember the end of the story: whether the man trembled and was shot, or whether he outlasted the guards and was killed anyway, or whether they took notice of his courage and let him live. But whenever he felt particularly tested, he would picture that man standing alone in the yard with heavy buckets for arms and would judge himself lacking. Sometimes he would even hold his arms out from his body until they trembled weightlessly to remind himself that on the scale of things his troubles had been small.

He had suffered bad moments before, but the trouble he'd known had always had an end. When his heart was broken, he knew it would mend. When he was hungry, he reassured himself by knowing that it was impossible for him to starve. And when he was lost in a strange place, he would stroke his wallet, knowing that no matter where he was, he had the money to get back home.

All his life, whether he was ill or lost, whether he was destitute or afraid, four words of comfort had saved him, no matter what happened: *you will not die*. With that security, he knew he could withstand anything. It meant the horror would end. It meant the trouble would become part of his story. And becoming part of the story meant that it was over, that he had lived to tell it. But now he had nothing, no net, no words of comfort, to tell himself: *you will not die*.

Once that was gone, he was astonished at how everything familiar vanished. Before he had been obsessed by age and failure, by time and money, by whether he had done enough with his life. Then suddenly, in one afternoon, it was over: all his worries stripped away to the one, great fear of death. He had heard that some people develop a lust for living at the moment they learn they're doomed, that each day becomes for them a wondrous thing. But he didn't see how that was possible, for every moment now seemed lethal and pointless, yet he held onto each without pleasure, because there was nothing more he could ever hope to have.

He assumed that Henry and Susan complained about his crankiness and petty rages, but they had no idea how much he spared them. For if he ever found a voice to express his dread, it would fly from his heart as a howl, just one, huge sound of mourning that would fill the city with its wail: telling them how he felt death eating at his body like insects gnawing on wood; how he sobbed hysterically into the night while they were sleeping, curled into a ball like a battered child; how life itself seemed so meaningless that he felt cheated, duped by lies; how he despised their silly optimism; how he wanted so badly to have the waiting over that he was blinded by fantasies of slitting his throat, sometimes to the point of bringing a knife to touch his skin, but he couldn't do it, because his fear of a world he didn't know was even greater than his fear of the one he was trapped so miserably within; how his unhappiness was so great that it knew no human bounds, until his body was split through with aching, like a wound opened and never closed.

And if he allowed himself to become so undone, who would be left to comfort him after that?

18

"*Archimime*," Henry said, pronouncing each syllable distinctly. He wrote A-r-c-h-i-m-i-m-e in large, bold letters on the board, then turned to face his class. "Does anyone know what it means?"

"Enemy?" a student ventured.

"No."

"A bridge?" another asked.

"No."

"I bet it has something to do with death," someone called from the back of the room. The students convulsed with laughter, even Henry's favorites, clustered in the front row of desks.

"Very funny," Henry said, his lecture notes flapping loosely in his hand. He had thrown away the lesson plan he had prepared so carefully that summer and begun instead to teach his students from the books he had read since William's illness, under the guise of Western Civ. The night before, he had prepared a lecture about funeral processions of the rich in ancient Rome. For the next day, he had an hour ready on burial customs in China. He found comfort in learning about the complex rituals and ceremonies reserved especially for the dead. He hoped that if he gave his students a foundation from the past, then death might not seem so freakish to them when it came into their lives.

He wanted to compel them with stories of China, where relatives built a paper house a year after a loved one's death and set it afire so that his possessions could join his spirit in the afterlife. Or of ancient Rome, where a corpse's eyes were left open on the funeral pyre so that he might watch his soul fly off in clouds of flame. But no matter how many stories he told them, Henry couldn't make them care. They barely paid attention when he told them of animals slaughtered on the steps of an altar, or of gladiators impaled by spears at their master's grave. Only suicide held their interest because it seemed romantic, something poets did.

"During the funeral," he continued, "a person masked to resemble the deceased walks in front of the procession, mimicking his mannerisms, wearing his clothes, surrounded by the family. He's the arch . . ." His voice trailed off when he noticed a secretary from the dean's office beckoning from the back of the room. He nodded once, then turned to the students, feigning indifference, though his body grew cold. No one interrupted classes except in the most extreme emergencies, usually an accident or death.

It's too soon, he thought, trying to remember his conversation with William the night before. He had seemed more tired than usual, but otherwise unchanged.

"Oh, oh, someone's in trouble," a boy called out, his voice bouncing off the walls. "Quiet!" Henry ordered, barely able to hear his words over the pounding of his heart. "Study chapter four until I get back." The class groaned.

He drifted through the rows of desks and chairs, focusing his attention on the knitted red of the secretary's sweater. As he grew closer, he saw she wore a ceramic pumpkin broach with lacquered scarlet lips and diamond chips for eyes. *Bitch*, he thought, remembering how she spent her coffee breaks spreading rumors and prying into people's lives. Once the door was closed behind them, he hissed, "What's the problem?"

"There's an urgent call for you in the office," she whispered. "That's all I know."

They walked past elementary classrooms festooned with Halloween decorations: cut paper goblins, witches on brooms, pumpkins slit with toothy grins scorched black by candle flame. Through the window in each door, Henry noticed his colleagues stop in midsentence and watch him pass, an expression on their faces as if they witnessed a neighbor's arrest. The secretary wore spiked heels that clicked on the tiles; Henry wore shoes with new silver taps. Together their footsteps echoed off the floor and walls, multiplying, so that it sounded as if they were chased by a mob.

The first thing Henry noticed when he entered the dean's office was the telephone receiver lying flat on the counter. The way its long cord looped in loose, black circles reminded him of something dead. *Maybe it's someone else,* he thought as he moved to touch it. He was so obsessed with William's condition that he had forgotten anyone could die at any moment, even members of his family. In the instant before he lifted the receiver, he made a mental list of all his relatives, shocked at how willingly he would have traded any of their lives, even his mother and father's, to buy William a reprieve.

"Hello?" he said. The telephone was cold against his ear.

"Henry?" The voice belonged to William's doctor.

"Yes, yes," Henry said, his mind jumping so far ahead of his words that he was blinded by an image of William's corpse covered in sheets, all the way to its head.

"I'm afraid you need to bring William in."

"In?" he asked inanely, sighing with relief. He wasn't sure what the doctor meant, but at least William wasn't dead.

"I just talked to him and I think there's something terribly wrong."

"We'll come tonight after my classes," Henry whispered, rearranging his schedule in his head. The secretaries stared full on, not even pretending to be busy with their work.

"No," the doctor said. "Now. I don't want to waste any time in case I have to admit him."

"Give me an hour," Henry said. As he put down the telephone, a shiver of efficiency rushed through his chest. He groped for the wallet in his pocket, calculating his available cash. He pictured his coat hanging in the teacher's lounge, just inside the door. It would take thirty seconds to grab it and sprint into the street. He imagined the route he would order the taxi driver to take — south along the river, then left at the exit a block from William's home — to avoid the afternoon traffic. If the local streets were jammed, he would jump out and run. With that plan firmly in mind, he turned back to the secretaries. "Do you think I might have a minute to see the dean?"

He ignored their raised eyebrows as he walked past the counter and knocked on the paneled door. "Come in," he heard, and didn't pause, not even to summon his nerve.

"What's up?" the dean asked.

"I'm sorry, but I have an emergency," Henry said. "William, my . . . *friend* is ill." He hesitated deliberately, so that the dean would read more meaning into the word.

The dean rose from his chair to sit on the edge of his desk. Up so close, Henry blushed, as if his face revealed the lie. But was he lying? He knew the dean assumed he meant his boyfriend, his lover, his companion, his mate — whatever term he used to describe a sexual relationship. William was none of those things to Henry, or not in the sense a stranger would intend it, but he wanted to leave that impression because there didn't seem to be a category of platonic friend who deserved the degree of mourning or care due a lover, a parent, a wife, or a child.

"Best friend," he often said when describing William to others, although the term sounded slightly defensive to him, as if he were unsure of himself. But without a family tie or a sexual bond to link them, Henry could think of nothing else that implied their closeness. If he were to say the things he knew were true — that William was his favorite person, as valued as a lover could ever be, that his death would leave him bereft, orphaned, crippled by unimaginable grief — then others would assume they were in love, or once had been, or at least that Henry nursed an unrequited passion that explained his devotion. None of it was true, yet the loss that William's death would bring was the largest of his life.

"I'm . . . I'm sorry to hear that," the dean said. "How long do you need?" He smiled kindly, but Henry was pleased to notice a slight twitch to his eye, a quiver to his lip. The dean would agree to any terms just to have the conversation over.

Henry stood, preparing to leave. "Today, at least. Perhaps tomorrow," he said. The weekend came after. He could worry about the future then.

"Take all the time you need," the dean said, holding out his hand. Henry barely grazed his fingers. He strode past the secretaries, grabbed his coat, and flew out onto the avenue to hail a cab. "Three oh five West Twenty-first Street," he said as he tumbled in. "Please take the outer drive." He leaned back against the springy leather, gratified by the feel of the speeding car and the lights blinking green upon green, as if by sheer force of will he prevented them from turning red. He counted one, two, three, four, five, pressing his foot to the floor. Six, seven, eight . . . feeling the car zoom unhindered over the pavement.

At William's building Henry spun through the revolving door and raced through the lobby, waving William's keys at the doorman. The elevator sat empty, waiting just for him. As he paused outside William's apartment to prepare himself, even for the most gruesome discovery, a neighbor poked out her head. "Is everything okay?"

"I hope so," Henry said. William hated his neighbors knowing his business, so he was afraid to admit too much.

"I don't see him go out much anymore," she said. "I hear the television late into the night. It hasn't been off for days."

"I'm sorry if it disturbs you," Henry said. He turned the key in the lock, but didn't push open the door.

"No, no, I was worried, that's all," the woman said. "I considered calling the super, but I didn't want to make more trouble than he already has."

Often Henry read in the newspapers about corpses left undiscovered in apartments for days on end. Only the week before he had read about a woman in the suburbs who had lain dead in her kitchen for four years. Her neighbors respected her wishes never to be bothered. They mowed her lawn. They bundled her mail. But no one ever knocked at her door. For a moment, Henry wondered who would be left in the city to keep track of him after William was dead. He didn't know his neighbors, even after years in the building. They barely said hello when they passed in the hallway. It would take days to raise an alarm if he went missing from school. *I must save him*, he thought, as much for himself as for his friend. "Excuse me," he said to the neighbor, then shoved open the door.

He blinked to adjust his eyes. The shades were drawn. The aquarium in the corner gave the room its only light, lending the shadows a lavender tint. At the far end of the room, William sprawled in an overstuffed chair with his face to the window. "Hello?" Henry called, but his greeting was lost in the blaring of the television, loud as an argument.

He walked into the bedroom to silence the volume, then back into the hall. Still William didn't move. The pendulum clock sat unwound above the foyer table, the time frozen at 5:37 from some night or morning days before.

He's dead, Henry thought, inching closer, averting his gaze by focusing on a cigarette burning in the ashtray beside William's chair. The smoke rose like the path of a fuse, bursting in thick clouds over his head. Suddenly the ash burned through to the filter and the butt rolled between the marble lips, falling onto the carpet. The quick spark of silken smoke engaged William's attention in a way that Henry's presence had not. When he leaned over to grab the smoldering ashes, Henry rushed forward, extending a hand, as if he had just arrived for lunch.

"Hello," he said calmly. "Why don't you give me that?"

William stared, then dropped the butt into Henry's hand. "The carpet's ruined," he said, brushing his fingers over the charred spot.

"We can fix it," Henry said, switching on the overhead light to get a better look. He dropped to his knees. A bug-sized mark was burned into the threads. "Don't worry," he said, looking up, then froze. A large gash, wide as a laughing mouth, split the center of William's forehead. Dried blood was splattered down his left cheek. Underneath, his skin was whiter than the walls, whiter than anything Henry had ever seen, sick white, the color of disease.

How can this be happening now? he wondered, in spite of everything he knew. No matter how many times he prepared himself, each change in William's condition upset him more than the one before. It was less than a month since they had traveled for the first transfusion. Only three days remained until their next appointment. His heart sank as he realized that he would be cheated of the illusion of even that small reprieve.

William traced the trickle of blood down the side of his face with a finger. "Am I a mess?"

"I've seen you worse," Henry lied.

"I felt this pain in my stomach, then my feet gave out." He blinked. "Did I call you? I forget what number I dialed."

"It doesn't matter. Let's clean you up." He led William into the bathroom and sat him on the toilet. He ran hot water over a towel and dabbed at the clotted blood. The wound oozed. He rinsed the towel and pressed it directly over the gash. William groaned. "Sorry, sorry," Henry said, stopping his work to grab at William's hand.

"No, my stomach, oh," William cried. He stared up helplessly, bunching his arms against his waist.

"We better get out of here," Henry said. He pulled a roll of gauze from the medicine cabinet and wound it around William's head. "Stay there," he said as he ran to the bedroom and snatched a black bandanna from the top bureau drawer. Even in his panic, he reeled from the room's musty, bitter smell.

When he returned to the bathroom, William lay moaning on the floor. Henry propped him against the tub and tied the bandanna over the gauze. "You look dashing."

William patted his head. He scratched his ear. "Are you taking me to dinner?"

"Yes, later," Henry said. "My treat."

He bundled William into his heavy coat and sweater and pulled warm mittens over his hands. When he turned out the lamp, the living room glowed again with the light from the aquarium. The four fish swam serenely, much larger than when he had bought them. An inch of food, fuzzy with mold, spread thickly over the coral bottom. As they walked into the foyer, William stopped and waved. "Bye, bye."

Henry wrapped William's arm around his neck as he tried to maneuver his dead weight into the hall. "Oh," William cried with a shudder, while Henry looked desperately around. The elevator seemed miles away. As he dragged William, Henry bumped hard against the wall, hoping the sound would summon the neighbor, but her door stayed closed. *I am in over my head*, he thought for the first time since William had fallen ill.

When the doorman saw them struggle, he rushed to the curb

and hailed a cab. He helped Henry lift William into the back seat and shut the door. "Good luck," he said.

"Party time?" the driver asked, without turning around.

"Fifteen West Eleventh Street," Henry said. "I hate Halloween." He spoke too sharply, for he was glad of the driver's company. If anything happened on the way to the doctor's office, he wouldn't have to face it alone.

The car inched through the traffic on William's block, then stopped dead. Henry heard whistles, sirens, shrieks from the crowd, but his view was obscured by the buses and trucks that clogged the avenue in front of them. He sat very still. William's breath made strange, hollow sounds, like the roar of a seashell pressed close against the ear.

"Has there been an accident?" Henry asked, for the cars seemed stuck and strewn over the pavement as if leveled by some catastrophe.

"Where you been?" the driver sneered. "The mayor gave those freaks a permit to parade."

Just then a whistle blared and a roll of drums with a funereal beat burst upon the street. A crowd of gawkers suddenly surrounded the cab. Through the side window, Henry saw as many masks as faces. A child or dwarf in a devil's suit pressed his face against the glass and screamed, *"Boo!"*

"Is there some way out of here?" Henry asked, imagining hours trapped in the car as William weakened, then stopped breathing.

"Not unless you can fly," the driver said and peered above the buildings to a corner of sunless sky.

It was ten blocks to the doctor's office, a distance Henry could run on an average day in two minutes flat. Even if he forced his way through the crowd alone, an ambulance could never make it back to rescue William. He remembered reading that twenty city blocks were equal to a mile, but he couldn't imagine how he could carry William half that far, when he had barely managed to drag him from the apartment into the hall.

He watched the traffic signal change uselessly from red to yellow to green. He held tight to William's hand. He tried to bolster his courage with images of superhuman powers, of plane crash victims trudging through miles of ice and snow to safety, of mothers lifting crumpled cars off the bodies of their children. "It's not that far," he said aloud, to no one in particular, but he didn't look outside again for fear he'd lose his nerve.

He dropped five dollars into the driver's lap and yanked on William's arm. "Let's go," he said and pushed himself backward through the door, dragging William after, not stopping until his sneakers touched the ground.

The bandanna slipped low over William's eyes, revealing a glistening bull's-eye of sticky red in the center of the gauze. A line of black-caped marchers wearing masks of skulls and bones turned the corner, stretching the width of the street. Around them presidents, clowns, starlets, preened while drunken teens hooted, heckled, and shoved. No normal person seemed to exist within that teeming crowd. Henry draped William's arm over his shoulder and trundled along, keeping his head low so that all he saw were feet and jeans and the hems of sequined dresses.

He counted cracks in the sidewalk, the poles of parking meters, the chipped yellow paint on every curb. His hysteria rose with each kick and push and curse it took to force their way through that awful human sea. With every block William's weight increased, until Henry thought his muscles would tear and his bones would crack from stress and pain. But every time he neared collapse, he told himself that his agony was nothing close to the suffering William lived with every day.

At the pillars outside the doctor's office, he gagged with exhaustion and relief. When they staggered up the front steps, William spun off Henry's arm and slumped against the door, his eyes wild and unfocused, his skin the color of cement. If it weren't for his terrible heaving, Henry would have thought him dead.

"Not now!" Henry cried. "We're almost there." He counted to three, then hoisted William from under his arms and dragged him through the lobby, not stopping until they collapsed on the elevator floor.

The receptionist leaped up when he saw them and helped Henry carry William into an examination room. They barely had him seated in a chair when the doctor rushed in, ripping open William's shirt, pressing a stethoscope to his chest, shouting orders to his nurse. Just as an IV pole swinging with bags of solution pushed him out of the way, Henry caught a glimpse of William's stomach, shrunken yet swollen with something round.

"Would you mind leaving us alone?" the doctor asked, not rudely, but with the confidence of a person who was never disobeyed. He turned his back and lifted William easily onto the padded table.

Henry heard shoes tumble to the floor, the rip of a zipper. Gloves, socks, shirt, sweater, followed after. "Yes, of course," he answered softly, but he might as well have addressed an empty room, for no one acknowledged his exit, not even with a nod.

I am useful, like a maid, he thought as he shuffled into the waiting room, dazed with hurt and shame. He had expected to savor some sense of triumph upon his arrival, but instead he felt worn out, merely dirty and unkempt. The doctor had barely noticed him. To the people on the street, they had just been two bodies out of thousands pushing rudely through the crowd. Even William, crazed with sickness, would have no memory of what his friend had done.

The other men in the waiting room were oddly quiet, their heads kept down, as if Henry's presence made them uncomfortable. He wanted to believe that a purity of heart had gotten him there, but with no amazement in the others' faces, he felt the sense of determination and love that had seized him in the cab vanish, leaving behind the vagueness of a fever dream.

Through the closed door of the examination room he heard a cry of pain, a stifled sob. He began to rise by instinct to go to William, but a weird inertia kept him still. William didn't need him, and when the force of that truth hit him, he felt suddenly as if he would disappear.

He clenched his thighs to ground himself and huddled silently within. He shouldn't leave before learning William's condition, but he couldn't bear to stay another minute in that room. And when he considered going out again to meet the swarming streets of drunken people, he felt his throat and skin and gut constrict, as if he would explode.

He considered calling his parents for the first time in weeks, but even as the thought occurred to him, he knew his homesickness was simply a response to his great unease. No matter how long he lived on his own, whenever he was ill or most unsure, his mind turned naturally toward home. His whole life so far had been an effort to replicate the quality of safety and care he had found there and nowhere else, not even with William.

He wondered if it could be true that William never secretly pined for his own family when he was most alone. But if not, to whom did he call out in the middle of the night? Even at his most grandiose, Henry never assumed it was him. He had always envied William his house because it meant he had claimed a part of the world that would always be his, an illusion of permanence, a place where one could take refuge from a sense of transience so acute that sometimes Henry believed he could feel the earth moving, trembling, slipping away. He didn't know anymore if it mattered, or even if, when William dreamed of returning, it was there he meant by home.

It came to him suddenly that if he were ever as sick as William, he would want to leave his life behind and go home. But his parents no longer lived in the house where he had been raised. His brothers and sisters were scattered throughout the country. When they visited at holidays, it was at a condominium on a golf course in a state in which they had never lived. Yet somehow, still, the space his parents inhabited seemed to hold within its walls a sense of the past that gave him comfort, an idea of a haven that remained present no matter where he was. It hadn't occurred to him until now that the place he longed for no longer existed, that when he dreamed of home, he had no idea what it meant or what he wanted or where he planned to go.

19

Susan leaned against the sill, blowing smoke through a crack in the window. Henry paced back and forth from the bed to the door, glancing into the corridor each time, as if expecting William's return. *Sit still*, she wanted to snap at him. The doctor had told them the operation would take four hours. They had waited less than two.

Susan had spent all day crammed in a chair against the wall while Henry reclined peacefully on a cot by William's bed. She had grown increasingly annoyed at the way Henry wordlessly anticipated William's needs: holding a cup to his lips, fluffing his pillow, changing the channels on the television. They seemed to enjoy an intimacy, almost an unspoken code, that she couldn't remember having shared with William. Or if such a familiarity had once existed, it had been lost too long ago.

Why do I care? she thought as she watched them. Although Susan had made the decision to change her life, she still felt left out and aggrieved, the way a person can when she sees a lover happily engaged with a new mate, even if she has been the one to reject him.

The night before, she had invited Stephen to her apartment for the first time after a date. They had been out to dinner four times over the past three weeks and had spoken almost every day on the telephone. From their first meeting, Susan had felt an ease with Stephen that surprised her. In the past when she dated a man, she had expected only doom and rejection, so she was bewildered by her sense of confidence and security. She was able to tend to her affairs without brooding about whether he would call.

Unlike the other men she had dated in recent years, Stephen made enough money to support himself. He had been married once, ten years before, and had an eight-year-old daughter, though Susan hadn't met her. He had custody on weekends and holidays and for five weeks every summer. He bore no resentment toward his ex-wife, despite her adultery with another man. In the intervening years, Stephen had lived with two other women and had been alone for only the past nine months. He seemed to have friends who loved him and a large family from whom he was not estranged. Unlike Susan, he wasn't ashamed to have met through a personal ad.

When she listened to Stephen talk so freely about his past, Susan had become humiliated by her lack of real affairs. She didn't know how to explain that she had gone on only three dates in the past four years without making it seem there was something wrong with her, something thwarted and cold in her personality. So that she would appear to have lived as full a life as Stephen, she invented two relationships of long duration: one with a married man who finally decided to stay with his wife, the other with a man who confessed that he was gay after they had been together for three years. To create this person, Susan used William in every detail: his physical characteristics, his job, his house, even his flight from his parents. At the end of the story, she even added, bitterly, "The only thing I've got to show for it is a mirror."

She didn't regret lying to Stephen. She was so sick of her life that she wanted to be rid of it entirely. She told him nothing about her real friends. As she added more details to her fabricated affairs, she grew almost exultant. For the first time in as long as she could remember, she believed it was possible to leave her life behind and begin again.

When they stepped into her apartment that night after dinner, Susan glanced at the answering machine on the small table in the foyer. By the blinking red light, she could tell there were five messages. Since it was rare for anyone other than Henry or William to call, she immediately suspected a problem with William. Certain that she would be punished for her lies, she made Stephen a drink, put music on the stereo, and excused herself.

She pressed her ear close to the speaker so Stephen couldn't hear, but even with the volume low, Henry's panic was evident. He had called twice from the doctor's office, three times from the emergency room, pleading for her to come. X-rays had shown that William's stomach was blocked with tumors. The surgeons planned to operate, the next day if possible, and Henry was afraid to be there alone.

Stephen seemed kind and understanding, but Susan didn't want to risk involving him in a drama so soon. She also didn't know how to explain the sudden existence of a close friend who was dying, when she seemed to have been so forthcoming about her past.

If she left for the emergency room and sent Stephen home, she was afraid that she might never see him again. Coming out of nowhere, the truth might seem an excuse for getting rid of him. For once, she resisted the urge to run to William. She convinced herself that he was safe in the hospital with Henry and the doctors. Nothing she could do would save him.

She returned to the living room without saying a word. She tried to behave normally, but she felt oddly disconnected, even as Stephen stayed the night. He fell quickly asleep after they had sex, his head nestled against her shoulder, his body naked above the sheets. She tried to settle against him, to enjoy the sensation of the touch of another's skin after so long, but she felt suffocated by guilt, growing angrier and angrier that William had managed to ruin her evening in spite of all her subterfuge and lies.

In the morning, she refused to answer the telephone. She knew it was Henry. Exhausted from sleeplessness and worry, she worked hard to appear cheerful and engaged so that Stephen did not think she was rushing him out. They read the newspaper over coffee. She even smiled as he climbed into the shower and soaped her shoulders, though his hands around her neck, the steady stream of water against her face, made her feel as if she were drowning. She gave him a lingering kiss at the door, remembering to look down modestly as he left, so that he would carry an image of her sweetness throughout the day.

When she arrived at the hospital, Henry didn't ask where she had been. William didn't seem to notice that she hadn't been with them all along. The doctors had given him tranquilizers in an intravenous drip, so he lay on the bed with a bemused buzz, betraying nothing of his true worries or fears.

They spent the day in mindless conversation. Morning became afternoon, then early evening, before the nurse came to take William away. With each delay, Susan became more distressed that she had behaved peculiarly with Stephen, despite her attempts to act enthralled. She replayed every moment of the previous night in her head: her conversation sounding more shallow with each repetition, her body seeming softer and fatter. Stephen had only said, "See you soon," when he left. He hadn't mentioned a specific plan or date. She was suddenly frantic that she would never hear from him again. If she were at home, she could be waiting when he called, but she was stuck in the hospital with William.

It should have been that she would become more sentimental

about William once she learned he was dying, in the way her parents became more perfect in her mind the longer they were dead. She found herself forgetting her father's drinking and dismal career, her mother's fretful letters about Susan's failure to marry, never celebrating her success, even as she asked for money.

Yet William irritated her more with every day. The aspects of his personality that once had charmed her now seemed evidence of an emotional shallowness they all shared. She blamed him for the wreck of her personal life, the demands of his friendship having held her back from any other chance for love. Even his refusal to contact his parents, which had once struck her as a kind of bravery, now seemed simply mean-spirited and self-destructive. She couldn't believe that they were as unfeeling as he claimed. Her life was getting worse instead of better. Everyone she loved best — her parents, William — had wanted only her care, and now they had left her, used up and alone, adrift in middle age.

She hated William for being ill. In her madder moments, she even believed that he should be able to beat his disease, as she had once beaten hers. She suspected something willful in his dying, a weakness in his character. Her view of things had become so skewed that she could see nothing worthy in anyone. Even Henry's devotion to William, which at first had been a relief to her, seemed somehow devious and slavish, another symptom of a sickness they all shared. She was frightened that something might be wrong with her, that some kind of poison was creeping into her nature, and it could only be stopped by starting again with Stephen.

Henry stopped pacing and sat on his cot. The book he was reading had a brown paper cover, so Susan couldn't tell its subject. Every once in a while, he looked up and smiled. His faithfulness seemed to accuse her. The longer she watched him tend to William, never betraying impatience or boredom, the more it seemed that her own friendship with William was a fraud. She was ashamed at the memory of how superficially they had spent their time together. Maybe something about her put people off. Maybe William was nothing like the person she imagined, maybe he had always felt freer to confide to Henry secrets he was otherwise unwilling to disclose.

"When you're alone," she asked suddenly, "what do you talk about?"

Henry looked up, startled. "I don't know," he said. "Life, death, doctors, drugs. And you, of course. Always you."

She beamed for an instant, then scowled. "Thanks, but I don't need any souvenirs."

"It's true," Henry said, closing the book on his hand.

She shook her head. She found it hard to believe he wasn't lying. "Last week he called me late at night. I figured he needed to talk about something important, so I said, 'What's wrong, William?' with my voice really gentle, like I'd tell him anything.

"He was silent for a minute like he was thinking back over all the years since we met, because that's what I was doing, and then he asked in that weak voice of his, 'Do you remember the name of that cheese you bought on Eighth Street? The one with blue bits in it like berries?'"

She glared so intently that Henry seemed almost to disappear, the way an image on film caught in a projector blisters on the screen. "I felt like he had hit me, but I spit out, 'Blue. Just blue cheese. But unprocessed. Sort of naturally rotten.' He even thanked me. 'I dreamed about it,' he said. 'I woke up this evening cleaning bits of it out of my teeth with my tongue.'"

"You know he's not always in his right mind these days," Henry said.

"He is when he wants to be," Susan said, her anger rising. "Sometimes I wonder what the hell we've been doing."

"He cares," Henry said. "He just doesn't know what to say. He'd be lost without us."

"Inconvenienced, maybe, but not lost," she said. "There's a difference, you know."

Henry looked up, puzzled. "I don't see why you're being so hard on him, especially now."

Saint Henry, she thought, flushing scarlet. She began to read from a magazine, turning the pages calmly, although she felt like ripping them in half.

After a silence, Henry asked casually, "You seeing someone?"

She shifted uneasily in her chair. "What makes you ask?"

He lay on the floor and cracked his back. "Out all night usually means something," he said. "You couldn't have gotten my messages or you would have come."

She considered telling him that she had heard every one of his pleas and still had decided to stay away, but the truth seemed too shameful. "Please don't tell him. It might not go anywhere." She looked at Henry in despair. "I don't know what I'm doing."

"You think I do?" he asked. "I don't know what the fuck any of this means. But every time I start to freak, I just make myself imagine what it's like for him, and then I come down."

An image of William naked on the operating table, like a body awaiting an autopsy, filled Susan's mind.

What must it be like? she wondered as she imagined him breathing the anesthesia alone, tended by strangers.

What must it be like? she wondered as she imagined the scalpel doing its work.

What must it be like? she wondered as she imagined him awakening, stitched closed, in the recovery room.

What must it be like? echoed over and over so that she might become saturated with the full force of William's suffering. She needed to conjure all the patience in her heart so that she didn't grow more frustrated with him through all the months ahead.

Henry did two sit-ups, then held out his legs, an inch above the ground. His T-shirt slipped partway up his chest. Underneath she saw the rippled muscles of his abdomen. He raised his shoulders again, curling his body slowly to his knees.

William has a hole right here, she thought as she rubbed her fingers along the soft flesh of her own stomach. *William has a hole right here.*

20

William's hospital room was in a corridor shared by patients who all had poisoned blood. Red plastic garbage bags were draped over every door to announce the peril. Placed in the corner by every bed were red plastic boxes in which orderlies carted the refuse away, as gingerly as a man might carry plutonium. William's food was served by nice, gloved ladies who volunteered their services five days a week. Except for Henry and Susan, he never felt the naked touch of another's skin. Even his doctor now prodded his glands with hands sealed in sheer latex that had the color of flesh, but was cold and stiff as a cadaver. Although Henry railed at the staff's caution, William didn't care. He had come to like his dangerous body. Sometimes he felt a kind of irradiated glow emanating from his skin, like an aura, that kept all others one step removed. Sometimes he stroked the contours of a vein, feeling the blood pulsing within, the way a hunter might caress the barrel of a gun. The hospital workers were often so afraid of contamination that they treated him with respect, as they would a murderous don who could turn vicious without warning.

William pushed the button by his bed and adjusted the mattress until his legs were lifted even with his neck. He groaned as he propped a pillow under them, trying to ease the pressure on his back. He pulled open his robe to examine the crisscrossed scars, thick as a bramble of thorns, slashed across his stomach. He remembered nothing of his operation but surrendering to the anesthesia like a little death. After he awoke, some memory of the days before was restored to him: his head smashed against the bathroom tiles; a cold wind; deafening crowds; painted faces; a giddy feeling as if he were lifted high above the street by someone's hand; then a blank until consciousness returned in waves of nausea, every face and object in the recovery room spinning before his eyes.

As he gently touched his incisions, he tried to imagine how the knives had loosened the outer layer of his flesh. He did not know what his body looked like underneath, but somewhere there were muscles, tissues, veins, that had to be cut through before the surgeon could find the mass of tumors coiled around his intestines like a colony of worms. She had cut them out, but without promising there wasn't other damage that couldn't be repaired.

William closed his robe and gripped the bed rail. A bullet of pain shot from his arm to his neck, then to his lung, before it was buried in the beating of his heart. It felt different from the constant flames that flickered from his tattered nerves: heavier, thicker, as if clots ran through his blood like stones.

After so long being ill, he had familiarized himself with the nuance of every twitch as his disease progressed out of anyone's control. He barely glanced at the x-rays his doctor hung over light boxes for his inspection. He didn't need them. He could feel things growing within him from the most solitary cell until they collected together like magnets, weeks before they became visible and hard. He believed he could describe every aberrant cell and flourishing germ, and the malfunctions that had not yet appeared on any screen.

He tried to view the ruin of each part of his body dispassionately. Since his operation, he had made mental lists of those organs he was willing to lose, in order of preference. A leg, a lung, an arm, seemed less important to him now than they might have the month before, but still he clung to those parts he couldn't live without. He cherished his brain, his ears, his remaining good eye, like remnants of a family fortune, for what would become of him if he couldn't think or hear or see?

When he felt most sorry for himself, he made lists of things he had done for the last time: had sex, had a drink; gone to work, to the movies, a restaurant, the gym, a museum; taken a run in the park, driven a car, left the country, flown in a plane. Even a trip to the lobby to buy a newspaper had attained a significance he couldn't explain to a person who did it without thinking. His world grew smaller, minute by minute, yet there was so much room for it to grow smaller still. The moment would come when he would leave his apartment for the last time, then the hospital, his room, finally his bed. Before too long he would be ticking off friends he would never see again. He was obsessed with knowing who the last person would be. He didn't want it to be a doctor or nurse. He didn't want the eyes of his corpse to be closed by a stranger, but lovingly, regretfully, by a friend.

Henry.

Time and again he told himself, *This is no life,* but despite his multitude of afflictions, he still didn't know how to decide when he'd had enough. He had always hoped that some clear sign of resignation, some peaceful feeling of surrender, would overtake his mind and show him the way out. It hadn't happened.

From the first day of his diagnosis, he had promised himself that he would not die a lingering death. He had often read of people who killed themselves before their suffering became un-bearable. He remembered a newspaper headline from years before about two lovers who bound their wrists and ankles together and leaped off a roof after being told they shared a terminal dis-ease. And a doomed woman who killed herself in a van with a doctor's assistance while her husband held her hand. William assumed his own doctor helped his most miserable patients to die, but not until they had suffered longer than he believed it was reasonable to do.

I could bear feeling worse, he told himself as he took stock of what was left, ticking off things he could still do that others couldn't: walk, wash, dress, read, feed himself. He had learned to bear the itches, the labored breath, the gray fatigue, the cloudy vision, the cramps that ambushed different parts of his body at will. He didn't know anymore if what he endured on ordinary days would be insufferable to the healthy, or if every moment marked a compromise with his disease that he wasn't fully aware he was making. A few years before he would have found just one of his symptoms intolerable; now pain had become a part of him in ways he couldn't explain to those who didn't share it. Bearing it took no tricks of bravery or courage. He had no choice once he surrendered to the fact that it was never going away. But how much more could he stand?

So many horrors existed within his body, dangers he had never dreamed possible. What frightened him most was the quickness with which new symptoms appeared. In the beginning his decline had kept a gradual pace. Now sores were born in the middle of the night — bloody, gaping pockets worn into his skin as deeply as if cut with a knife. He had seen patients struck dumb with brain seizures that flashed out of nowhere like electrical storms. No minute was safe, despite his vigilance. Every second he stayed alive only increased the odds of losing to a catastrophe.

"You have to have hope," his doctor told him, as if hope were the miracle that would save him. But hadn't he noticed the patients William saw every day in the hospital ward, dying in pieces? Hadn't he watched them endure months of useless treatments, pricked and poked and poisoned with no observable effect? Often William shared the treatment room with a man named Juan. Over recent weeks he had watched Juan's eyes overtake his face, growing hugely black and round. The last time Juan had come there, spittle thick and yellow as yoke was dried on his chin. He had mouthed "hello" silently, terror pinching his face, as in photographs William had seen of prisoners in cattle cars. William was too smart not to know that he was on the way to becoming just like Juan, but each time he had given up, hope would creep up on him again, like the germ of another disease.

Still, he was plagued by fears of waiting until he was too weak or feeble to find the means to take his life. Already he felt so unreal sometimes that he forgot where he was; often in the middle of the afternoon, he couldn't tell the difference between waking and sleeping. What he dreaded most was his body hooked to a respirator: gagging on tubes, listening to the steady *whoosh whoosh whoosh* as each breath was forced out, while he lay speechless, locked in the machine's embrace more tightly than in a strangler's hands.

Months before, he had looked up the best ways to kill himself in a book. He knew he could never use a knife or a gun, or throw his body in front of a speeding train. As miserable as he felt, he was still too accustomed to comfort to choose a painful death. The book claimed the sweetest way for him to die was to swallow a lethal combination of pills, then tie a plastic bag around his head. The bag should be loose at the face but tight at the neck, secured with two rubber bands. The instructions included the required number of pills, more than enough for a good night's sleep, but not so many that he would awake vomiting, brain-damaged and still alive. So far William had endured his suffering with the knowledge that he had ten times the number of pills he needed, hidden in the nightstand by his bed, a secret pharmacy he had made Henry bring from his stash at home. William liked to have them near because the nurses were often grudging about doping his misery or letting him escape into a dreamless sleep.

*

He leaned down and pulled the plastic liner from the wastebasket. He poured a glass of water and selected a bottle of sleepers from the drawer. It was midnight by the clock on the wall, hours before an aide would come to draw the morning's blood, even longer before Henry stopped by on his way to school. All he needed to do was swallow two fistfuls of pills, and soon it would be too late to save him. For years he had taken more vitamins than that during a normal day. Before he grew too groggy, he would wrap the bag around his face and settle into the pillows. He imagined waves of a familiar, drowsy blackness, almost a giddiness, as unconsciousness slammed upon him. Only this time, somewhere between night and morning, the sleep would drift away to death.

He swung his feet off the bed and raised himself up by leaning on the IV pole. Although his stomach cramped violently, he struggled to the window and rested on the arm of the chair. His sight was best at closer range, so the opposite towers of the hospital building were as indistinct as mountaintops in fog. Up so high, the lights from the street split and shattered in his kaleidoscope eye.

He stared at the pills, shiny as marbles in his hand, and began to drop them into his mouth, first one, another, then three, four, until they rattled against his tongue. He raised the cup of water to his lips and sipped.

Do it, he told himself, but his throat seemed to seize and close by instinct, as if his muscles were beyond his control. He tried to force himself to keep the liquid in by imagining something irrevocable: either aiming the barrel of a gun at his head or stepping off the roof of a skyscraper into midair, but still he coughed and retched. Scattered sounds blew up at him — an accelerating engine, an isolated shout — but mostly the peculiar silence of the city filled his ears, a static buzz like the hum of high-tension wires. He closed his eyes, mesmerized, and in that instant he knew he would trade anything to feel his feet touch those streets again, even just to lie in bed and imagine the life below as it had once existed, with him still part of it, if only in a dream.

He spit the pills into his lap, their blue coating melted in places by his saliva. *I am making a mistake*, he thought in despair, but still he drowned their bitter taste with gulps of water. When he had first considered killing himself, he recalled the night he heard his parents whisper about a cousin who had thrown herself off an overpass into the path of an oncoming truck. During his months of careful planning, William had marveled at her courage to run headlong and never stop. Now he wondered if it wasn't courage at all, but a kind of indifference he didn't share. Despite everything that had happened, he still cared deeply about his life. It was just possible that one day soon the doctors would discover the proper combination of pills to save him. After all, most discoveries were accidents. Or maybe one morning his body would awaken to a remission that would buy some extra time. It had happened to others before.

That day in the waiting room when he had watched Juan being wheeled past, William heard a man whisper to his companion, "Promise me you'll kill me before I ever get that bad." At the time, William had silently agreed. He had always believed he would rather be dead than crippled from a car crash or maimed by an explosion. When he saw photographs of men charred in fires, their features melted, he never understood why their doctors hadn't let them die. Even when he heard stories of families killed in burning houses, four children and a father dead, he always believed that the measure of the mother's heartbreak would outweigh any reason to survive. The choice had seemed simple when he still was blessed with the mind and body of a healthy man, but now he understood how a person could cling preposterously to life without ever wanting to let go.

He turned away from the window and struggled to the bed. He

placed the bottle of pills in the drawer and wadded the plastic bag into a ball. As he slipped between the sheets, he reassured himself that the same way out would still be available the next day, or the day after, whenever his hope or his energy ran out, whichever came first. At the very least, he didn't want to die in the hospital, but back at home, where he belonged.

He waved his hand over his stitches, trying to ease their burn. The nurses had told him that itching in his incisions was a sign of healing, so he savored the sensation as it sparked across his stomach, then traveled back repeatedly, as if he were pricking his pores with hot pins, wanting to believe his body was still fixable.

A few weeks before, he had heard a story on the news about a graveyard excavated beneath the foundation of a building in the heart of the financial district: a cemetery of slaves, the poor, the bleakest cases, dumped into a mass grave in what had once been beyond the farthest borders of the city. The archaeologists discovered that all of the bodies, stripped of any adornment but buttons and bouquets of desiccated flowers, were pointed east so that they might sit up and face the morning sun on Judgment Day. If hope remained even within the most hopeless lives, maybe William, too, might join that clatter of skeletons with rough sockets of bone for eyes, rising up again on Judgment Day to be blinded by the light of the Lord.

PART THREE

The entrance seemed to be by a long narrow pass, like a furnace, very low, dark, and close. The ground seemed to be saturated with water, mere mud, exceedingly foul, sending forth pestilential odors and covered with loathsome vermin. At the end was a hollow place in the wall, like a closet, and in that I saw myself confined. . . . Those walls, terrible to look on themselves, hemmed me in on every side. I could not breathe. There was no light, but all was thick darkness. I do not understand how it is; though there was no light, everything that could have given pain by being seen was visible.

— A vision of Hell, from *The Life of St. Teresa of Avila*

21

No matter how often he is washed, he reeks of spoiled food. His mouth, his pores, every orifice and opened hole, even the stitched scars from his surgeries, exhale a rank, putrid air. He never feels clean.

Inside his mouth, fungi flourish like seeds in a hothouse. His esophagus, his throat, his tongue, his gums, are smothered by layers of creamy white fur. His breath whistles past its obstruction, more wheeze than air. Often in his bedroom, he stares helplessly at the damage with a flashlight and a hand-held mirror. Even with his failing sight, he can tell that his mouth resembles the entrance to a snowy cave.

His teeth rattle loosely within it, like pickets stuck in melting snow. His gums bleed at a touch, his skin bruises, until his body is not a normal color, but all reds, blues, purples, yellows, a palette of disaster. Soft foods, liquids, even weak streams of saliva, make his throat feel raw as a salted wound. He dreads each swallow, collecting spit in mouthfuls to delay the acid burn, until he chokes, like a drowning man.

This damage is nothing compared to the horror he senses within. Although even x-rays cannot reveal the catastrophe, he feels veins, arteries, the ventricles of his heart, collapse like rain-soaked dams. He imagines that if he were cut open, his organs would look softened and wrecked — ruined pieces of their original architecture. When *he turns over in bed, they slosh within him, pressing against his skin, like a sack brimming with garbage.*

The more his body dies, the more his mind becomes alive with fear. He has learned a whole new language to describe what is waiting for him. At night he repeats the words in his head, as if memorizing a new vocabulary:

> *lividity*
> *rigor mortis*
> *putrefication*

He has read that after death, the abdomen is the first part of the body to turn green, inflating with gases that eat away at everything solid. Blood, water, the seas of the interior, ferment into alcohol, as if by magic, the levels rising higher and higher until nothing is left of him but a drunken corpse. Then the skin that has been his torture becomes suppler, stringier, before it turns to bubbling fat, like meat cooked on a spit. It melts from the bones, piece by piece, taking with it the brain, the eyes, the heart, the lungs, leaving only teeth, finger-nails, clumps of hair clinging to a leathery hat of skin. To the naked eye, what is left could be anything, human or animal, a stick figure of crumbling bones.

He is tormented by suspicions that death is more terrible than even he has imagined, that the mind's afterlife is a special kind of hell. He fears that all dreams of escape are a lie, that consciousness remains trapped, mute and blind, while the body decomposes, sens-ing each moment of its demise. He fears he will feel the cuts of the autopsy, the burning fluids of the embalmer, the fires of the cremato-rium oven. Most of all he fears awaking in the dark, half suspended but still aware, buried six feet underground for all eternity, learning at last the truth the living can't know: that death is a blindfold, a straitjacket, a pine box with no holes for air.

22

William couldn't see clearly out of his hospital window unless he arose from the bed. The top of the blinds obscured all but a sliver of black or blue, by which he judged the time of day. To give him a view other than the white cinder-block walls when he lay alone, Henry had brought a photograph of the house to hang above the nightstand. On the opposite wall, he had pinned a multicolored poster of the planets taken from his classroom. Jupiter's moons were drawn within its orbit, Saturn's rings spun around its greenish globe, and on and on until Pluto sat at the edge of the visible universe, nearly hidden by a splatter of stars.

Henry had meant well, but the pictures only reminded William of the ways in which his world had become no larger than his room. Even the vastness of the hospital complex meant nothing to him, since he never ventured farther than one loop past the nursing station to the lounge at the end of the hall, then back again, a routine as familiar now as his nightly walks from his apartment to the river's edge once had been.

Despite the news that Henry and Susan brought during their visits, the television had become his most treasured link to the world outside. Without a job to go to, with only doctors' rounds to anticipate, he had little else to break his preoccupation with his disease. Of his many regrets since he became ill, he minded leaving his job the most. He had loved to work twelve, sometimes sixteen hours a day. Each project completed and each new one planned gave him a satisfaction he had known in no other part of his life.

Other than watching the news, he had always scorned television as a waste of vital time. But with nothing else to ground him, he lay for hours, mesmerized by game shows, often crying when contestants won prizes or money. He watched sports for the first time in his life and cheered when a particular team won. He followed soap operas and found that the daily dramas of betrayal, accidental death, and adultery gripped him in the way that once had the crises of his friends.

Late at night, when demons ruined his sleep, he would reach for the remote control to dispel his panic, the sound as pacifying as if he had shaken awake a friend. After dark, he preferred live programs, not prerecorded or canned, as if the electrical connection from the studio to his television brought real people into his room. Sometimes after midnight his attention wandered to a religious program hosted by an evangelical minister. The only remarkable feature of the man's slick, good looks was a manic grin that never left his face, even when he was deep in prayer. At first William watched because the minister's intensity amused him, but over time the studio audience began to enthrall him. Overweight, badly dressed, and long past middle age, they appeared ordinary in every way except for the rapture of their belief.

Until he became ill, William had found it easier to believe in creatures on other planets than to believe in God. As his future grew bleaker, he found himself hoping for the first time that another life might exist beyond his own. He didn't know if it was simply fear that changed his heart, or a special yearning that came to the hopeless, and opened his mind in a way it never had before.

Throughout his life, he had heard stories that made him question his view of the world. For years Susan had told him about a man named Scott, whom she believed to be a healer. He had once been a minister in a city church but had become addicted to drugs and lost everything except his faith. When Susan met him, he was working in an insurance office and living with a woman he met in a rehabilitation program. Although she was embarrassed by her faith in him, Susan had called upon Scott several times to help her friends. Even William couldn't deny that there was a mystery to his character that simple trickery couldn't explain.

William had seen enough exposés of charlatans who claimed to use their eyes as lasers or their hands as scalpels not to doubt Scott's power, but he knew one story he could prove for himself. Years before, Susan's friend Frances had developed a tingling in her fingertips that quickly worsened. Within a month, every muscle in her body began to fail. After a series of tests, her doctor determined that she showed evidence of a crippling disease. Frances called Susan in despair. Soon after, Susan called the healer. He asked questions about her symptoms, her appearance, her personality. He even had Susan describe the decor of Frances's apartment so that he could imagine her moving within her own space.

Neither William nor Susan knew what rituals or prayers Scott performed, but over the next week the numbness left Frances's extremities. When she went to the doctor for further tests, all of her symptoms had disappeared. Five years had passed, and still she remained in perfect health. No one knew what to make of her recovery. A remission? A misdiagnosis? The power of suggestion? William had tried so often to wish his own disease away that he couldn't believe Frances had hoped for a cure more fervently than he. Like him, she claimed not to believe in God. Like him, she prided herself on her skepticism and irreverence about all things. But after Susan called the healer, Frances didn't ask questions. She took her cure and ran.

William knew that after he became ill, Susan had searched for Scott, but he had moved without leaving a forwarding address.

Sometimes he prayed that Scott would return in the nick of time to save him. Or if not, he hoped that he would find another person who could work a similar magic on his disease.

On the religious program every night, he saw evidence of people being cured: men throwing off neck braces and leaping into the air, women healed of deafness, children freed from blindness. The minister held up written testimony from viewers who swore to the miracles they had experienced in their lives. They seemed so contented and sincere, William couldn't believe that all of them were frauds. Their ecstasy seemed too real to be merely a performance. He found it difficult to conceive of a conspiracy so vast that millions of viewers took part in it every day, but it was impossible to know what to believe. When he was young, his mother's best friend, Mrs. Ellerbee, the kindest and most reasonable of women, was convinced that no man had ever walked on the moon. She claimed the scenes from outer space were staged in a crater in Arizona. When William listened to her, the theory sounded plausible. How could anyone know for sure?

Miracles could happen. He had read stories of visitations from heaven, of paintings that wept tears, of statues that bled from marble wounds. Surely not all of them could be dismissed as psychotic delusions or sleights of hand. He remembered the nuns at school speaking with awed reverence of Saint Teresa's body, placed in a wooden coffin covered with chalk and stone, and how the air above her grave grew redolent with jasmine and violets. When she was exhumed, her features remained perfect and untouched after thirty years beneath the ground.

William couldn't understand why the saint's body should have been different from any other, just as he couldn't understand how the psychic could see beyond the limits of time or how the healer could change lives irrevocably through the miracle of prayer. He had begun to wonder if there was a wild power to the mind — to predict the future, to levitate the body, to cure an illness — that those with faith could touch at will, and those who didn't believe, like William, had let wither and die.

Every night on the minister's program, he heard testimony from people who had been struck by God during times of anguish and despair, often without searching. They described dazzling lights, sometimes even a physical presence, a bearded figure appearing in midair, overwhelming them with faith. He wanted so much to believe, not simply in God, but in paradise, guarded by angels, its gates opening specially for him at the moment he died, if only because there was nothing else left in the world that could take away his fear.

William flicked on the television and watched the minister walk in front of a photograph of olive trees in the Holy Land blown up to the size of a wall. Dirt roads wound up a mountain slope with small, stone buildings clustered at the highest rise of hill. In the distance beyond, he saw a corner of pure, blue sky. The minister flung his arms wide, as if to invite the audience into the studio, then pressed his hands together and began to pray. "I feel a hunger out there; I feel a heat," he murmured, so quietly that William pumped up the volume with the remote control, louder and louder, until he seemed to shout from across the room.

"I feel a hunger; I feel a heat; I feel a hunger; I feel a heat," he chanted until William became hypnotized by the rhythm. Suddenly the minister snapped open his eyes and stared directly into the camera. "I feel a man out there who is hurting. He has been sick a long time." He smiled reassuringly. "Rise up, my friend." He beckoned gently with his hand. "Your trouble is ending."

William looked from left to right to make sure no one hovered outside his room. He lowered the mattress with the electric switch and limped over to close the door, dragging his IV. He waved as a nurse passed in the corridor, carrying an armful of sheets and towels. "Nap time," he said, then tucked his head back in.

"Come," the minister called.

As he gazed at the screen, William hoped that the minister's words were addressed to him in particular. At the same time, he imagined a hundred, maybe a thousand, suffering viewers inching toward their television sets, each praying with their hearts to be the one who was saved.

He watched transfixed as the minister's face twisted in rapture. "I feel a man out there with a tumor. Lord, you gave me that word. Yes, a *tumor.*" He nodded twice, as if addressing a person whom no one else could see. "Love God and He will end your trouble. Let God be true."

William ran his hand over the tumors on his arm. He pictured their lumpy shapes on his back. He looked to see the red blotches encircling his fingers like rings. He sucked in his breath until the air whistled painfully past the obstructions in his lungs. He had tumors to spare.

"Come close, pray with me," the minister said, lowering his head.

Even if the program only promised lies, William would never get any better by resisting. When he knelt before the screen, the cement floor stabbed the bones in his knees, but he forced himself to bear the pain, worried that he might break the spell if he only surrendered partway.

"Take my hand," the minister said, holding his open palm before the camera. It filled the picture completely, obscuring his face. William could see each groove and crooked line, as if the skin had been placed under a magnifier. When he touched his own hand to the glass, it zapped from the static.

"To my friend out there who seeks a cure, make a vow and pay it, and in the day of your troubles God will hear your prayer. Make a covenant with Him, and He will make you well to establish His kingdom on earth."

William summoned the full force of his concentration, filling his mind with images of Jesus he had seen in sculptures, icons, paintings, in churches, on crucifixes, in stained glass windows, a face pinched with exhaustion and despair, bleeding from wounds. He pressed harder and harder against the screen, until it hurt, his bones so brittle that he worried they might snap. He tried to will the image into being, desperate to feel a change come over his mind and engulf his soul. He could only remember fragments of prayers from childhood, so he mumbled after the minister's words, conjuring the red shape of each tumor until it pulsed in his sight; he imagined a divine light flooding through his body, eliminating all traces of disease like blasts from a laser.

"Feel the sickness leave you," the minister said. "Peace won't come until you release your life: that's what making a vow is all about. That's what's killing you. Make God true in your heart, and He will deliver you."

William promised to do good. He promised to go to church. He promised to give his money to the poor. He promised everything he owned to atone for the emptiness of his existence, as if it weren't already too late for a miracle to give him a chance to begin again.

"Close your eyes and imagine God's hand," the minister said, purring with certainty and calm. "Know that it is everywhere about you. Salvation isn't a dream if you see it with the eyes of God. Surrender your life and let Him take you to the promised land. Let His eyes be yours."

William watched the camera shift toward a photograph of

mountains dwarfed by a cloudless sky, the peaks seeming to glitter through bursts of a perfect sun. "I'm just showing you how big God can be," the minister said. "Is my God too big for you?"

William stared, blinking, at the television. The shimmering image was quickly replaced by a commercial. He remained kneeling, feeling foolish now that the minister had vanished from the screen. He removed his hand from the glass. It felt numbed from the pressure of holding it there so long, but nothing else had changed. If anything, the angry rise of tumor near his wrist looked darker and more pronounced. He leaned back on his haunches, still hesitant to stand up and quit. Maybe he hadn't prayed hard enough. Maybe some unconscious part of his mind resisted being cured. Or maybe in time he could rid himself of doubt and learn to believe, as the minister's audience did. He hoped it was possible, for he didn't want his death to be the desolate black hole he imagined, yet his reason stopped him. How could he hope to expect more from death than he had ever found in life itself: punishment for the wicked, reward for the good, reunion with a life's worth of lost souls? An ending that beautiful could never be true.

He looked from left to right. He turned on the light. The frame around the picture of his house shimmered with gold. The night sky on the poster beside him pulsed with stars. He tried to find comfort in imagining them as something larger than the tiny flickers of light they seemed from earth: the uncharted territories of planets, barren moons, an endlessness he had read about in books that went on and on forever, as he had once imagined his own life would. Although he could take on faith the rocks, dirt, and gaseous clouds he had been told existed within the darkness out there, he lacked the imagination to know what might lie beyond it.

Once Henry had told him about a new theory that claimed the universe was always receding, the darkness at night reflecting the distance it traveled every day, leaving us farther and farther behind. The force of the life William held onto was nothing compared to that. Although he wished for more, he knew that when he died he would simply vanish within it, no substance, no weight even to ruffle the air as he drifted off, less than a whisper in the storms of a billion galaxies, each with its own network of a trillion stars. Black, cold, and vast, even the words used to describe its nature — *infinite, timeless, a world without end* — only served to make him feel more acutely that it was not a place where a soul might live.

In his heart he knew it was too late for rescue. If he hadn't been ill, any idea of another life would have meant nothing to him, except in the way he had once prayed for his parents to come when he awakened from nightmares in the middle of the night. In times before, the world he was given had seemed enough for any man. Only now did it seem that with nothing after, he didn't understand the meaning of anything he'd done. He felt suddenly as if for forty years he'd been a visitor in another's house, and the reasons for his journey there had been left behind with all the things he had planned to do but had never done.

He rose from the floor and climbed into bed. He pressed the mute button on the remote control, but the sounds of horns outside, other voices, sirens that seemed unceasing, howled from down the street and up into his room.

A dizziness swept over him, like that of a person who awakens the moment he is falling out of bed. He pulled the sheet over him, wrapping it tight against his legs. The blue-gray shadows flickering from the television made the fabric seem to glow, too white, against his skin. When he looked down at his arms, his thighs, the knobs of his knees, his flesh seemed shriveled and burned. He felt his body to be the most lifeless thing of any object in the room.

What do I do now? he wondered, knowing sleeplessness would haunt him. Should he call someone? Read? Write a letter?

He was so afraid.

23

William rubbed his back crazily against the mattress. He shrugged off his robe and scratched at the crusted circles of blisters that covered his shoulders like small white targets. As he picked with his nails, they flaked to the sheets in a blizzard of scales. The only relief he found from his constant itches was the few minutes each day he lay immersed in a tub. No matter how many ointments or creams he slathered on his body, he felt as if he were trapped within nests of stinging insects whenever he was not submerged.

Go to hell, he thought as he watched Susan idly thumb through a glossy architectural magazine. He could see her eyes alight on her watch, deerlike and furtive, each time she turned the page. He sighed more loudly, letting out a moan.

Susan dabbed at a lipstick smear, then cleaned her teeth with her tongue. It had not escaped his notice that she appeared to bloom in perverse proportion to his own physical demise. All winter she had been losing weight. He was concerned at first, thinking the demands of his care were affecting her health. Then he began to notice how toned her skin had become and how her new haircut flattered the contours of her face. She arrived for hospital visits as if dressed for a party. Tonight she wore a sheer white dress that clung to the curves of her body and shoes with heels so spiked that she tipped at an angle when she walked. Henry, too, grew bigger and pinker, his bulk apparent even under baggy sweatshirts and jeans.

I'm glad I'm such an inspiration to them, he thought as he scratched his chest. He could feel hard, round knobs rooting beneath the skin. He hadn't mentioned these new growths to his doctor, but they felt to him like the fetuses of tumors.

Susan caught his eye and fanned the magazine over her lap. "Can I help?"

"No!" The boom in his voice surprised him, a thunder of old.

"Maybe you'd feel better if you ate something," she said, pointing to his untouched dinner on the table by the bed. "You need your strength."

The tips of pink meat swimming in milky rice looked to him like severed tongues. He would rather starve than taste it. "No."

"More water?"

"Thank you, no."

"Maybe take a walk in the hall?"

"No," he said. Seeing the other patients wheeled along the corridors only made him feel more hopeless about the future of his disease.

"Do you want me to call your parents?"

"No," he started to say by rote, but as her words sunk in, he snapped his head around.

Susan laughed. "I figured I'd get your attention." The four diamond hoops in her ears jiggled with a rainbow of sparks.

"Why not go into the hall and shout 'fire'?" William said. "Maybe you can cause a riot and amuse yourself no end." He glared at the ceiling above his bed.

"Sorry." She leaned over and squeezed his hand.

Her fingers were soft and newly manicured, with perfectly painted tips. William lifted an arm so that his IVs dangled like broken bracelets. "Leave me alone," he said. "I feel like shit and I don't want to be talked out of it today." He brushed her scarlet claws away.

"Then maybe I had better go." She did not say the words unkindly, but her face was set, hard-eyed and unsmiling.

"Wait," he said, stopping short of a full apology. Even if he seemed to spurn them, these days each departing visitor left him feeling more lonely than before. The quiet in his room was never peaceful, but upside down and charged with panic, like being locked in a closet during an acid high. The more he reflected upon his operation, the more he realized how much it had thrown him. Until then, his disintegration had seemed distant and unreal, no matter how bad he felt. After his body had been cut open, it seemed ruined in ways it never had before. Even his fear was different: less shrill, but heavier and more distressed. Once it had struck, then vanished like a mood. Now it never left him, gripping tightly, like rubber gloves over skin.

Nothing could stop it, especially not a conversation. Any language he knew increasingly seemed ridiculous to him, for when he felt terror race through his body like a fever, leaving him sprawled across the mattress in pools of dripping sweat, the only words he could find to express it were those any child might utter:

I feel so bad.

Help me, please.

I don't want to die.

Despite months of lying naked while strangers examined his body, he refused to be humiliated by leaving himself so vulnerable and exposed. Any fool could guess what he was thinking. The only person he looked forward to seeing was the fat, blond nurse from Ireland who bathed him every night in alcohol, her hands caressing the cool liquid into the recesses of his body, probing as lovers once had.

But Susan was as stubborn as he was. In recent weeks he had watched her impatience grow with every visit. If he didn't meet her halfway, he would poison her last memory of him. He didn't want that to happen, since she and Henry would be its main trustees.

He watched her suck an imaginary puff from a cigarette, then stroke two fingers along its edge. The paper broke from the filter and fell into her lap. She jumped up, brushing the curls of tobacco from her dress as if they were small, brown spiders. *I'm driving her crazy*, he thought, not pleased the way he might once have been.

"I'm sorry," he said. "I want you to stay."

She fiddled with the gold clasp on her purse, snapping it back and forth. "It's just that I can't keep going on like this, pretending nothing is happening. You're too important to my life."

"I'm not pretending," William said.

"You forget, I know what it's like to feel awful all the time. I was sick once, too."

It wasn't the same. William resented people presuming they knew how he felt just because they had been ill in the past. He didn't believe anyone alive could understand the depth of his suffering. Susan had only a child's memory of disease. It couldn't possibly have held the same sensation of dread. "You recovered," he said.

"So could you."

"Not now. I know my body too well." He didn't have the patience to explain the ways in which the daily doses of drugs had turned his insides into a cesspool. Or how twice a month the blasts of chemotherapy sent him hurtling into the blackest, rattling despair. For days afterward, he was crazed with madness and rage, incapable of judging which horrors were real and which were simply part of a chemical reaction. Either way, it was killing him.

"Well, I hope you're wrong," Susan said. She walked over and stroked his head, her fingers lingering at the base of his skull, then moving to the deep lines in his forehead. He settled back and closed his eyes. Because the light above the bed was on, from behind his lids he saw electric orange streaked with black, like the last of a sinking sun.

Despite his pleasure, he sensed a tenseness feeding the strength of her touch, as if she were softening him up before giving bad news.

"What is it?" he whispered. "You might as well say."

She released his head and played her hand along the IV, leaning to within inches of his ear. "Would you kill me if I found your parents?"

Up so close, her breath was foul with smoke. He ripped the tubing from her grip and let it hang loosely from the pole. "Visiting hours have ended," he said, turning his face to the wall.

"But wouldn't you feel more resolved about your life, even in a small way?"

"They've got nothing to do with my life," he said. He twisted the collar of his robe around his neck, then choked, his body a shudder.

Susan did not go to help him. She sat, knees together, hands crossed at her stomach, as if to protect herself. "Well, this will really piss you off, but I tracked down the number and called your house late one night. I hung up when a woman answered." She inhaled deeply. "Sorry. I was never going to tell."

A stone house, rolling hills browned by drought, his parents' faces, whirled through William's mind. "How do you know it was my mother?" he asked to halt his sense of slipping away.

"I don't for sure," she said. "But the name, the place, were all the same. I just called information."

William had erased his family so completely from his mind that he was amazed to learn they still existed in a directory somewhere, only a telephone call away. He felt no real longing to return, but he couldn't stop from asking, "How did she sound?"

"Old, I guess, but after all, I only heard her say hello." Susan pulled a piece of folded paper from her pocket and held it before his eyes. "Here's the number. You could call and find out for yourself."

"I really want you to stop," William said. "This is none of your business."

She crumpled the paper in her palm and dropped it to the floor. "Okay. Sorry."

"I don't understand why people are so sentimental about their families," he said, unable to let go.

"Maybe because mine wasn't so bad."

"They're not all the same."

"Sometimes that's easy to forget," she said. "I'm sorry, really." She returned to the bed and kissed him sweetly on the forehead. "We'll start over tomorrow. I promise. I'll try to think of a thing or two to amaze you, something that won't make you mad."

"You've got news?" he asked. "Tell me now."

"Tomorrow," she said, laughing, halfway out the door. "Just think, maybe the waiting will give you another reason to live."

He watched her go, then watched an orderly come to take his dinner tray away. He heard bells ringing softly in the hall, a bustle of other visitors leaving. He longed to follow, to walk the streets all night, as he would have done in another time to absorb the things that Susan had said. She had meant well, but he felt ambushed by her, his mind so alive with the past that he couldn't bring it under control. He hated the way others sought to orchestrate his dying, as if he had no role in deciding which parts of his life to leave unfinished. He knew no one believed him, but he had never missed his family, even at his most despairing. Years before, they had ceased to be an integral part of his heart or his mind. Or else his longing was buried so deeply within him as to be incidental to the normal course of his day. Even in sleep, they had never invaded his dreams.

If a stranger were to look at the few photographs that existed, William did not appear to be related to any member of his family by blood. He shared none of their features, but was bigger, darker, more intense. From childhood on, he had sensed a coldness in his parents' touch, as if he were an orphaned relation they were compelled to raise by duty, not love. Although his recollection had become skewed and more ingrained the longer he stayed away, he remembered a different connection between his parents and his sisters, a warmth and pleasure in each other's company that only made him feel stranger and more outcast.

He should have been cherished. As the only male heir, he was meant to ensure that the family's name survived into the next generation and beyond. Those 1,400 acres owned for over one hundred years were to be his reward for procreation, as if the only immortality that mattered was carried in the land. But once his parents learned that he was gay, he would watch them study him from across a room and believe they were thinking, *Where did you come from? And when are you going to leave?*

The longer he stayed, the more their house oppressed him, until all his energy was spent trying to keep out of their way. He caught their attention only when he was sick, so he came to crave illness as a blessed state. Love and disease became so ingrained in his mind that sometimes now he wondered if he had been doomed before he left. But back then, he had wanted nothing but escape. He had foreseen only more unhappiness coming from prolonging a relationship that would never have naturally lasted on its own. He left before their image of him could ruin his life.

And never once in twenty years had he been stopped by more than small regrets.

William reached across the bed and took the picture of his house from the wall, as if to reassure himself that it alone was the place he missed. Maybe it was the fact that his disease had made his body irrelevant, but increasingly he had come to see his past in terms of the places he had lived, no longer in the way he had looked, as if they alone marked his passage through life. Although his family's obsession with their land had been the cause of so much grief, he understood the comfort derived from a sense of physical space, especially something that could be *owned*, for the rooms he had lived in were more vivid to him now than any body, the only things he had ever possessed that were tangible, that had given his self a home.

He couldn't believe how long it had been since he had last gone to his house. The rooms must be covered with dust, the gardens ruined. In better times, whenever he had left on vacation he had hired a local boy to tend to it. He had arranged nothing since he was ill. Every weekend he had planned to return, even as the months became a year. It was time to sort through his things and put the house in order. He wanted it to be perfect when Henry brought him back.

He leaned over and picked up the paper Susan had left crumpled on the floor. He remembered how his mother had coached him before he left the ranch for his first day at school, drilling the telephone number into his head so that he could call if he was ever lost or in danger. He had learned it before he learned to spell his name.

I am in danger now. He laughed, but when he tried to summon the numbers into his mind, he wasn't sure of any of them, not even the prefix with which they had begun.

Before he threw the paper into the trash, he unfolded it to see 408-327-4891 written in Susan's familiar scrawl. He waited to feel some start of recognition, some nostalgic pull of desire that would weaken his resolve and compel him to call. Nothing happened. It could have been the number of any place on earth.

They could have found me, too, he thought as he imagined his mother answering hello into Susan's silent phone. He wondered if sometimes, when his parents' telephone rang in the middle of the night, they had ever prayed it was him. He didn't know if simply stubbornness or pride had kept him from contacting them all these years, or if he had lived in dread of the shame he would feel if he had made a gesture and been again rejected.

It didn't matter anymore. But the closer he got to dying, the more William did have one regret about leaving. He dreaded having an obituary that read as its last line, *There are no survivors* — as if it would announce to the world that he had spent his life alone; as if he had come from nothing; as if he had made no mark on anyone, anywhere.

24

Henry hovered by the edge of the bed, holding a tray piled high with food to tempt William's appetite: pasta dyed with squid ink, a steaming miso broth, four flavors of ice cream, a crème brûlée. But now the choices he had made seemed ridiculous and overdone, merely evidence of his fear that William was slipping away.

William didn't seem to care. He ignored the food entirely as he reached for Henry's hand, lifting it up to rest against the rocky glands in his neck. "Feel," he said.

Underneath the stubble of William's beard Henry felt something hard, as if a handful of pebbles were sewn under the skin. "Do you think they're getting larger?" William asked.

Henry wiped his fingers against his pants, but the sensation lingered in his palm, like an aftertremor. He stroked his jaw to assure himself of its angular grace.

"The tumors are growing in my mouth like stalagmites," William said. His pallor was more green than white, with chalky blisters bubbling on his lips.

Henry had long since ceased to respond when William described his newest symptoms except to try to look him full in the face without flinching. Any words of consolation seemed ridiculous in light of the magnitude of his suffering. But he couldn't resist stealing a peek into William's mouth to glimpse the thick magenta lump behind his teeth. Henry's tongue darted nervously over the smooth roof of his mouth, then flipped back toward the well of his throat. To distract himself, he tried to remember whether stalagmites grew up from the bottom of a cave or dripped down from the ceiling. Either way, what William had said must be true. When he spoke, his tongue seemed caught by some obstruction; then the words flapped from his mouth with a flutter, like bats.

Henry had hoped William's death would be a gradual fading away, not this torrent of ever-changing symptoms. In the last month his skin seemed to have melted on his bones. His hair was falling out in tufts. Two nights ago Henry had come upon him holding a brush and staring at the matted bristles, as if each hair were a year.

"I need a favor," William said, but his sentence drifted off as he scratched his arm vigorously. Henry was fascinated at the way he could dig at his flesh without disturbing the tubes. The fabric of his sleeve moved up and down with the rhythm, exposing muscles grown loose and stringy as dough. Even as Henry stared, William paid no attention. He seemed to have lost all self-consciousness, as if his body no longer belonged to him.

Henry reached across and stilled his hand with a touch. William's eyes darted from the ceiling to the window to the door before they landed on Henry, blinking. "Oh, hi," he whispered as if seeing him for the first time that day. He whipped free the twisted tubes and dragged himself up with a grimace, then closed his eyes and seemed to fall asleep.

Henry slumped in the chair. Did William even realize he was there? He couldn't tell anymore. Some days William seemed to have no memory of his visits, yet if he stayed away for only an evening, William reproached him for his abandonment. His energy seemed to flow, then ebb almost to unconsciousness, then spark back to life, as if jerked by a malformed current.

As Henry watched him sleep, he imagined a battle of opposing cells within him: a few shrinking, healthy clusters besieged by deadly armies, fighting, then hiding, grouping and regrouping, each time retreating to a farther part of his body. And each erratic burst of energy marked a small victory of the healthy cells over the dark advance of the others, spreading like an oil slick through his blood. He could even see evidence of this in William's extremities: round, fleshy feet swelled from the sticks of his legs; his hands were of an even, ruddy color so unlike the rest of him that they hung from his wrists like gloves.

Henry stood and began to clean the clutter of Styrofoam cups from the table. He switched off the television and padded softly about the room, folding towels, discarding newspapers, wiping clean the sink and counters with a wadded dressing gown. He liked the moments best when he was alone in the room while William slept. It was like caring for a baby or a pet, no longer a creature with impossible demands teetering on the brink of death.

Three nights a week, he slept by William's bed. They watched TV until dawn, rarely speaking. Sometimes Henry slipped out to buy whatever William wanted at the market down the street. He loved walking through the hushed hospital corridors after hours, coming and going with his special pass. It was like having a deserted museum or a theater all to himself. The nurses treated him with respect, as if he were one of them. Whenever he was home, his apartment felt less and less like the place where he lived.

"Oh, oh," William groaned. He sat up panting, squinting in the light as he fumbled for the call button. He seemed startled when Henry rushed into his line of view. "William, what's wrong?"

William gasped for breath. He brought a cup of water to his lips with a palsied hand. "Things happen when I'm asleep. I don't know what it's from, but I get these rushes of panic that jolt me awake." He hugged the sleeves of his robe tight around his shoulders. "Even my bones are cold."

Henry pretended to work. So little needed to be done that he rubbed at a brown stain worn into the paint of the windowsill. "It's not surprising, dear," he said over his shoulder. He wiped at the wood with wide, circular strokes. He was tired; it was late; he wanted to leave. He had run out of ways to respond to William's misery. He could neither talk nor wish it away. He couldn't even say that he understood, because any sympathy he felt was merely a guess at how he would feel when his own time came. Yet he was called upon to make a hundred such leaps every day. No matter how hard he tried, William's death wasn't something they could share like a broken heart, a ruinous depression, or a battle against nerves, troubles Henry had known often and well. It wasn't even like a common grief at a loved one's death, because William was the one who was dying: and Henry imagined that sorrow for the self bred an endlessness that obliterated anything the living could know.

More and more he had discovered that there was an abyss he could not cross with William, one that had nothing to do with love or caring for his needs. He had learned to distance himself from the horror of William's wasting body: its strange colors, tumors, and sores were as alien to him as when he watched actors transform into monsters in movies. Its menace still seemed far enough from his own life as to be impossible. But worse than the physical ravages were the ways William's mind seemed visited by unspeakable fears. Sleep had become a place of ruined dreams, as if at night his consciousness were abducted by spirits and forced to witness the torments of eternal hell. Henry didn't want to learn too soon the secrets the dead know, in case they took root in his brain like the germ of another disease. If he got too close, their contamination would spoil the rest of his life. He would never be able to forget.

He gathered up his coat and bent to kiss William good-bye. "See you tomorrow."

"I need a favor," William said, his eyes still closed as though he were talking through a dream.

"Of course." Henry flung his coat over his shoulder. It slapped against the wall, too hard.

William opened an eye and scowled. "I was wondering if you could find the time to go with Susan to clean the house. I've been thinking how full of junk and dust it must have gotten. It's probably time to throw some of it away. Anything you think is best. It's up to you, especially now that it's almost yours."

Henry stiffened as he always did whenever William mentioned his will, but he scanned his friend anxiously, trying to see if he'd missed a sign that William was closer to death than he had realized, ready to surrender everything he owned. Through the folds of his opened robe, Henry saw the zippered scars from his surgery, the skin translucent as wet paper. Underneath, his heart fluttered with quick, fragile beats. He forced himself to ask, "Why now, William? I mean, you're not feeling any worse, are you?"

"It's not possible to feel worse," he snapped. "I just want to lie here and think of the house being clean. Ready for anything. Simple enough?"

Henry felt a weird relief as William's anger filled the room, as it had in the old days, when Henry would agree to anything simply to appease him. He was pleased to see that even lying shrunken on the bed, William still seemed powerful enough to fear.

"And throw out the flowers on your way out," he added, glaring at the vase of yellow lilies Henry had brought the day before. "They're dead."

"Yes, William," he answered, pulling the dripping stems into his arms. "Anything you want."

25

Susan gripped a cigarette tightly between her lips and clutched the steering wheel with both hands as she maneuvered her car through the sharp turns of William's driveway. The tires roared over the stones.

"Looks like nobody's home." She laughed as the house loomed up at them around the corner of the last curve: three stories of white clapboard with shutters framing every window, some latticed and square, some small and round like portholes. A widow's walk surrounded by knee-high posts crowned the roof, reached by a ladder hidden in the eaves. A sea captain's house built far enough from shore that no waves could touch it, even in the most violent storm.

Henry got out of the car and leaned against the fender. In the beams of the headlights, he saw pieces of cast-iron furniture tumbled in piles over the lawn. Already William's house seemed haunted by the silence of a place long deserted. The slate of the patio was broken and cracked, and farther out, pale clumps of grass lay scattered over the stones by the empty swimming pool like uncombed wigs.

Susan followed him up the steps that led from the drive. They approached the house as cautiously as trespassers. "Hello?" Henry called at the back door. "Hello? Hello?" He slipped the key into the lock, but its tumblers held fast. "We've got the wrong ones," he sighed.

"Does this mean we get to leave?" Susan asked.

"I wish," he said as he wrapped his fist in a rag and rammed it through the window. He had never broken glass before. He had never even been in a fight. He was surprised at the strength in his arm, at how easily the glass sprinkled around his wrist like confetti. He unlocked the window and climbed up on a milk crate set in a corner by the door. Then Susan pushed him, tumbling, into the room.

When he stood up, the air inside the kitchen was so stale and cold that he felt it displaced by his body, as if it hung about the room in sheets. He unlocked the back door, then ran from room to room flicking on lights and shouting, "Let's get some air in here," as his voice caromed off the walls.

He hovered by Susan's side as she unpacked a bag of cleaning supplies. He was afraid to touch anything. He wondered if he felt the way thieves did when they first stole into a house: absorbing the silence around them, then picking their way furtively through the cupboards and drawers until they found a pattern to the places where everything valuable was hidden.

"I've got it covered in here," Susan said, ripping at the cellophane wrapping of a new yellow sponge with her teeth.

"See you later, I guess," Henry said as he turned slowly toward the door.

From the center hallway, he had an unobstructed view of the ground floor. In the dining room, the straw hat William wore in summer lay on the table like a centerpiece. In the den, a cast-iron rack was layered with coats for every season, each in different shades of blue: a navy slicker, a stained down vest for cutting wood in winter, a sharkskin raincoat with a quilted satin lining, a denim jacket with a severed cuff hanging by a tangle of threads. Mismatched gloves were stuck on knobs around the rack, like hands without bones.

Henry paused, suddenly uncertain of the task before him. He felt simultaneously as if he were preparing the house for William's return and readying his tomb. Although he knew it was unlikely William would ever return, he couldn't risk seeming to take possession. He tried to imagine how he would behave if William were already dead, but even then, he couldn't conceive of ever thinking of the house as his own.

He reinforced the bottom of a box with tape and moved to William's desk in the alcove by the living room. He made neat stacks of bank statements, receipts, bills, and placed them in a folder to take back to the city. He filled a garbage bag with yellowed stationery, pencils, pens, envelopes, rubber bands, boxes of unused checks, emptying every drawer. He vacuumed the floor and moved into the living room, yanking the machine behind him as it sucked balls of dust and cobwebs from every corner. He polished the wooden surfaces with lemon oil. He cleaned clouds of cigarette smoke from the windows and mirrors. He flooded the plants with water and picked handfuls of dead buds from the pots. He snipped free the withered blooms and cracked stems clinging to the roots. Here and there a green shoot struggled to grow. He sprayed each gently, holding it between his fingers, as if he were handling the most delicate fabric.

On the sofa he could detect the spot where William's head had rested when he napped, with two indentations at the opposite end, one for each foot. His body was exactly as long as the couch. Each time Henry fluffed the cushions, their centers sagged the moment he turned away, as if William's ghost slept upon them still.

After two hours, the center rooms were perfectly in order. He leaned against the wall, marveling at what he had accomplished. He could hear Susan singing in the kitchen. Every few seconds he heard a crash as she plunked bottles, cardboard containers, packages of food, from the refrigerator into the trash.

He climbed the stairs that led to William's private quarters: his bedroom, his bath, and a smaller room lined floor to ceiling with books. Even when he stayed for weekends, Henry had never ventured past this threshold. He hesitated now, uneasy in his freedom to walk inside.

He lifted the corner of the bedspread. The fabric felt unnaturally warm and slick. Its whiteness had turned beige, with brown stains splattered across the center. He dropped it with a shudder, remembering the last time William had made him dinner in the city. He sat at the kitchen table slicing vegetables for their salad. When juice and pulp ran from the knife onto his hand, William had licked his fingers clean and continued to cut, coating the food with a thick layer of saliva. Although Henry knew it was impossible to catch anything from William, his stomach had seized as he imagined every morsel poisoned with his disease, just as now he imagined the bed swimming with deadly germs.

He rummaged through a cupboard for a pair of latex gloves, slipping them on before he stripped off the blankets and sheets. He piled pillows on the floor and removed even the inner zippered covers. Feathers fluttered in the air and stuck to his pants, so many flying about that he felt as if he were caught inside a paperweight in flurries of plastic snow.

For a moment, Henry let himself imagine the walls hung with his own pictures, the windows free of the dark, heavy curtains that blocked out the sun. In his mind, he positioned his favorite chair in the corner with a view out onto the garden and through to the woods beyond.

Will it really be mine? he wondered, ashamed again that he could dream of a more comfortable life before William's was even over. He walked down the two steps into the bathroom and opened the windows to let the breeze take away the dank, musty odor. The walls surrounding the bathtub were covered with streaks that stood out against the ceramic, bluish gray over white. He hitched the gloves past his elbows and secured the ends with rubber bands, then tied a bandanna over his mouth and put on his sunglasses, letting the room grow dim in the algae-colored light. He turned on the hot water full blast, and poured ammonia into the tub. He breathed deeply, imagining the germs burning in that molten layer of suds.

He swabbed the sides fiercely with a brush, soaking his clothes. He stood on the rim and scrubbed the bristles against the tiled walls and ceiling. Water dripped onto his lenses and into his hair, running in rivulets down his face. The air grew so thick with ammonia that he choked, but he kept working. To spur himself on, he shouted along to a song on the radio downstairs, so he didn't notice Susan sneak up and tap his leg.

"Everything all right?"

He jumped down. "Look!" he cried, skating along the slippery floor. "Almost clean."

"I can see that. And are you planning a robbery on the trip home?"

"Oh, this," he shrugged as he untied the knot, letting the bandanna swing loosely around his neck. "Too many fumes."

Susan took the sunglasses and set them on the tip of her nose. "You know, I read somewhere that during the plagues in the Middle Ages, people believed that even seeing was dangerous. If somebody saw a sick person approach from down the street, they'd turn away because they believed you could get infected just by looking too closely." She laughed. "You and I couldn't have made it to the corner to buy cigarettes."

Henry pulled off the gloves and crushed them into a ball. "Somehow it gets worse the sicker he gets," he said. "I know it's awful, but he didn't look so diseased before."

Susan drew open the thick linen curtains and flicked off the light so that the room grew dark and seemed part of the open air. "Don't worry," she said. "I feel the same."

Through the window Henry saw moonbeams streak across the lawn, a sight as inviting as it had been on any of the nights they spent there, back before anything had happened. Only the smell of cleaning fluids and the deadness emanating from the rest of the house reminded him of how much had changed.

"Hard to think about anything but him, isn't it?" Susan said, as she turned away from the glass. "I don't mean just here, but anywhere. Weird to think that soon we're not going to have him anymore."

"Hmm," Henry muttered. He dug his fingers into the wood around the latticed pane, for he felt swept away by an unbearable longing he couldn't explain, not just for William, but for all of them. The closer William got to dying, the more uncertain Henry felt about his own life. Something had befallen them that couldn't be dismissed as simply part of William's disease, as if a trap door had been kicked open under all their lives. Standing so close to Susan, he could hear her breathe, he could smell her perfume, even feel the warmth of her body rising against him, but still he felt more isolated than he ever had before.

"I need to finish up," he said, moving away. He tossed the gloves onto the counter and walked into the bedroom. All its surfaces glowed in the lamplight from his cleaning.

When he went to the closet for new sheets, he found such a jumble of things that he began to straighten them. Buried among the clothing and linen were a few of William's secrets Henry had no desire to know: pornographic magazines, brochures for body-building equipment, order forms from tabloid magazines promising miracle cures, a packet of envelopes in several different hands addressed to William at a post office box in another town. Henry blushed at the thought of the objects in his own apartment he didn't want anyone to see. *They can find out anything after you're dead*, he worried as he listed what he needed to discard the moment he returned home.

He stuck his arms deeper inside the closet, groping blindly, the way he had once done in a neurological exam to test his reflexes. He felt plastic, cotton, leather, and all that paper pass through his fingers. He stashed everything haphazardly in the dark so that even he couldn't swear where it was.

He stood back and smoothed the sleeves of William's shirts. They hung on the pole like thin pink and white and blue-striped men. Folded and stacked in the other closets were just a few of the thousands of things William had collected: ten changes of sheets, blankets, towels, candlesticks, vases, enough clothes for twenty men, dinnerware for thirty, tools for every emergency. The house was waiting for him to reclaim possession and bring it back to life. Nothing had changed from the last time William was there, yet his absence had changed it forever.

When William first became ill, Henry began to collect odd mementos: notes William had written, a few photographs, theater stubs from evenings out, postcards, even a rubber stamp of his signature that he found buried in a drawer. Henry kept these objects in two large envelopes under his bed. He worried that years from then there would be no evidence to point to when he spoke of William. After the funeral, his plan had been to divide everything he had saved among their friends so that they would each have a small part of William to keep.

But that was before Henry became familiar with the complex damage a disease could do. William had floated in limbo for so long that Henry had lost all sense of what he had been like before. He seemed always to have been part of that hospital bed. There was only a haze of scattered anecdotes and half impressions to hold on to, nothing tangible like a body, just images evaporating like fog.

Months ago, he had thrown the envelopes away.

He moved deeper into the closet, crouching among William's shoes. He held one shirt to his cheek and breathed deeply. The fabric was cool and soft as skin. He pressed the sleeve to his face and breathed again. Everything about it had William's particular scent, still as strong as if he had just left the room: nicotine mixed with soap, hair gel, burnt wood and weeds, even the faint aroma of cooked garlic and spices with an undercurrent of simmering meat. The odor clung to William's clothes as it no longer did to his body. Now he smelled rank and medicinal, like the corridors and rooms anywhere in the hospital.

He wasn't going to have him anymore. Wasn't that what Susan had said? Only as he grew more absent did Henry understand the ways William had given his life a shape it hadn't possessed before: something his other friends, his lovers, had never accomplished in quite the same way. He had come to take for granted the way William championed his smallest desire or made even listening to the evening news seem part of a private conspiracy. Without him, Henry would have to learn everything from scratch, and he no longer felt he had the time.

He shut the door and carried fresh linen to the bed. He took his time layering the mattress with sheets, blankets, and a new cotton cover. He fluffed the pillows and turned out the light. From the wall he took a framed photograph from another time: eight years ago that spring on the first weekend he had visited the house. In the picture, he and William stand on the front porch surrounded by suitcases and bags of groceries. Henry's smile obscures the nervousness he felt alone with his new friends, but William's arm loops lazily over his shoulder, drawing him in. Henry remembered how Susan had pulled a camera from her purse, crying, "Wait, wait," as she caught them just outside the door.

They had stepped inside the house, and there began for Henry what had been a perfect day, the memory of which he had used in subsequent years to gauge his degree of happiness. Until that weekend, he had never felt the spark of human connection strike with such revelatory power. It was completely unlike the unhinged swoon of desire he had felt on sight for countless men. Rather his whole mind and attention were engaged; even a new kind of hopefulness became palpable while William and Susan were in the room. The years since had only strengthened their weird yet enduring bond, but never again had friendship seemed to possess the unqualified magic it had during those first three days, as if love alone could rope the whole world into harmony and make life seem possible in ways it never had before.

He did not know what the next years would hold for him, but he couldn't dispel the belief that despite everything William had collected, even with the honor and good will he had earned in abundance, it was all vanishing too easily, as if no matter the caution or care they each had taken, the life they had built was nothing but a house of cards that had been set outside in the wind.

26

No lights were on by William's bed, except for a dim glow from the hospital corridor that made his walls gleam as if lit by candles. He heard patients moan from other rooms. Somewhere a clang of metal against wood, beating one two, one two.

A nurse entered wordlessly and bound his arm with rubber tubing. William did not know her name, but over the past weeks they had come to perform this nightly ritual dutifully, like a married couple long strained past conversation. He had developed an intimacy with his nurses that was different from anything he had ever allowed with his friends. Since they expected nothing from him, he felt freer to admit to pain or to shed self-consciousness about his body. He was careful never to moan, because even the kindest nurses had limits. He had heard them complain about the man who screamed all night across the hall. Whenever they were summoned to his room, they shouted at him to shut up. Sometimes William heard a slap and a muffled, gauzy sound, like a person being gagged. He had trained himself to bite hard into his pillow so that he never cried out, even when his suffering was intolerable, trying to delay for as long as possible the moment when he couldn't stop himself from letting go.

When the nurse pulled the strap tight, he felt no pounding in his veins as he once had, only a slight racing of his heart as the needle slipped into the skin. After she had drawn his blood and capped the vials, she placed a thermometer under his tongue. The alarm sounded the instant the tip touched his lips — five, six, seven times — as the beeps tracked the heat of his body. She scribbled briefly on his chart, then padded out as silently as she had entered, keeping his temperature secret. He didn't need her to tell him. His eyes bubbled in their sockets; his skin lay over his body like hot towels. He was so light and dazed with fever that he felt the way he imagined he would as a ghost returned, years from then, to wander through his house.

He pushed a button to release the morphine drip into his body. His legs and arms were so cramped and knotted, they felt as if someone had taken a hammer to his bones. As he waited for relief, he cruised the channels on the television, but his mind kept wandering to the projects he wanted to start the moment he got home: new kitchen cabinets, screens for the summer porch, slip-covers for his bedroom sofa. What he loved best were the ways in which the house was never finished. By the time one task was done, another wall would need a new coat of paint or develop a crack in the plaster, and he would begin again. He could have spent an eternity there, moving from room to room.

For a moment he mused with pride on the wonderful home he had created. He closed his eyes and pictured the decor of every room, the arrangement of the furniture, the view from the windows, especially the one through the skylight in his bedroom, where he liked to watch the rain pound during storms. His mind drifted with images of the birdhouse with the burnished copper roof on the shelf in his room, the rectangular tin box with floating cupids in which he kept needles and extra thread, the carved wooden rabbit from a turn-of-the-century carousel that stood at attention by the front door. He reveled in the pleasure he derived from even his most useless things.

After he left his family, William swore he would never be dependent on another person for shelter, never again feel outcast in the place where he lived. When he looked back on his life, he despaired that in this alone he had succeeded. But sometimes in the right light, when the sun shone through the cracked red and blue stained glass window in his study, he would stand alone and feel a serenity he had known in no other time or place, the kind some people find in the mountains or at sail in the middle of a warm, blue sea. He had no illusions about the world outside, for it seemed to him a mean and terrible place, but he had built a haven in spite of it, and what he had accomplished surpassed his wildest dreams.

Where are they now? he wondered, as he imagined Henry and Susan sorting through his possessions. He had given them so little direction that he wondered what things they were choosing to discard. He pictured closets filled with clothes unworn for twenty years, the junk in his drawers, broken bits of tools, shutters, a whole basement of spare parts he had never had the opportunity to use.

He imagined Henry entering his bedroom, opening drawers, checking closets, looking under the bed, dusting the top of the bookcase and finding the shards of glass from a broken candlestick he kept in an ashtray. *That's mine*, he thought childishly, as he saw Henry throw it into the trash. *No, no, I want it back.* He had always meant to repair it, one day when he had the time. Henry and Susan couldn't be trusted in the house alone. Neither of them understood the uses of things nor his reasons for keeping what he had. They didn't know all the projects he had planned.

He wanted "William" inscribed on everything he owned, indelibly, just like the name scratched into the glass of his attic window: *Paul Baer, July 14, 1893.* A boy, he had always imagined, who one day had used a nail to inscribe the brief graffiti of his presence. But it came to him suddenly that no one would know any more about him than he knew of Paul Baer at that moment. It was no better than reading a name written in a guest book or spray-painted on a highway overpass. There would be no trace of the life he had made, no matter the years he had taken to build it.

He needed to call Henry and Susan to stop them. He didn't

want to leave his possessions to anyone, not even to them. He wanted to blow the place up and have his property planted and seeded and covered with grass like a grave.

He reached for the telephone so quickly that his IV tangled in the cord. He waited four rings, then heard his clipped message of only four words on the answering machine, a voice from a lifetime ago: grave, confident, and deep, as foreign to him now as a photograph an old man might see of himself when young and feel no connection beyond the certainty of loss.

He heard the beep, then a long silence. "Henry!" he shouted. "Henry! Susan! I've changed my mind."

The machine cut off, leaving only the dial tone echoing back at him. He looked down at his arms, the crooked sticks of his legs, the tubes seeming to run from every orifice of his body, binding him to the bed. Even the shadowy light, even the faded dressing gown and crumpled sheets, could not disguise his ruin. Until that moment, he hadn't realized what he was doing when he asked Henry and Susan to go to the house. He had seen it dispassionately, as a practical matter, but now the full meaning struck him more vividly than it had that first day when the doctor told him he was dying.

"I am never going home," he cried, his fear as pure as the fear he imagined a person would know the moment before being murdered: the heart-stopping daze when the glint of a knife slices toward the body, the second he realizes there is no way out.

His teeth began to clatter with such force that he gripped the bed rail as a charge rushed through him, from his feet to his head. "Oh God, help me," he cried as he flopped against the mattress, lungs seizing, arms thrashing so wildly that the needles were torn from his veins. As blood pumped in sprays from the holes, he felt something let go within him, and he wailed, a sound as perfect and pure as the one he remembered when his father cut a pig's throat. But William's cry went on and on, because there was still life left in him: each breath flying from his body as a scream until they came together into one sound that would not stop. And even when the doctors and nurses ran to his side to beg him, he would not stop, because for all their pleas and words and hopes and drugs, not one of them had come with the power to save him.

27

Henry arrived freezing, complaining of the weather and delays on the subway, but he stopped in midsentence because William was looking beyond him, uninterested in any news he might have brought into the room. Outside the window, the city was nothing but the burnt reds and browns of multileveled brick, shimmering barren trees, a blue-gray sky swollen with clouds pinking to sunset, streets dizzy with people, dogs, taxis: from that distance a dream of a place, rooftops spreading out, infinite as a hope, a call to life. A city a man would lose anything to live in.

William had lost many things, but if it helped him to believe that the city he remembered lay waiting should he ever return, Henry didn't want to disappoint him. He stopped ranting and kissed William lightly on the cheek.

"How are you feeling?" he asked, suddenly taking in William's half-shaved head, sparsely tufted. He recoiled, thinking, *How can he have gotten so much worse in just one day?*

William looked at Henry and cracked a smile. "Like my haircut? I did it myself." Only then did Henry notice his body, stripped except for a dressing gown pulled up to his navel. His right hand held an electric razor; his left fondled his genitals, idly, the way an infant might as his mother changed his diapers.

As Henry stood transfixed, William banged the railing by the bed. "Get my clothes," he said. "It's time to go."

"Go?"

"Home," William said, as if it were the most natural thing in the world.

Henry spun toward the door with hope that a doctor might interrupt them. Two passed in the corridor without looking in. "It's cold out today," he said, as if that were an explanation. He poured some water and slowly sipped.

"Not if you've got a fever," William said, pointing at the metal closet.

Henry shrugged as if he didn't care and turned the handle. But he silently prayed, *Please let it be empty, please*, as he imagined shelves and hooks hanging with William's clothes.

"Nothing's there," he exclaimed as he braved a look. "I swear, William. See for yourself." He flung the door open so wide that it clanged against the wall. The closet was empty except for a gym bag and a striped pillow crumpled on the rusted floor. Henry didn't know how many other people William had asked for help in leaving, but clearly someone had taken his belongings while he slept unaware.

William seemed oblivious. He shit, loosely, a bubbling stream. "Shouldn't have had that ice cream," he announced, pleased, as he settled lower into the bed.

While William napped, Henry moved to the chair to read the newspaper, but he couldn't focus on the words. He spent every moment of repose in a kind of stupor. With each day, more of his own responsibilities were left undone. Bills for the telephone, utilities, his student loan, were two months overdue. It was weeks since he had been grocery shopping, longer since he had done his laundry. Even his visits to the gym were slipping, down to less than once a week. He told himself it didn't matter, but already he could feel his clothes droop around parts of his body. The air felt different when he moved, almost like it had before.

*

An aide Henry had never seen entered the room carrying a tray neatly arranged with cups of pills. Henry smiled and indicated the bed. "I know you're busy," he whispered, "but he needs new sheets."

The woman stopped and broadly sniffed. The cups rattled on the tray. "I changed that bed an hour ago. He can just wait until I've had my dinner." She shook William by the shoulder and pressed two pills to his lips. Henry saw a strange flash in William's eyes as he opened his mouth to swallow. As soon as the pills hit his tongue, he snapped at the woman's fingers with his teeth, just missing her skin.

She made a fist, then forced her hand to her side and strode indignantly from the room. Henry stood and found a fresh set of linen in the bureau. "Let's get you up," he sighed as he lifted William under the arms and settled him in the chair. When his feet emerged from the blanket, Henry saw that he wore slippers with bunnies' heads and long, floppy ears.

He pulled the nightgown over William's head and bunched it into a ball, wiping at his soiled skin. *This is no different from cleaning up after a baby or a dog,* he told himself, but still he gagged from the smell. He ripped the sheets from the mattress and tossed them into the corner, removing as well several layers of blue, plastic pads. When he finished, he helped William back to bed.

William stretched out flat, kicking his legs so that the rabbits flew in the air. "So where were we?" he asked.

"Nowhere," Henry said, washing his hands in the sink. He eyed the bathroom, wondering if William would be insulted if he stopped to take a shower.

William rubbed his hand over a patch of newly shaved scalp. "Oh, I remember," he said. "You were going to take me home."

Henry looked at the stinking pile of linen, the stains and splatters on the floor. He tried to think of ways to convince William that the hospital was a better place for him to be: treatment for his sores, regular meals, a vigilant staff. The week before, his brain had shaken with a seizure that left him lying senseless for two full days. If he had been at home alone, he surely would have died. But in his heart, Henry knew his real concern was that he couldn't imagine what would become of his own life if William didn't stay where he was. It could be months before he died. The hospital was the only barrier to his complete surrender to William.

He couldn't face the thought of being alone with William in the house while he lay dying. He didn't know how to comfort him. He didn't know how to take him in his arms and hold him as he died. He was terrified to be left alone with the body, to be the one to watch it stop breathing.

"I can't help you do that," Henry said simply, without bothering to explain. He tried to reassure himself that no one he knew would expect him to give up his life for a friend, as a son might do for a parent. Most friends, even most family members, wouldn't have lasted as long as he already had. Yet he had always assumed that his own family would welcome him with open arms if he were ever in trouble, without considering their own lives. But maybe he was deluding himself with the illusion of a bond that didn't exist. He remembered that when his grandmother was sent to a nursing home after a series of strokes, she lay moaning all day, tied to a bed. When his father visited, he sat whispering in a chair, "Shut up, no one can hear you," until Henry believed she had died of a broken heart.

To his surprise, William only nodded. "At least you don't lie. Everybody else says they'll come back to get me, but they never do. I'm keeping score."

Henry didn't know how William could remember broken promises when sometimes he believed that France lay outside his window. He longed for the day when all he had to do to appease William was smile at him and lie.

William stared at the ceiling, his brow furrowed, as if he were studying something that Henry couldn't see. Then he looked down, directing his gaze at the railing around the bed. "Would you at least let down the bar?"

Henry couldn't believe that the six-inch bar could be a real barrier to William's flight. He seemed unable to figure out that he could release the catch with a flick of his wrist. Or else he simply didn't want to leave without Henry's complicity.

"But what will you do if you get there?" Henry asked.

William stared back, blinking, confusion clouding his face. "I don't know," he said. "Be there."

Henry took in William's rabbit slippers, his half-shaved head, his hospital gown tied with a bow at his neck. "But you look ridiculous," he said.

William shrugged, pulling the gown around him, almost daintily. "I don't care."

Suddenly Henry was swept away by an unbearable tenderness for William. He wanted to take his hand and lead him into the streets and leave this life behind, as if there might be some available magic waiting for him there. He had been taught to believe that there was nothing that couldn't be changed with work and a strong will, that no act or decision was ever irrevocable. But now he had no ideas left, nothing that could make a difference.

I should help him, he thought. He shouldn't care that the doctors would yell at him or that people on the street would stare at William, but he did. William didn't care about anything. He was like a wounded animal dragging its body to some hidden nest in the woods where it might die in peace. Or maybe he was nothing like that. Maybe the part of him that was not yet dying wanted to run away to prove he could still do it. Maybe if he never stopped, then nothing else could ever catch him.

Henry let down the bar with a crash.

William swung his legs over the edge of the bed. He stumbled as he worked his feet into his slippers, but he righted himself, the old determination hardening his face. "Thanks," he said.

Henry swung an arm around William's neck and hugged him so hard that they tumbled backward on the bed. William kissed him, coolly, on the cheek. "You first," he said.

Henry took off his coat and left it draped on the chair. "Wear this," he whispered as he stepped into the hall. He considered detouring to the nursing station to report William, but changed course and walked to the elevators instead. Henry couldn't betray his friend when he was one of the last people William trusted. He shifted impatiently from foot to foot, waiting for the elevator to come. A bald, moon-faced child stood next to him, holding her mother's hand.

He heard a shout, then a soft stampede as the nurses raced in the direction of William's room. Even after the elevator doors had closed, William's screams still echoed in Henry's ears.

Outside, the city streets seemed like a maze of darkened alleys. Henry felt as if its inhabitants were gathered in their apartments, hiding from some catastrophe. Footsteps echoed behind him. Near the entrance to the subway, a homeless man jumped from a doorway and blocked his way.

"Give me a match," the man demanded, expecting fear.

Henry grabbed his arm and bent it backward roughly. "Fuck you," he shouted, inches from his face.

The man backed off, stunned, but soon he was replaced by one, then another, until it seemed as if men were holding out their hands from every corner and unlit stair. Henry ducked into the subway station and onto the train, trying to distract himself by reading the newspaper he found on the seat beside him.

The headline told of a man shot dead while making a telephone call on the street as his wife watched from a window up-stairs. Henry put the paper down, trembling. The train careened dangerously on its track, screeching at every stop. Each person who walked through the doors seemed more sinister than the one before.

When he arrived at his station, Henry stumbled upon an old man leaning off the platform to piss upon the rails; another snored loudly across a row of plastic chairs. When Henry breathed, the musty, humid air stank more horribly than the air in William's room. The odor clung to his skin, following him down the street, even as he closed the door to his apartment.

He switched on the light and looked around. Cockroaches scattered from under an unwashed plate and disappeared into the wall behind the sink. Dirty clothes were strewn over the floor. Newspapers, magazines, bits of paper he couldn't identify, covered the surface of his only table. If he were introduced to a person who lived in such squalor, Henry would not have wanted to be his friend.

How have I let things go this far? he wondered, but he was stopped by the ringing of the telephone. He heard the machine click on and William call his name. "Henry? Henry? Pick up. It's me." His voice was harsh and rough, more like exhaust than human breath.

I will never be rid of him, Henry thought as he reached for the receiver. William would never be satisfied until he actually shared his disease.

Often lately, Henry thought of a movie he had seen as a child in which the residents of a town were possessed by aliens as they slept and woke up as pod people. Soon only one woman and one man remained untouched. They fought to stay awake so that they would not end up like their neighbors, but they grew exhausted from all their days of running. The woman fell asleep as they hid in a sewer and awoke with that dead smile that told her companion she had gone to the other side. And then she did something with her eyes, a kind of look, that let him know that he, too, was about to be gone.

Somewhere in the movie Henry remembered another scene in which trucks full of pods were driven into town. There was a long shot panning down the rear of the caravan. One truck jiggled on a bump and its doors swung open. Pods spilled into the street and split open, scattering the heads of all the smiling new dead people like handfuls of giant peas.

28

Susan lifted her fork and paused, mid-bite. "He bought a car with his credit card," she said.

"Really?" Henry could barely see her face through the wild blooms of the centerpiece and the blazing beeswax candles. Despite the years they had known each other, he had never been to her apartment before. He had always assumed that she was ashamed of it, so he was astonished by the comfort of the large, well-appointed rooms. The city seemed miles away. Watching the assured way Susan moved within her own space made him wonder if he had ever truly known her at all.

She seemed unaware of his discomfort. "I don't know what we're going to do," she said, leaning back in a wooden chair that had the look of a throne. "He can still get that authoritative tone on the telephone, so strangers can't tell he's nuts. His super called me. There are boxes and boxes all over the lobby. A new stereo, a VCR, a complete set of china. He's spent a fortune. Today a truck brought the biggest dining room table I've ever seen, with sixteen upholstered chairs."

Bigger than this? Henry wondered, gazing across the long, gleaming planks at Susan, fifteen feet away. "What difference does it make?" he said. "I don't think he has much longer anyway; his energy's bound to run out soon."

"You didn't see his apartment. It looks like a loading dock. When is he going to use that stuff?"

"Who cares?" Henry said, too sharply. They had more important problems than how William spent his money.

Susan looked up, startled. "I guess that's true," she said. "I just didn't have anyone else to tell."

"Sorry," Henry said. "It's been a long day."

"That's okay," she said, beginning to eat again. "The fish are dead, by the way. I found them floating in the tank this morning. I guess it's a miracle they lasted as long as they did."

"Dead?" Henry said, gulping back the lump that rose in his throat. He had bought them so long ago that they had come to seem a fixture of William's life. "It's my fault. I've been so busy, I haven't taken proper care of them."

"It's not that big a deal," Susan said, kindly. "We've got enough to worry about." She dabbed with a napkin at her bottom lip. "Speaking of which, I've been thinking that maybe one day soon we should talk about you coming to work with me. Meet new people. Make some real money for a change."

The last thing Henry wanted was another disruption in his life. At school he lectured in a state of constant panic, speaking extemporaneously because he didn't have the concentration to prepare. The week before, the dean had sat silently in the back of the room, observing his performance for the first time in years. His students did not betray him. They pretended to be animated, asking questions with an energy he had rarely seen. The dean left mollified, but still Henry was nervous. There were only six weeks left to the term. If he made it that far, he would have all summer to worry about what happened next.

"I have more than I can handle for now," Henry said, "just taking care of William."

"Well, think about it," Susan said. "I think you'd like selling real estate. I still get a thrill going in and out of strangers' apartments with the extra key, especially when they aren't home. I like pretending that I'm them, or at least imagining what their lives might be." She leaned over and blew out the candles.

"I'm in no hurry," Henry said. Clouds of smoke wafted toward his face, filling the air with a sweet, sick smell. He looked out through the alcove into a corner of the living room. Silver-framed photographs sat neatly on a table around a vase of flowers. Often lately he envied the life that would be waiting for Susan after William died. She was settled in her career. She had a boyfriend. William still didn't know he existed; it was the first secret she and Henry had shared. He was pleased she had confided in him, but it also reminded him of everything that was missing in his own life. Susan had lived alone for years. He was stunned that she had managed to find a man just before they were about to be without William. Henry couldn't imagine having the energy to make friends again, much less fall in love.

He had liked to think that the bargain he made in surrendering to William was to trade the ruptures of the past that once plagued him for days that slipped easily into the next. But now he felt that he was becoming lost along with William, or that he might be falling even faster, because he held onto a life that spun recklessly about him, while William slept to his own, final end.

Susan stood with her plate in hand. "Now probably isn't the time," she said. "I just don't want you to get stuck, you know? We're both going to have to make some decisions soon, with or without him."

Susan's kitchen was larger than Henry's entire apartment, with reddish brown paneled walls. The cabinets above the counters were made of a similar wood, with stained glass doors that gave the room a subtle glow, like daylight inside a church.

"Do you mind if I sit?" Henry asked, looking at the square oak table with four matching chairs.

"No, I'm sorry. You have to stand." Susan laughed by the sink. "What's the matter with you?" She put water on for tea.

Henry blushed. He felt that he would break something if he moved, or that he was intruding, in a way he never had in William's house.

Susan stacked the dishes, chatting easily. Henry was pleased that she had forged a new alliance by inviting him into her home, but he couldn't imagine what it would be like to spend time with her alone, after William. Without William as a bond, he couldn't trust that their feelings for each other would survive. He returned her smile, but in the way he would after spending a night with a man he wasn't sure he would ever see again.

"We're going to have to stick together," Susan said without turning around. "There's going to be such a mess after he's dead."

"Of course we will," Henry said. Then he added, "What mess?"

"His relatives for starters. I'm afraid they're going to start popping up all over, especially once they learn he doesn't have a will. I see it happen at work all the time. Families have this weird antenna, even if they've been estranged for years."

"What?" Henry asked. The room tipped, sickeningly.

When Susan turned from the sink, her mouth seemed huge, grotesque, all thick maroon lips and yellowed teeth. Her voice sounded too slow, like a recording on the wrong speed, when she repeated, "Since he doesn't have a will."

"But he told me you were the executor," Henry said, trying to muffle his shrillness. "He claimed you were the only person he could trust to make sure his family inherited nothing."

Susan wiped her hands with the dishtowel and shrugged. Henry tried to decide if her indifference was real or feigned, but his mind was racing — shame, anger, confusion, greed, rushing upon him.

"He says lots of things, but I've never seen a piece of paper," she said. "I think he only mentioned it because he wanted me to feel important."

"But he promised," Henry said.

"Don't be upset. I don't care." She tossed the towel playfully at his head.

"That wasn't what I meant," Henry said, but went no further. He couldn't admit his sense of disappointment and betrayal. He had always assumed that Susan knew of William's promise, since she was supposed to have a copy of his will. Henry could never claim possession if William had left no record of his intentions. *Then it's all been for nothing*, he thought, but even at that moment, he wasn't sure if he meant it.

The kettle shrieked on the stove, hissing sprays of steam. "You're shaking," Susan said. "Let's warm you up with some tea."

She opened the cabinet door. "What do you like best?" she asked, pointing to shelf upon shelf of cans and boxes.

Henry saw nothing but a brightly colored blur.

"Earl Grey, Lipton's, Morning Thunder, Sleepy Time, Red Zinger. Just pick it out. I've got anything you need."

29

When he was seven, Henry dreamed that his grandmother died and shook his mother awake to tell her. When the telephone rang in the morning, his grandmother was dead. Sometimes, still, whenever his mother got him alone she whispered, "Do you ever dream of me, sweetie?"

Henry never did. But every night for weeks he had dreamed of William's death: once under the wheels of a car; once as the prey of a gang of thieves; once in a plane blown out of the sky; once thrown from a horse as it leapt a silvery pond, his body crushed among the limbs of a tree. The night before, Henry dreamed he murdered William himself, smothering him with a pillow while he slept so deeply that he never woke to resist.

As he dipped a brush into a can of white paint, Henry said to himself, *Dreams don't count; dreams don't count,* to ease his guilt. He began to cover a new section of wood along the windowsill, erasing nicks and cigarette burns accumulated during his four years in the apartment.

The telephone rang.

For the fourth time that day, he heard a woman's voice, with a slight southern accent, speak into his answering machine. "Mr. Nichols? Mr. Nichols?" She paused, as if hoping Henry was rushing toward the telephone, then let out a sigh. "This is Judith Ferris, the social worker at the hospital. Will you *please* give me a call?" She nearly brayed at the end, her tone both exasperated and pleading.

Henry guessed she was calling about William, but he didn't know why. In all his time at the hospital, he had never met a social worker; he didn't know what role they played in patients' lives. Once the administrator left a message at school when there was a problem with William's insurance; once a grief counselor asked that Henry intervene after William had ordered her from his room. Usually doctors and nurses were the ones who called, always with questions about drugs or changes in William's treatment.

Henry dabbed the brush along the window frame with exaggerated concentration, trying not to surrender to the temptation to answer the telephone. He came to a gash on the lip of the wood that he remembered William had made two summers before when he opened a beer bottle against the sill, a souvenir of one of the three times he had visited the apartment. Henry dipped the brush again and covered the mark sloppily. A glob of paint splashed from the bristles onto his shoes, then splattered across the floor. He stepped down from the ladder, disgusted. No matter how hard he tried, it was impossible not to worry about William.

After Susan told him that William didn't have a will, Henry tried to go about his life as if William had never existed. He cooked dinner for himself every night, three-course meals complete with vegetables and salad, after stopping at the most expensive grocery store in his neighborhood on his way home from the gym. In the mornings, he arrived early at school to prepare for his classes, writing out his lectures with the same dedication he had shown in the old days. He left his stacks of books about death untouched on his desk and reverted to a more traditional curriculum, emphasizing historical dates and territorial borders, important rulers, battles and wars.

He wrote notes to old friends he hadn't seen in months. He even asked an old trick out to dinner. He tried to behave as he imagined a person would after the death of a loved one or after a divorce, trying to enjoy his freedom from taking care of William. But any relief he hoped to find was spoiled by the outrage he felt. After everything he had done and everything that had happened, he couldn't believe that William had lied.

Several times Henry started for the hospital to confront William, going so far as putting on his coat and opening the door, but he always found himself standing frozen in the hall. No matter how many times he rehearsed the conversation in his head, anything he wanted to say sounded base and self-serving the moment his thoughts were formed into words. He worried that if he came face to face with William, he would be made to feel that he was angry simply because he wanted the house. It would be impossible to explain that what he had lost was much less tangible, and therefore more troubling and more profound.

William attacked most viciously when he knew he was wrong. In the best of times, Henry had never won an argument with him. Even in his diminished state, half in and out of reason, William would sense Henry's ambivalence and twist the meaning of anything he said. Before he knew it, his years of devotion would be dismissed as merely part of a larger plan of calculation and greed. Henry could not prove that if he had wanted anything, it was to believe in an impossible selflessness to love, in no barriers to human kindness, so that maybe he would get the same thing back one day when he was in need. He could not prove that he would have behaved as generously if the house had never existed, although he hoped he would have.

The house was never something he would have expected on his own, but once William told him about the bequest, the fantasy took hold of him. It seemed that luck had come his way no differently than it came to friends or former students whose parents bought them houses and cars and made their lives as comfortable as it was in their power to do. Henry had wanted to believe that the promise of the house had a similar quality of a loving gift, a natural inheritance, that affirmed his importance to William. Without it, he felt cheated out of everything he had believed their friendship to be. The past eight years now seemed like little more than an endless series of humiliations.

What troubled him most was that he had learned about the will by accident. If Susan hadn't told him, Henry would not have discovered William's lie until after he was dead. What seemed most unforgivable was that William cared so little about him that he was willing to die and leave Henry feeling so betrayed, hating him for all eternity.

The more he tried to make sense of what had happened, the more confused he became. Hour by hour, his outrage changed to guilt, then to a kind of fragile indifference, as he went about his day. Just when he would begin to make excuses for William and become convinced of his own pettiness and corrupted motives, waves of hurt and shame would overwhelm him and he would find himself again frantic and speechless with rage.

He didn't know whom to talk to. He couldn't call his parents. William was only a name to them; they knew nothing of his illness. An instinctive caution had stopped him from telling them that he had a close friend who was dying. They would only become more anxious about the life he was leading, and pressure him to come home. In the old days when he suffered through a crisis, he always called William. Now William was the one person whom it was impossible to see.

Henry had spoken with Susan frequently since the dinner at her house. She seemed bewildered by what was happening, yet strangely unwilling to press him for details. Her own days were overwhelmed by the violence with which the hospital staff had started to complain about William. He was on his best behavior whenever she visited, but the doctors told her stories of dishes thrown at every meal and of screams late into the night. The week before, he had even flung his bedpan at the midnight nurse, who had once been his favorite. During their last conversation, Susan begged Henry to return. "I don't know what's going on with you two, but it's a strange time to have a fight. Please come back. He misses you."

Henry had heard nothing from William, which he interpreted as evidence of a guilty conscience. Sometimes late at night his telephone rang, but no one spoke when he answered. He assumed it was William by the sound of labored breathing followed by the loud clatter of the receiver being hung up that was peculiar to him.

In another world, Henry wished he might run into William on the street and be forced, by accident, to speak. Maybe then they might begin to see each other and find a way to mend their friendship. But William would never leave the hospital again. To see him, Henry would have to go there, and he refused. He wanted William to call and apologize. For once in his life, Henry didn't want to be the one to give in first and lose the remnants of his self-respect.

He was losing it anyway. Every time a colleague at school asked politely after William, he felt monstrous and uncaring. It seemed impossible to explain why he had stopped seeing a friend who was close to death, especially when everyone he knew had praised his loyalty for so long. "There's been no change," he always answered vaguely, and no one ever pressed him to learn it was a lie.

Henry believed he might have broken off all contact with William, purely, if he hadn't been ill, but it seemed that the rules of forgiveness were changed when a person was dying. As a healthy man, his own grievances were supposed to pale in comparison to William's death. Henry's suspicion that William was playing this card to assure his silence, only made him madder.

The telephone rang again.

Henry looked at the blinking red light as the machine clicked on, waiting to hear the social worker call his name. She was as relentless as a bill collector. He knew that if he didn't make her stop soon, he would develop a phobia about answering the telephone and burrow further underground, just when he was supposed to be surfacing. As he listened to her now familiar voice, it occurred to him that she might be calling to apologize in William's stead, to plead with Henry to come before it was too late. It wasn't impossible that William would have asked a stranger to intervene so that Susan wouldn't learn what he had done. When Henry reached for the receiver, he felt elated for the first time in weeks, as if he and William might find their way to a truce after all.

"Hello?" he said, making his voice sound deeper and more mature, as if he were an executive with only a moment between meetings.

"Mr. Nichols?" the woman asked hesitantly, as if she were unsure whether she was finally speaking to a person rather than a machine.

"Yes."

"I'm so glad you're there. I was worried I might never find you."

"Sorry," Henry said. "I just came in. I've been out of town."

"You gave me quite a scare," she said, then retreated behind a more businesslike air. "As I said in my messages, I'm Judith Ferris, Mr. Addams's caseworker, and I understand you're his next of kin."

There would be no apology.

"In a way," Henry said, stiffening. He hadn't heard that term since William's first admission to the hospital. The idea seemed preposterous to him now, yet some of his past concern returned as he asked, "Why? Is anything wrong?"

Henry heard a rustle, as if the woman flipped through a large stack of papers. "Not *wrong*," she said, "but we need to make arrangements for Mr. Addams's discharge."

"From where?"

"From the hospital," she said quickly, running the words together almost as though she hoped Henry would miss their meaning.

"Why would you do that?" In his confusion, Henry wondered for a moment whether William had been cured.

"Because at this time there's nothing critical about his condition, and, frankly, we need the extra bed," she said, as if she were reading a script printed on a card.

"But he's dying," Henry said, almost laughing. In the hospital he had often seen patients kept in the corridor for days while they waited for a room, but none of them had ever looked as critical as William. He also knew that William's insurance would pay his bills for as long as he needed to stay.

"Unfortunately, that may be true," the woman said, "but at present Mr. Addams can be treated just as well at home. Of course, if circumstances should change and he were to return to a state of extreme distress — *physical distress* — and it's a condition we can treat, we would welcome him back. Until then, I'm afraid he needs to be discharged. And you're the guardian of record."

"That was just a formality," Henry said, flinching at how hollow his protest sounded when he heard his words aloud.

"Mr. Addams doesn't think so," the woman said. "And well . . . I mean, I've seen your signature on the form in his file, so I can't believe this hasn't come up before."

Henry ripped a corner of the tarpaulin free and sat on the couch. Paint fumes made his head grow dizzy. He had signed the document simply to make William feel secure; he hadn't thought he was leaving behind a trail of incrimination. "But that was just for decisions about his medication and treatment," Henry said, looking helplessly at the four walls that made up his entire apartment. "He can't come here. There must be somewhere else for him to go."

"I didn't mean it had to be the place where you lived, exactly," the woman said. "I understand Mr. Addams has his own apartment in the city and a house in the country. Maybe you could go there?"

"I wouldn't know about his house," Henry snapped. "Besides, I'm not trained for that kind of care."

The woman paused. Henry heard her fingers tap against something hard. "If that's the problem, I'm sure his insurance policy will cover the cost of an aide. I'd be happy to help you arrange it."

"But I never told him I would take him," Henry said, his voice as much moan as whine.

"I don't understand," the woman said, not insincerely. "When I explained the circumstances of his discharge, Mr. Addams suggested that I call. He said he was certain that he could come and live with you."

Henry imagined her disgust at his callousness. But just as he considered agreeing to take William in so that the social worker would soften her opinion of him, fury overtook him again. William had no regrets about anything he had done. Nothing had changed except that now he was using a stranger to do his dirty work.

Henry couldn't believe that five minutes before he had grown almost maudlin at the idea of William's apology. He rose and stormed back and forth across the room, the space growing smaller and smaller with every step, something in him snapped. He was overwhelmed by a desire to punish William. In eight years, at least, he had learned how to play the game.

"I mean, it's not like I'm his lover or anything," Henry said, nearly spitting the words. "The real problem is that he doesn't have any friends. And his parents hate him. He's refused to speak to them for twenty years, no matter how many times they've tried to make amends."

The woman seemed thrown by the harshness of his tone. "I'm sorry," she said. "I never would have bothered you if . . . I mean, I just assumed that you and he . . ."

"It isn't your fault," Henry said, softening. "You don't know him well enough to know. He has all kinds of fantasies that aren't real."

"Maybe you'd better call him," she said, nervously. Henry imagined her dread at having to tell William that she had failed.

"I will, of course," he said. "But will you do me a favor and talk to him first?"

The social worker coughed, then cleared her throat. "Okay, but I have to say I saw him just this morning, and I can't tell you how confident he sounded. He didn't seem irrational at all. If anything, I'd say he was serene."

Already Henry felt sick with regret at what he was doing, but he couldn't stop himself. He only wanted the charade to be over.

"You don't know him like I do," he said. "Most of what he says isn't true. Just tell him that he made a mistake."

30

Henry left the subway and walked past William's apartment without looking up, then headed farther west, toward the river. He pushed his cap down over his ears and adjusted his sunglasses. Crusts of black snow lined the curbs. Here and there the trees were dotted with green shoots and closed, purple buds.

William had been moved to a hospice built in an abandoned hotel only two blocks from the bar. The interior had been decorated to appear as little like an institution as possible, with touches of home: polished wooden floors, brightly colored carpets, plants, bookshelves, pictures on the walls. No one wore uniforms. A staff of volunteers was on call twenty-four hours a day to do anything a patient wanted: play cards, go shopping, sleep by the bed, hold hands, talk about God.

Henry rode the elevator to the eleventh floor and waited in the hallway outside William's door, gathering his nerve. He hadn't told anyone he was coming. He hoped that if he caught William off guard, they might meet on more equal ground and avoid recriminations.

The longer Henry stayed away, the less he knew what he wanted. Any resolution seemed impossible when William would never return to a normal life to have his faithfulness reproven, a test over time. They had no time, and this pressure only added to Henry's confusion.

He had tried to hold onto his sense of righteousness, but increasingly his dreams were haunted by death and fire. He was afraid that if he didn't see William before he died, he would be crippled by regret for the rest of his life. William's betrayal would recede over time, just as everything Henry had loved about him was receding, leaving him with nothing but an image of himself as a person who had abandoned his friend.

Through the door Henry saw two feet, covered by a blanket thrown carelessly at the foot of a bed. There was no television or radio playing. He couldn't hear a sound.

He counted to three and walked briskly in, rustling the paper around the bouquet of flowers he had brought, panting so that he would seem harried from countless chores. "Hi," he said loudly as he rounded the corner, imagining that he would find William sitting up, his eyes fixed in a glare.

He saw a body lying across the bed: a head on a pillow, a spotted back, a leg tangled in sheets. He blinked several times, then looked again. A wound on William's buttocks so assaulted his eyes that he stifled a retch. It resembled a photograph from an anatomy textbook: the skin cracked open, revealing layer after layer peeled down to the bone. The hole was broken by two fleshy sections, like bloody lips.

Henry dropped the flowers onto a chair and rushed forward, ripping the sheets free to cover William's body. He struggled to regain his composure so as not to alarm his friend, but William did not stir or sigh, even when Henry kissed his ear. The skin wasn't feverish, as he had expected, but moist and cold, like refrigerated meat.

Henry sat, dazed, in the chair. William had been so bad before, he hadn't thought it possible for him to get any worse. In all his weeks away, Henry had imagined William being much as he had last seen him: diminished but still formidable. Now asleep, there seemed to be no personality left, just something that breathed.

Henry tried to distract himself by looking at William's new surroundings. His room was on the top floor of a turret, with two rounded walls and a dormer window that had a view clear across the river. The decor was pleasant, if austere: a chest of drawers and a small pine desk much like the ones in Henry's childhood room, a small round vase of orchids and lilies, with a card from Susan hanging by a purple ribbon.

William sneezed, a sound as small and pinched as a cat's. He rubbed his head against the pillow. He groaned. Henry fixed a smile on his face and stared at the bed, ready to greet William, yet also hoping that he wouldn't awaken. He considered arranging the flowers and taking his leave, but just as he stood, undecided, a gray-haired woman dressed in jeans and a pink cashmere sweater walked through the door.

"Good afternoon," she said. "It's nice to see you here." Her voice was friendly but hushed, a tone a person would use in church.

Henry watched her fill a pitcher with ice and set it by the bed. "He doesn't like —" he started to say. William drank his water warm, room temperature, even in summer. It wasn't his business anymore.

The woman tucked the sheet closely around William's shoulders and mopped his brow with a towel. There was something assured and intimate in her movements that reminded Henry of the way his mother used to tend him when he was ill. With her ponytail and double strand of pearls, the woman even resembled his mother. "He was trouble at first," she said, almost admiringly. "Now he sleeps most of the day. His woman friend comes almost every night, but I'm glad to see another visitor here."

"I only just returned from vacation," Henry said. "I came as soon as I heard." He turned to look out the window at the traffic increasing on the road below.

The woman seemed to accept his lie. "It's terrible," she said, meeting his eyes, then seeming to draw them to the bed. "He can't be much older than my son. Half the time he doesn't know where he is, so I try to tell myself it isn't so bad."

"It's nice here," Henry said, feeling the sun beat through the glass against his face. The room was of a kind a person would be pleased to stay in for a night on vacation, but nothing more, no sense of a place that had been lived in, nothing to make someone forget the desire to go home.

The woman arranged Henry's flowers in a vase and crumpled the paper neatly in a ball. "Sometimes late at night he seems to think he's at the beach," she said. "I don't know what your plans are, but if you've got the time later, I'm sure he'd love to have a bath."

Henry borrowed a pair of shorts and took William to the basement in a wheelchair. The water bath had been constructed from the room that once housed the hotel's swimming pool. Plaster gargoyles were set on pillars in every corner. The walls were of dark blue tile, their plane broken every few feet by gold tiled flames. Everything had a chipped and battered opulence, except for the gleaming metal ramp covering the stairs.

An inflatable mattress floated in the shallow end of the pool. Henry pushed the wheelchair down the ramp until William was submerged to the neck. He locked the wheels and laid William across the raft, amazed at how easily he could lift him in his hands.

The water was warm, almost soapy with foam from the pressurized jets. As William floated on its surface, his face relaxed, losing all signs of age. His wrinkles seemed flattened and pressed, almost glowing, like cosmetic surgery gone slightly awry.

Henry splashed water over William's stomach, then pushed him deeper, until only his head bobbed above the surface. Under the lids, his eyes were still, like the glass eyes of a doll. Henry dragged the raft back and forth across the pool, a few feet in each direction, keeping his head above water by standing on his toes. With the fog and heat and clouds of steam, he felt as if he were caught in some other dimension, the rest of life so far away as to be unbelievable.

Swirls of water took William's gown away so that the material floated to his neck. His skin flapped against his bones like a baggy suit of clothes. Henry looked at William's thighs, his chest, the scarred droop of his stomach, the map of stretch marks and wattled flesh. The hot water raised the patches of rash a blistering red, as if they were singed by the heat. He remembered reports he had read of people burned in fires; they always listed the proportion of charred to undamaged flesh as a percentage: burns over twenty-five, fifty, seventy-five percent of their body. William must be close to eighty percent. He had more rashes than skin.

The more Henry stared, the more he grew afraid. He kicked off from the bottom and began to swim, turning on his back to stare up at the domed ceiling, pale and vaulted as a sky. *You can leave*, he thought, to calm himself: go out to dinner, to a movie, talk on the phone, walk the streets, pick up a stranger in a bar, even call his parents and get a ticket home. But still he felt as if he were looking out upon the world, trapped in a place against his will. He fumbled blindly and dragged himself up by grabbing the corner of the plastic raft.

He glanced down at his own body, glistening in the heat and wet, and for the first time he felt no reassurance from the strength of its smooth, undamaged lines. In the past his sympathy for William had always been tempered by a kind of giddy relief. The more grotesque his illness had become, the more removed it had seemed from Henry's life. Often he left the hospital guiltily pleased by his youth and good fortune, feeling more alive. Now the sound of his breath in his ears, the beating of his heart, even the beads of sweat slipping from his pores, all seemed to be warnings of a danger he had never understood before: that his whole life was held together by a fragile layer of skin.

He reached out and took William's hand, the bones nearly visible beneath his white, puckered knuckles. William opened his eyes and jerked his head around, moaning, as if trying to remember where he was. Henry wrapped his arms around William's neck and pulled him close, until his lips touched his ear. From that perspective, the small ripples of water seemed to extend forever past the tips of William's feet. He whispered, "Sshh," over and over, his breath whistling like wind over a deserted beach. He rocked the mattress gently so that William might be lulled by the rhythm of the waves.

William kicked his arms and feet about, weakly. Something white poured from his nose and curled around his face like string, catching in his soft wisps of hair. "I want to go home," he coughed as water slapped over his chin and into his mouth. Steam rose from the jets around them, as loud as pounding surf.

Henry moved his arms down William's body, holding him suspended by the curve of his spine. He reached over with one hand and closed William's eyes. "Imagine you're there," he whispered, as if to let William believe that the sound he heard was the sound of waves crashing through his bedroom window, no different from any night of the thousands he had spent there. Until he found a way to bring them back, Henry hoped its echoes might transport him to another place and time, before anything happened, just sound and water lifting his body so that it lay free and weightless, wave upon wave.

He dreamed of swimming through rivers, across seas, in pale green ponds, in blue cement pools the size of lakes, his limbs moving freely, as of old, cutting through the water as easily as air, every muscle toned and perfectly in sync.

No matter how deep he dove, he swirled and turned in circles, blowing out his breath so that bubbles burst from his mouth and glided upward, like spheres of hand-blown glass. In his dream, his oxygen lasted for hours, flowing from his arms like gills, as if he were the most fluid of sea creatures, surer below the surface than he had ever been on the ground.

Henry sat on the porch, watching great wafts of steam and clouds smoke over the lawn. He looked out at the white picket fence marking the property line along the strip of pine trees William had planted his first year in the house, grown taller now than the telephone poles lining the road below. Beyond them, the lights of the nearest neighbors twinkled brightly, like cities seen from the sky.

Susan and Stephen came out the front door and stood awkwardly by Henry's chair. The royal-blue stripe in Stephen's patterned silk tie was the same hue as Susan's dress. With the gel gleaming in their short, slicked-back hair, they looked less like lovers than fraternal twins.

Susan held a square, brown paper package under her arm. "I guess that's it for today," she said, smiling, but her features were drawn from exhaustion.

Henry rocked back and forth. "Yes," was all he said. He couldn't wait for them to go.

"You sure you don't want to come to the motel?" Susan asked. "It has an indoor pool." She looked up, as if she could see through the porch roof to the two stories looming above, white against the gray-black sky. "I'm sure the aide could manage one night alone."

"I gave him the night off," Henry said. "Besides, I wouldn't be comfortable so far away. There's a lot I need to do." He forced himself to his feet and shook Stephen's hand. "I'm sorry if it's been a little strange for you. I hope we can spend more time together soon, once everything calms down."

"I'd like that," Stephen said, with the same polite demeanor he had shown for the past three days. He walked down the steps and waited at a discreet distance in the yard.

"So," Susan said, embracing her package. Her eyes reddened; her cheeks began to quiver. Henry noticed for the first time a path of fine lines around her mouth and eyes.

Henry reached into his pocket for a cigarette. He flicked a silver lighter expertly, savoring the smell of the quick burst of lighter fluid as he drew the smoke into his lungs. "So."

"I can't believe you started just when he made me quit," Susan said, rubbing her hand along the outside of her empty pockets.

"It helps to pass the time," Henry said, vaguely. He inhaled deeply again, blowing out a stream of perfect, smoky O's.

"Is he watching?" Susan asked, looking from Henry to Stephen walking toward the car. "I'm dying for a drag."

Henry took the package from Susan and turned to block her body. She bent down for two quick puffs, letting the smoke escape slowly through her nose.

"Already cheating," she said, with an echo of her once familiar sarcasm. "Do you think the first lie is the beginning of the end?" She laughed, then waved at Stephen across the yard. "Actually, it's my hundredth." She popped a mint into her mouth. "He's sweet, though, don't you think? I guess I better go," she added, slurring her words.

She kissed Henry, then stared hard into his eyes. "Are you being weird or do I just feel guilty?" she asked. "I don't want you to be mad."

"Probably both," Henry said. "But I'm not mad."

"Promise?" she asked, not letting him go.

"Promise," he said. He kissed her back, then hugged her close, feeling his composure begin to crack. "Enough for now. I'll see you soon," he said, looking down at the ground.

He watched her run down the steps, then stumble once as her heel sank into the sodden grass. She caught herself with one hand, waved, then ran laughing to the car. The horn honked twice, and Henry saw Susan's hand rise from the window and wave again, her fingers opening and closing in the air, still visible as they drove through the gate and out onto the road.

Henry stretched his arms wide and yawned, each movement deliberate and slow so as not to disturb his hard-won sense of calm. Then he turned and went back into William's house, locking the door behind.

Henry had spent the last two weeks with William, waiting for him to die. He had returned to his apartment after leaving the hospice, packed a bag, and checked William out. They were safely in the country by noon the next day. Henry had never gone back to school. Though he knew he had probably destroyed his career, it had given him a thrill to say nothing and simply disappear.

He hired an aide to help care for William, a silent man who worked the midnight shift. William's hospital bed was set up in the living room, surrounded by machines. He had an oxygen tank and two IVs: dextrose to keep his body hydrated and morphine to dull his pain. The fluids for the IVs were kept in the refrigerator on a separate shelf. An hour before changing the bag, Henry would set it on the counter to warm so that the infusion wouldn't make William cold.

Usually Henry slept on the couch. When the aide convinced him to sleep upstairs, Henry climbed to the guest room on the third floor, as he always had. He entered William's room only for changes of underwear and towels.

For all Henry's dread, so far William's dying had been one long sleeping. Sometimes they watched TV, or Henry read aloud. Once or twice William had the strength to play children's games on pads of paper: ticktacktoe or hangman, using simple, one-syllable words.

Henry was surprised at how easily he had gotten used to the ruin of William's body. Before, coming and going from his life at school or home, Henry's horror had increased with every hospital visit. Now that he never left, even the most savage damage had become routine. He learned to stop comparing William to the person he had been.

For the first week, Henry had been so happy to be reunited with William that he found himself forgetting all the trouble that had followed them. He began to fantasize that they might continue as they were forever, that maybe if nothing disturbed them, the peaceful rhythm of their days would keep William alive.

Soon that hope went like all the others. One afternoon William had a seizure, then two others in quick succession. He lost the power to speak. Even to this change, Henry adjusted. William answered his questions by squeezing his hand once for *yes* and twice for *no*. If Henry couldn't understand, William scrawled what he wanted on a legal pad kept by the bed. *Pain, water, heat, cold*, a few other words, were the only vocabulary he needed.

As news of William's deterioration spread, long absent friends and former coworkers called to tell him good-bye. Their guilt made them stilted and awkward, but Henry took great pains to put them at ease. He held the phone next to William's ear, but he never gave a sign of recognition unless Susan called. Sometimes then he made a sound, part howl, part moan.

Three mornings ago, William suffered an attack so violent that his body seemed to levitate above the bed. After it was over, Henry dressed him in a clean flannel robe and washed his hair. William stared back at him, blinking, a new kind of blankness in his eyes, as if he were already a ghost watching from the distance of stars.

Later, when Henry changed the sheets, he found a piece of

paper stuck between the mattress and the rail. William had written his own name all over the page, the way a person doodles when daydreaming about a lover. William's handwriting had always been illegible, but this was wilder than Henry had ever seen — huge, shaken letters, as if someone had tried to write in a moving car.

William did not awake again, even when Susan arrived with Stephen. Henry never questioned why she had checked into a motel instead of joining them in the house. He preferred to spend his last nights there alone. For the first two days, Susan and Stephen kept a vigil with Henry and the aide as William slid away: two strangers and two friends, faithful, in their way, to the end.

Stephen read quietly in another room or roamed around the yard. The aide did his chores. Susan made arrangements for William's cremation and memorial service. She even wrote a draft for an obituary and a eulogy. Mostly Henry stayed by William's side. Sometimes he played selections from William's favorite music on headphones to choose the perfect songs for his service, something between a dirge and a lullaby, some Mahler or Brahms. At night he listened to the hush of William's body, and tried to settle into grief and mourning. But even as William lay dying, what was left of their life was slipping out of Henry's control.

The night before, Susan had discovered a small photograph album in a box in the foyer closet. Glued on every page was a record of William's past before they had known him: pictures of him as a boy with horses and guns, with his sisters in a pasture on the ranch, in grammar school, on family vacations. William, who claimed to have severed his ties so completely, had never been able to throw all of it away.

When Susan returned to the motel that night after dinner, she called William's parents without consulting Henry. He didn't know that she had found their telephone number months before.

A few hours later she drove back to the house, weeping, to confess what she had done. They squared off in the living room while William lay unconscious between them, his face covered with an oxygen mask, his IV beeping. Of all the betrayals, both large and small, that they had each endured over the years, Susan's was the most inconceivable to Henry. When he shouted at her, he felt as if he were possessed with the spirit of William's rage.

But it was too late. The next afternoon, William's parents were coming to take him home.

Henry walked into the living room, the carpet so thick that his feet moved over it soundlessly, like boots through sand. Through the stained glass window by the foyer door, he could see out to the lawn and trees, distorted by the blue, beveled glass, as if he were peering through a kaleidoscope. He stood for a moment looking at the main floor of the house that had meant so much to them and been the cause of so much trouble.

He turned the stereo on loud and lay next to William, holding his hand. William's breath came in quick, strangulated bursts, as if someone held a pillow over his face. Henry pushed the release on the morphine drip and let the medication flow. He rested his hand over William's heart and felt its flutter slow.

Inside the garage Henry turned on the light, a bare bulb in the middle of the ceiling, dim with dust and cobwebs. Half-used cans of paint, tools, storm windows, discarded tires, a workbench, lawn mowers, shovels, and rakes neatly covered the floor. In one corner sat the five metal cans of gasoline Henry had bought that morning from the harbormaster. From a drawer in the workbench, he took a handful of rags and stuffed his pockets.

He lugged the containers through the garden and back into the house. He uncorked one can and drenched the dining room carpet, sprinkling gasoline on the curtains, the table, the side-board, the picture frames, anything that would burn. He pulled the arched doors to the living room closed without looking in, then turned a fresh container upside down as he walked through the foyer and climbed the stairs. He hesitated on the landing outside William's room, then entered quickly, splattering the bed-clothes and upholstery, the mahogany shelves of books, reeling from the way the fumes flew back at him in the shuttered air. He covered his face with a handkerchief as he moved up to the attic, soaking the floorboards and boxes stacked against the walls, taking care to drench the underside of the eaves.

Outside in the garden, he doused the kitchen windowsill, then tipped a can along the shingles at the top of the foundation, splashing liquid everywhere. He hurled the empty container to-ward the cedar roof and watched it falter halfway there, then smash against the bathroom window. The crack of glass split the silence like a gunshot. Henry shuddered as he saw a car drive slowly past in the distance, but against the darkened house, he was invisible. Even the sky was barely lit by the moon.

He didn't know how much gasoline he needed, but he poured out each can as he ringed the house twice, wrapping it with an invisible bow. He left the back door open and laid a trail of gaso-line a few feet into the yard, then stepped back and threw a lighted match onto the ground.

The grass burst into flames, which ran up to the house and broke in two, like a battalion dividing: one fiery trail racing through the kitchen and into the front hall, the other licking across the wood of the exterior, at first thin and light, like alcohol burning over a stove, then gaining fury as the flames began to blister the paint. The blaze spread along the back wall and inched around the corner, searing the shoots of wild bamboo that pushed against the living room window.

The inferno grew, loud as a windstorm. Henry heard a roar as a fireball exploded inside, the sound like a detonation. Shingles sailed off the roof, first one by one, then several at a time, glowing red as they landed on the lawn. He saw lamps flick on in houses down the street. A horn shrieked in the distance, long, steady cries, raising the alarm; then a trio of red and white lights flashed in the darkness as fire trucks rushed onto William's street. Henry knew he had to run for the train station before someone caught him, but he was stuck to that place, mesmerized as windows shattered, curtains vanished with a hiss — a conflagration, timbers falling, the fire snapping like bones, as the neighbors came, running.

At his grandmother's funeral, Henry remembered the priest reading a prayer about the soul's journey to the valley of death, the congregation echoing the appeals for angels to lead the way to paradise. Henry knew such things were impossible, but still he hoped that somewhere among the smoke and burning embers, one angel might come out of hiding to usher William on his way.

Henry melted into the crowd, exclaiming along with the others, their "aahs" and "oohs" and moans mingling in an agitated murmur, like voices speaking in tongues. As he backed into the shadows and prepared to leave, he turned to look one last time at William's house. Everywhere around him sparks burst in the sky and shot off into the night like the souls of the dead, flying. And the ground under his feet nothing, nothing at all.